FOLLYFOOT FARM

MONICA DICKENS

FOLLYFOOT FARM

containing *Follyfoot* and *Dora at Follyfoot*

HEINEMANN : LONDON

William Heinemann Ltd
15 Queen Street, Mayfair, London W1X 8BE

LONDON   MELBOURNE   TORONTO
JOHANNESBURG   AUCKLAND

First published in this form 1973
© Monica Dickens 1971, 1972
Photographs © Yorkshire Television Limited, 1971, 1972, 1973
434 93451 8
Photographs by Brian Jeeves and Alan Harbour

Printed in Great Britain by
Cox & Wyman Ltd, London, Fakenham and Reading

Follyfoot

I

On these early spring Sundays, there were usually a few visitors who came to the farm at the top of the hill.

Some of them were regulars, horse-lovers and children with carrots and apples and sugar for all the horses, and special snacks for their favourites. Peppermints for Cobbler's Dream. Soft stale biscuits for Lancelot, who was too old to have much use of his teeth.

Some of the people who came into the yard under the stone archway were strangers who had been driving by, saw the sign, 'Home of Rest for Horses', and stopped to see what it was all about.

'What's it all about then?' The two boys who had roared up on a motorbike were not the sort of people who usually came to the farm. Nothing much doing here. Daft really, the whole outfit. 'What's it all about?' The taller boy swaggered across the yard as if he had come to buy the place: cracked leather jacket with half the studs fallen out, cheap shiny boots, long seaweed hair, a scrubby fringe of beard that wouldn't grow.

'Saving lives,' Steve muttered, not loud enough for them to understand. They wouldn't understand anyway, that kind. Steve went on sweeping the cobbles, his head down, dark hair falling into his eyes.

'Huh?' The shorter, thicker boy looked as if his mother should have had his adenoids out long ago.

'Horses that are too old to work, or too badly treated – we give them a good life.'

'Daft, innit?' The boys went jeering towards the loose boxes that lined three sides of the yard.

7

'Willy. Spot. Ranger. Wonderboy.' The younger boy, about sixteen, with a stupid hanging lip, spelled out the names above the stable doors, to show he could read. 'Cobles Dram. Whoever heard of a name like that?'

'Cobbler's Dream.' Callie came out of the stable, where she had been brushing the mud off the chestnut pony, whose favourite rolling places would delight a hippopotamus. 'And everybody's heard of him. He was on television. He was in all the newspapers for catching a horse thief.'

'Thrills.' When the boy hung his big cropped head and looked up at her with his slow eyes, she thought for a moment she knew him. Where had she seen that broad earthy face with the thick lips hanging open, because he could not breathe through his pudgy nose?

One of the boys threw up a hand and the pony flicked back his ears and jerked his head away.

'That's not the way to go up to a horse,' Callie said. 'Especially Cobby. He's half blind.'

'Don't tell me about horses,' the boy grunted. 'We've got dozens of 'em at home.'

'Bad luck on *them*.' Usually Callie was polite to the visitors. Her mother was married to the Colonel, who ran this farm, and Callie loved to take people round the stables or down the muddy track to the fields, and tell them the history of each of the twenty horses, or as much as they would listen to.

But these boys would not listen to any of it. When she started to tell them about Wonderboy, who had been her father's famous steeplechaser before he died, and Ranger with the ruined mouth, and Spot, the circus rosinback with the rump as broad as a table, the taller boy said, 'Oh shut up, you silly kid,' and the younger one stuck out a boot and tripped Callie up as she turned to go on to the mule's box.

'What the hell are you playing at?' Steve was there in

8

seconds, holding the broom like a weapon, his clear blue eyes hard with anger.

'Don't touch me,' the boy whined, 'or I'll call the coppers.'

'I'll call them myself if you don't get out of here.'

'Can't wait,' the older boy said. ' "Visitors Welcome", it says on the sign. Some welcome. Come on, Lewis.'

Willy the mule stared sadly over his door, a pocket of air in his lower lip, lop ears sagging. Callie, inspecting her grazed hands for blood and disappointed to find none, yelled after them as they ran under the arch, 'Don't bother to come back!'

'Don't worry!' Lewis yelled back over his shoulder. Yes... there was something familiar about him. Where on earth – ?

'Lewis.' She wiped off her hands on the seat of her patched jeans, as if she were wiping off the disgustingness of Lewis.

'Louse,' Steve said.

The motorbike snarled, spat foul smoke and roared away.

2

Dora, the girl who worked with Steve in the stables, had been home for the weekend, but she came back on an early bus, to help with the feeds. She would rather be here than at home anyway. The Colonel had to force her to take an occasional weekend at her parents' flat in the industrial town which sprawled along the valley, to keep her mother from storming up the hill to complain.

Steve's mother did not come, and he had no father. This was his home, and his family. Cobbler's Dream, the pony he had rescued from a spoiled and vicious child, was the horse he loved best.

It was going to be a wet night, so Dora brought the rest of the old horses in from the fields. She was coming round the corner of the barn with the two Shetlands, a handful of shaggy mane in each hand, when a car stopped in the road and a man walked into the yard. A worn-looking horsey type of man, with bow legs and a lean brown face.

'I'm sorry, we're closed to visitors.' Dora shoved one Shetland into its stable with a slap on its bustling bottom, and made a grab for the long tangled tail of the other, as it ducked under her arm and headed for the feed shed. 'Shut that door!'

The man moved quickly and shut the door in Jock's square face. Dora got her arms round his neck and practically carried him back to the loose box he shared with Jamie and the tiny donkey. They had tubs on the floor because the manger was too high, and they nipped each other round and round the box, going from tub to tub like a buffet lunch.

'I've come to see the manager,' the bow-legged man said.

'The Colonel?' You were supposed to say he was not at home on Sunday afternoons, but Dora always stated facts, even when they were ruder. 'He's in the house, but he can't see you.'

'Why not?'

'He's probably asleep.'

The man bit his lip, which was cracked and dry, like badly kept leather. 'Could you possibly. . . . It's an emergency. About a horse.'

'Another customer?' Callie came up. The stables at the farm were full, but she always wanted more.

'It's a hard case.' The man looked sad. He looked defeated, as if he had known a lot of disappointments and could not stand any more. 'The mare is in bad trouble.'

'I'll get the Colonel,' Dora said, but Callie said, 'Let me. He hates being woken up, but at least I do it gently.'

The last time a horse was down at night and thrashing in its box, and Dora had shouted in the Colonel's ear, he had sat up and yelled, 'Messerschmitts – take cover!'

The Colonel came out of the back door with his yellow mongrel dog, pulling his worn tweed cap over sleepy eyes. He was a tall thin man with a slight limp from the war, and a scar by his eye where a kick from one of his horses had left him able to move the right side of his face more than the left, so that you could not always tell if he were serious or joking. He limped down the cinder path in his socks because he couldn't find a pair of shoes, walking on his heels with his toes turned up, because the ground was damp.

He and the bow-legged man leaned against posts with their hands in their pockets and talked quietly. Callie put a wheelbarrow in a doorway and pretended to be cleaning out Lancelot's clean stable, so that she could hear.

'. . . but I can't do any more,' the man was saying, 'because I lost my job.'

'I'm sorry.' The Colonel waited. He was a good listener.
'Down at the Pinecrest.'

The Pinecrest was an unattractive shabby hotel outside the town, with no pine trees in sight and not on the crest of a hill, but in a swampy valley where a polluted stream ran sluggishly through, gathering more pollution from the garbage that the Pinecrest cook threw out of the back door.

'I was in the stables there. They hire out riding hacks, you know.'

'Yes, I know.' The Colonel made a face as if he would rather not know.

'It's been on my mind,' the groom said. 'I done my best for my horses, but they want to get the last scrap of work out of them, and they're not fit for it.' The Colonel waited. 'Well, you can't feed more than the owner will buy, can you? The pasture is all grazed out and the hay he bought – you wouldn't use it for bedding.'

'They got a licence to run a riding stable?'

'Must do, or they couldn't be in business. I don't know how they got it though, unless they bribed the authorities, *which* I wouldn't put it past them, the kind of people they are.'

'Why did you stay with them?'

'Work's not easy to find.' The groom shrugged. 'I kept my mouth shut, because I needed the job, and my horses needed me. But then I couldn't hold myself in any longer. When I hit that boy of theirs – he was lucky I didn't kill him – they said, "Pack your bags and keep walking." '

'What happened?'

'They've got this old mare, see? A good one once. They got her off the track because she wouldn't race, and they've always kept her down and very poor, so she'd be quiet enough to ride. Quiet! The poor thing can hardly raise a canter. She gets a saddle sore, of course, with that thin thoroughbred skin and no flesh on her. Well, then it's my day

12

off, and this fat lady comes to the hotel. "I want to ride Beauty Queen," she says. Beauty Queen, that's what they call her, though she'd win no prizes anywhere. I come back early with a bag of cracked corn I'd managed to scrounge from a friend of mine who has some poultry, and someone yells, "Hey you! Saddle up Beauty for this lady." "Her back's not healed," I says, shutting the door of my car quick, so they wouldn't see the bag of corn and grab it to make porridge for the guests. "Saddle her up, I told you!" That was their eldest son, name of Todd, very ugly customer. When I refused, he gets the saddle himself and thumps it on that poor old mare's back' – the groom winced, as if he could feel the pain of it himself – 'and leads her out. I grab the rein and start to lead her back inside, and when the boy gets in the doorway to stop me, I knock him sideways.'

'Into the manure heap, I do hope.' Callie was frankly listening now, standing in Lancelot's doorway with a foot on the barrow handle and her chin on the fork.

'Right.' The groom smiled for the first time, then turned back to the Colonel with a long face. 'So I lost my job, and the horses lost me, and Beauty – well, God knows what will happen to her.'

'What about the RSPCA?'

'The Inspector is away. I can't wait, because I'm leaving for Scotland first thing tomorrow. I've a pal up there might have a job for me. So I came to you, because I'd heard what you do here for horses. Will you help?'

'Oh Lord,' the Colonel said. 'I'll try.' He hated trouble and this looked like trouble, but for a horse, he would get into trouble with both feet. Last year, he had got himself knocked out at Westerham Fair, taking on a giant of a man who was dragging off a mare in foal tied to the tail gate of a lorry.

3

'Remember when you pulled that chap out of the driver's cab and found out how big he was?' Steve laughed, remembering, as they drove next day down the long winding hill and headed towards the Pinecrest Hotel.

The Colonel grinned with the agile side of his face. 'I wouldn't have tackled him if I'd known.'

'You would.' Steve drove fast and cheerfully. He liked to drive the little sports car, which the Colonel wasted by driving too cautiously, and he loved to go on rescue missions like this. It made his nerves hum and his body feel light and strong at the same time. If he had lived in olden days, he would have gone off hacking at dragons with a two-bladed sword.

'Don't drive so fast,' the Colonel said. 'I've got to think out how I'm going to handle this.'

'Why can't we just march in, demand to see the horses, and if the mare's condition is as bad as the groom said, take her away? I could start leading her home while you go back for the horse box.'

'And get charged with – let's see: forcing an entry,' the Colonel ticked it off on his fingers, 'breach of the peace – that's if you get into a fight – trespassing, horse stealing. No, Steve, we've got to be very careful to stay on the right side of the law.'

'Oh that.' Steve shifted impatiently. When he was younger, he had got into a lot of trouble for not caring which side was which. 'The mare is in a bad way. That's what counts.'

'We've got to do it right.' The Colonel bit at the skin

round his nails, a habit that Callie's mother Anna had been trying to get rid of since she married him. He remembered, and put the hand down into his jacket pocket. 'I've got twenty other horses and ponies to think of. No help to them if I get my stable closed down.'

'No one would do that. Everyone's proud of the farm.'

'You'd be surprised, Steve. There are people round here who'd be glad to see us go out of business. They think the farm is a waste of money and a waste of land. Unproductive. Plough it under and raise wheat for the starving millions.'

'Couldn't grow much wheat in our chalky soil.'

'Face it, Steve,' the Colonel said gloomily, biting his nails again. 'There are people who don't like horses. Incredible, but true. Horses smell. They bring flies. They give you asthma. One end kicks and the other end bites. They get through gaps in hedges and go across people's land.'

'Old Beckett.'

'If a brewery Clydesdale with feet the size of Stroller's went over *your* lettuce seedlings, you wouldn't be so keen on horses either. These people at the Pinecrest sound very tricky. I can't risk any trouble. So back me up, Steve. Try and look like the assistant to the Agricultural and Domestic Animals County Surveyor.'

'Who's he?'

'I've just invented him.'

'Good morning to you!' The Colonel was always at his most polite when he was nervous. 'Am I speaking to the lady of the house?'

The elderly woman who was crouched over a weedy flower-bed outside the hotel looked up, brushing back wild grey hair.

'If you mean Mrs H.,' she said, 'I think she's in the kitchen discussing menus with the cook. Listen – you'll hear plates and saucepan lids flying. I merely live here. But there's nothing to do and the garden is so run down, I thought I'd give myself some bending exercise, at least.'

She began to get up, clutching her back and groaning, and the Colonel gallantly helped her to her feet.

'If you've come about taking rooms—' she looked suspiciously at the Colonel and Steve.

'No, we – er, we've come to see—'

'"—my advice to you is forget it.'

She paddled off in grey gym shoes with her toes turned out. The hotel door had opened, and an anxious little woman with nervous hands and a twitching mouth had come out.

'Dear Mrs Ogilvie.' She tried a laugh. 'Quite a joker. No need to take any notice of what she says. She's a bit – *you* know.' She tapped her head, which was done up in pink rollers.

'Too true.' Mrs Ogilvie spun round in the gym shoes. 'Anyone must be to stay in this dump.'

'She's been here for five years,' Mrs Hammond whispered. 'We can't get her out of the bridal suite. But come in, do. Mustn't keep you standing. It looks like rain.' She put out a hand and squinted suspiciously up at an innocently blue sky. 'Come into the office and let's see what we can do for you.'

She was all smiles and pleasantries, and so was her husband when he came into the office, summoned by a maid who opened a door and yelled down an echoing stone passage, 'Mr H! You're wanted up front!'

After what the groom had told them, Steve and the Colonel were surprised to find him quite an agreeable man, a bit soapy and smiling too much, with an oiled wave in his hair and small pointed teeth like a saw, but not the mean and brutish tyrant they had expected.

16

The Colonel was thrown out of gear. They chatted politely about nothing much, and although he kept trying to start his piece about the Agricultural and Domestic Animals County Surveyor, he could never quite get it out. Instead of being put at his ease by the smiling Hammonds, he was even more nervous. He shifted his feet. He blew his nose. He bit round his nails – what a giveaway. Steve wanted to slap at his hand as Anna would have done.

When Mr Hammond finally stopped vapourizing about the weather and taxes and asked him, 'And what can I do for you, sir?' the Colonel lost his nerve completely and blurted out, 'Well, it's like this. I'm from the Home of Rest for Horses, up at Follyfoot Farm.'

That did it. Steve had told him at least twice. 'Keep quiet about the farm, till we see the mare.' But Mr Hammond said without relaxing his smile, 'I know that, of course.'

'You know the Colonel?' Steve asked, surprised.

'Oh yes, I've heard a lot about the Brigadier.' Mr Hammond deliberately upgraded him. 'It's wonderful work you're doing up there.'

'Yes indeed, very wonderful. The poor dumb beasts.' Mrs Hammond's anxious eyes misted over slightly under the rollers.

'Of course,' said the Colonel, trying to get the talk round his way, 'most of my horses are past working, but in a stable like yours, they have to earn their keep.'

'You've hit it on the nail, Brigadier,' Mr Hammond complimented him as if he had said something clever. 'I'm not a rich man, but I feed the best. Hard food, hard grooming, hard work, and what do you get?'

The Colonel's eyes were glazing over. They were all sitting down, too comfortable, and Mrs Hammond had sent the noisy maid for coffee. Would they ever get out to the stables?

'What do you get? I'll tell you what you get.' Mr Hammond, with his long glossy sideburns and his smiling sharp teeth, was an unstoppable tap of horse hokum. 'You get a fit horse, as you and I, sir, very well know, eh? Eh, lad?' He winked at Steve, as if this was a chummy secret.

The Colonel cleared his throat desperately. 'How about stable help? Hard to get these days.'

'You've hit the nail again, Brigadier. I'm not a rich man, but I pay the best. But they don't want to work, that's where it is. Had to get rid of a chap just the other day. Lazy! You've no idea. And when my son had to speak to him about neglecting the horses, he went for the boy. Like a madman, Brigadier. He had to go. I'm running the stable now with my boys, though one's still at school. Too much for me, with the hotel as well, but the horses come first.'

'I'd love to see them.' The Colonel stood up quickly and moved towards the passage door, but Mr Hammond was quicker.

'Flattered, Brigadier, flattered.' He moved casually but swiftly in front of the door. 'A man of your experience, interested in our modest—'

'I am,' said the Colonel firmly. 'Let's have a look at 'em.'

Still smiling, still soapy, Mr Hammond managed to say No without saying it. 'Feeding time . . . highly sensitive animals . . . nervous when they're disturbed. . . .' The coffee arrived right on cue, and the Colonel and Steve had to sit down again and drink it. It was as soapy as its owner, with scummy milk and bitter grounds. Steve's cup had lipstick on it.

They left in a flurry of smiles and compliments. 'So kind of you to drop in . . . always nice to swap horse yarns. . . .' and a shout from the grey-haired lady who was back in the flower-bed, cutting everything down with a pair of rusty sheep shears, 'I didn't think you'd stay!'

Steve drove out by the back gate, past the stables, a patched together, rickety line of uneven sheds with a couple of thin horses in a yard outside, nosing sadly about in the trodden mud. Bales of mouldy hay were piled in an open shed. A boy was leaning against them, a cigarette smoking on his hanging lip.

It was the boy Lewis, who had tripped Callie up in the yard at the farm.

4

'He bluffed me out,' the Colonel said.

'That wasn't difficult,' Steve said glumly.

'Don't talk to the Colonel like that,' Anna said, and the Colonel said, 'He's right. I was a flop.'

They were all sitting round the kitchen table at the farm-house, trying to work out the next move. Anna, the Colonel's wife and Callie's mother, with her long pale hair pinned on top of her head. Callie in her school uniform, trying to do homework and be part of the talk at the same time. Steve disgusted, but eating slice after slice of home-made bread as Anna cut it. Dora with her untidy hair and brown blunt face, two puppies snoring in her lap. Little Slugger Jones, ex-jockey, ex-boxer, who worked with Steve and Dora in the stables.

'He wants to keep his nose out of trouble,' Slugger said. 'That's what he wants to do.' He had been punched about so much in his boxing days that he could no longer talk directly to anybody, only to himself.

'That's no help to that poor mare,' Dora said.

'There she goes again.' Slugger munched cake with his gums. He was losing his teeth and hair at an equal rate. 'All excited over hearsay talk.'

'Slugger might be right, you know,' the Colonel said. 'Sometimes he is. How do we know that groom was telling the truth?'

'Of course he was. You heard him.' Callie drew beautiful lines under her Earth Science heading, but could write nothing more.

'Suppose he was trying to get back at them for sacking him?'

'But *suppose*—' Callie was having an idea – 'suppose those boys came up on the bike yesterday because they thought the groom might be here?'

'Good grief, she's brilliant,' Dora said.

Steve said, 'She's almost human.'

'That boy Steve saw at the Pinecrest. Lewis. Louse. I've seen him too, but I can't think where. He's no good. Oh, Colonel.' She still called him that, although he was her step-father. 'Please – you must go back!'

'When the Cruelty to Animals man gets home—'

'It can't *wait*!'

'That wretched mare—'

'An infected sore on a thoroughbred—'

They rounded on him, Dora, Steve, Callie, even Anna, who was quickly moved to pity.

'I can't get in. He'll bar the way with those teeth.'

'Pretend you want to hire a horse.'

'I can't. They know me.'

'But they don't know *me*.' Dora stood up, spilling sleepy puppies. 'I wasn't here when the boys came. "Good morning, Mr Hammond, I want to hire a hack" (anyone got any money?) "Certainly, madam." "Let me see all your horses, and I'll choose."'

'They'll rumble you,' Steve said. 'One look at your hands, and they'll know you work in a stable.'

'No they won't. I'll go disguised as one of those silly women who say they can ride and then don't even know how to hold the reins. Anna – lend me those pink flowered pants.'

'Yes, and that nylon top with the frills.'

'What on my feet?'

'Those plastic sandals Corinne left.'

'Long dangly earrings.'
'Lots of makeup.'
'Nail varnish.'
'Scent. My "Passion Flowers".'
'Love beads.'
'A hair ribbon.'
'You're putting me off my tea.' Dora pushed away her plate. 'But I'll do it. For poor old Beauty Queen, I'll do it.'

Steve drove her in the farm truck to a crossroads half a mile from the Pinecrest Hotel, and got her bicycle out of the back.

'Be sure and wait for me,' she told him. 'I'm not going to ride this thing ten miles home and up that hill. Especially in this outfit.'

Dora never wore anything but jeans and sweaters and old shirts of Steve's that had shrunk in the wash. She had one skirt for going home to her mother. She felt ridiculous in the flowered pants and the earrings, with the garish eye make-up and the pale shiny lipstick and silver nail varnish with which Anna and Callie had prepared her as carefully as if she were a film star going on the set. The 'Passion Flowers' scent made her slightly sick. Horses were her natural perfume.

She approached the Pinecrest stables doubtfully, but the man who came out greeted her without surprise.

'Looking for someone, dear?'

'I want to hire a horse to go for a horseback ride,' said Dora in the kind of voice someone would have who would go riding dressed like this.

'All right, dear,' said the man, still unsurprised. First bad mark to him. If he ran a decent riding stable, he would have said, Go home and get a proper outfit.

'My friend told me you had beautiful animals here.' Girls who looked like this always had 'my friend' who told them this or that fantasy. The man was grinning as if he liked girls who looked like this, so Dora risked a seductive smile and a bit of a hip swing through the muddy yard. 'Might I see them all?'

'Come along in, my dear.'

Steve had said, 'Yuch!' when Dora got into the truck with him, but Mr Hammond ('Call me Sidney') seemed to find her divine.

The stables were what you would expect of a second-rate riding school just managing to sneak in under the law. Outside, a scrubby paddock with a trodden ring and a few flimsy jumps made of oil drums and old doors. Inside, jerry-built loose boxes with no windows, and narrow standing stalls, with a clay floor stamped into holes and hillocks. Woodwork chewed from boredom – or hunger. Scanty, dirty bedding. Flies. Thin horses with dusty coats, many of them with tell-tale patches of white where the hair had grown in over an old sore. As far as Dora could see, most of them needed shoeing.

'What a pretty horse. Oh, I like that spotted one. Why is he waving his head like that? What's he trying to say? Ah, the wee pony. Got the moth a bit, hasn't he?'

As Sidney Hammond showed her round the stable, she made stupid remarks to disguise what she thought. Some of the horses were fat enough, the chunky, cobby kind who wouldn't lose weight if you fed them diet pills; but many of them were ribby and hippy, gone over at the knee, and you could tell by their eyes that they had lost hope. Dora wanted to untie all their broken and knotted rope halters, let them all out, and herd them slowly back to the farm, wobbling behind them on her bicycle.

But, as the Colonel said, 'Face it, everyone isn't like us. If we took away every horse that wasn't kept by our standards, we'd have half the horses in the county up here.'

And she was here to look at Beauty Queen. That was her job.

And Sidney Hammond, although ignorant and probably miserly, was quite nice to his horses. He slapped them on their bony rumps and thin ewe necks, and told tall tales about their breeding and performance.

'This little grey. Irish bred. What a goer across country! Now here's a bay mare. Perfect lady's hack. Suit you all the way, she would. Todd!' He shouted towards the tack room, where a transistor radio was blasting.

A tall weedy boy with a feeble growth of beard appeared in the doorway. 'What do you want?' he shouted back. He inspected Dora from head to foot and back up again, and favoured her with a breathy wolf whistle.

'Get the tack for Penny.'

'Oh, just a moment, there's one horse I didn't give a sugar lump to.' In a dark corner box, Dora had spotted an un-mistakable thoroughbred head beyond the cobwebby bars. She ran down the littered aisle, stumbling in the loose sandals. Before Sidney could reach her, she slid back the bolt and went into the box, where a thin chestnut mare rested a back leg in the dirty straw, wearing a torn rug.

'Why is she wearing pyjamas?' Dora looked innocently up at Sidney. Anna had put so much black stuff on her lashes that she could hardly see.

'Keep her warm, love.'

'But she's sweating. Let me—'

'Best not touch her,' Sidney said quickly. 'She's nervous.'

'Oh, I'm not afraid of her.' She reached up and quickly but carefully folded the rug back on to the neck of the mare, who jumped away in pain.

24

No wonder. The saddle sore on her high withers was two or three inches wide, oozing and raw.

'Oh God!' Dora said in her normal voice, but Sidney Hammond was too busy explaining to notice.

'Looks worse than it is. All my groom's fault. I sacked him for letting it get so bad. It's clearing up with this new ointment.'

'Have you had the vet?'

'Of course, love.' When he was telling a full scale lie, his mouth went on smiling, but his eyes did not.

'He can't be much good. I know someone who could help.'

'I'm not a rich man, you know. I can't afford these huge fees.'

'No, I mean at Follyfoot Farm. The place where they have the old horses.'

'But Beauty Queen isn't old.' If Mr Hammond guessed at a connection between Dora and the Colonel, his soft-soaping smile didn't show it.

'They might take her though. I know a boy—' Dora lowered the heavy lashes coyly – 'a boy who works there. Shall I ask?'

Mr Hammond sighed, and surrendered. 'If it's best for Beauty. I'm up to my neck here, short-handed, all these animals and a hotel full of guests. . . .'

He started to cover the mare's back, but Dora said, 'Let's take off the rug and put ointment on, and a clean rag or something.'

'You're a great girl.' Sidney squeezed her hand. 'A real little Samaritan.'

When they left the box, the bay mare was drooping between pillar reins, with a long-cheeked curb bridle and an ugly old saddle that made Beauty's back understandable.

'You pay in advance,' said smiling Sidney.

'How much?'

25

'Seventy-five pence to you, my dear.'

'Oh, I'm afraid that's too much.'

Some other people had come to ride, three women in tight jodhpurs who looked as if they were housewives hoping to lose weight, and other horses were being saddled.

Sidney lowered his voice. 'Fifty pence then, but keep it dark.'

'Oh *no*,' said Dora, glad to find a way out of riding poor Penny, although she would only have taken her round the nearest corner and let her graze for an hour. 'That wouldn't be fair on you. I'll come back when I'm not so broke. I'll ring up the farm about Beauty. Don't worry.'

She ducked under Penny's pillar rein and got herself out to the yard, where one of the housewives already had her stout thighs across a hairy cob with its eyes half shut. Dora paused briefly to let out a couple of links in its curb chain, and ran – slop, slop in the plastic sandals – to her bicycle.

'Don't forget to come back, my dear!' Sidney Hammond was in the stable doorway, smiling and waving.

5

'And perhaps I will,' Dora said. 'Don't laugh, but I quite liked him. He was nice to me.'

Beauty Queen had been brought up to the farm, Sidney Hammond profuse with thanks, blessings, promises to pay whatever he could ('though I'm not a rich man'), and make endowments in his will.

'I've got to laugh,' Steve said. 'You had him cornered and he knew it. He had to be nice.'

'He fancied me.'

'Hah!' said Steve. 'Listen to that, Callie. Get her all dressed up, and look what happens.'

'It was the Passion Flowers.' Callie was standing on a box, very tenderly smoothing the ointment the vet had prescribed on to the chestnut mare's back. 'It went to her head.'

Callie had inherited from her mother a natural gift for caring for sick or injured animals. Beauty Queen, rechristened Miss America, was in the foaling stable behind the barn, and since Steve and Dora and Slugger were busy enough, it was Callie's job to clean the wound with warm water and hydrogen peroxide, and put on ointment and antiseptic powder.

She got up earlier to take care of Miss before she went to school, and rushed straight back to the mare as soon as she got home on the bus, so that her uniform was always smeared with ointment and powder and her school shoes full of bedding.

When Anna complained, Callie said, 'Then don't make me go to school.'

She had never liked the big rough school on the outskirts of the manufacturing town which lay farther along the valley; but it was the only one, unless she went to boarding school, and Callie would not hear of leaving the farm.

This year, school was worse than ever. There was a rotten gang of older boys who were always in trouble, except with those teachers who were afraid of them, and who got themselves through the boredom of the day by terrorizing some of the younger children. The sneaky kids sneaked, and got beaten up. The fighting kids fought back, and got left alone. The others simply tried to keep clear of the bullies. Callie was one of the others.

But one day when she was sitting on the playground wall reading, because she got all the exercise she needed at the farm, and she hated games with balls because she was short-sighted, a foot suddenly came up underneath the open book and sent it flying.

Three big brutish boys scrummed for it, knocking each other down, and when they got up, howling like inane hyenas, the book and cover were in shreds.

It was a library book and she would have to pay for it, but Callie walked away in silence, stretching her eyes to keep tears back.

'Hey!' A hand took her arm and spun her round. 'I know you, stupid cry-baby!'

'Let me go. I'll scream.'

'Try it.' The boy guffawed. 'We'll give you something to scream about.' He had a broad stupid face, with a pudgy nose and thick hanging lips. It was Lewis the Louse. This was where she had seen him before. Hanging about with the bad crowd. This school was so big that you couldn't know all the names, nor even all the faces.

'Yeah.' He dropped her arm, staring. 'I do know you. You live up the hill, doncher?'

Callie nodded, sick with fear. The three large boys stood round her. With such a shrieking mob in the playground, no one would see or hear whatever they did to her.

'You belong to that chap with the gimpy leg – haw haw, jolly good show and all that sort of rot.' The Louse did a rotten imitation of what he thought would be the voice of someone like the Colonel.

'My mother is married to him.'

'Oh girls! It's too romantic.' Lewis snuffled in his horrible blocked-up nose. Then he leaned forward and put his face so close to Callie's that she could see all the pimples and open pores. 'You know who I am, doncher?'

She nodded, staring at him like a rabbit.

'Your lot tried to make trouble for us. Remember that, you guys.' He jerked his head at his friends, who were even uglier and stupider (if possible) than him. 'We don't like this person.'

'But I'm taking care of your horse!' Callie was bolder, thinking of poor Miss America, who was her life's purpose at the moment.

'Quite right,' said Lewis, 'quite right. And we'll take care of you. Don't forget it.'

He snapped his thick grubby finger in Callie's face and sauntered off, his friends behind him, singing a crude song, whose key words they changed briefly while they passed a teacher, and then took up again.

When Callie was really upset, she couldn't talk about it. All she could do was to say she had a bad headache the next day, and all this got her was that Anna made her stay in bed and would not let her go out to the stable to take care of Miss America.

She knew that Callie had not got a headache. That was why she did that. And because she knew she hadn't got a headache, she sat on Callie's bed in the dark that night and asked her what was wrong.

'Oh – nothing. It's just school.' Callie tossed about, and the kitten who was on the bottom of the bed made a pounce at her toes.

'Was there trouble? Work, or what?'

Usually Callie did not like to have her hair touched, but when her mother stroked it at night, it was all right.

She shook her head under the stroking hand. How was it you could manage not to cry until someone gave you sympathy? It ought to be lack of sympathy that made you cry.

'What then?'

Callie sniffed. 'It's just – oh, I hate the kids.'

'Aren't there any friends?'

'I'm not the type that makes friends, you know that. All my friends are here. Most of them have got four legs.'

'You ought to have friends your own age.' All mothers worry once in a while that their child is 'different', though they wouldn't really like it if they weren't. 'Perhaps we should think about boarding school.'

'Mother, you promised.'

'Let's see how things go then.'

6

But things did not go any better. They went worse. Wherever Callie went, Lewis and his gang seemed to be there, jeering at her, tripping her up, jumping out from behind lockers, tweaking a pigtail as they ran by.

One day she was changing classrooms, going upstairs as Lewis was coming down, and he bumped into her so hard that he knocked her back down the stairs. She caught the rail and steadied herself against the wall. The rest of her class went on up the stairs. In this school, if you saw trouble brewing, you got out of the way.

'What do you want?' Callie stood against the wall with her hands spread out as if she was going to be shot. When she was afraid, it went to her stomach. She thought she was going to bring up her lunch all over the Louse's elastic-sided boots.

'Don't be afraid, little girl.' He put on a kind of leer which he thought was a smile. 'I got a present for you.'

Callie managed to say, 'Oh?' and swallowed her lunch back down.

'Knowing how much you love our four-footed friends—' from behind his back he held out a parcel wrapped in newspaper – 'I brought this for you.'

Callie took it, watching him.

'Go on. Open it. You'll like it, really.'

It smelled peculiar, but Callie gingerly unwrapped the newspaper and saw that she was holding the hoof of a dead horse. Where it had been cut off, it was congealed with black blood and dirt.

She wrapped it up again quickly and handed it back to Lewis. She could not speak.

'Don't you recognize it?' he jeered. 'You should do. I thought you was so fond of poor old Beauty Queen.'

'You couldn't—' she whispered.

'It's still our horse, ain't it? Too bad you didn't take better care of her, for we had to have her destroyed this morning. Very 'umane. A merciful release.' He shoved the newspaper bundle back into Callie's hands and ran away.

She could not believe him. Yet she had to believe him. It was a narrow, well-bred hoof, the pale colour that goes with a chestnut's white leg. She must telephone her mother. Yet she could not telephone her mother. As long as she didn't hear the truth, it still could be not true.

After she had been sick in the cloakroom, she went down to the basement furnace and got a shovel, and buried the hoof in the newspaper under the bushes behind the goal posts. Then she went back to her classroom.

'Where on earth—' Miss Golding began, then saw Callie's face.

'I was sick.'

Immediately there was a clamour from the class of, 'I knew that sausage was off', 'It was the spuds, they boil 'em in the dish-water', 'You won't catch me eating their treacle roll.'

'Do you want to lie down? Shall I ring up your home?'

'I'm all right.' Callie sat down.

At the end of the day, she went to the bus like a sleep-walker, and sat at the back, staring straight ahead, not looking out of the window all the way to ride a cross-country course alongside the road, as she usually did. The bus climbed the hill and stopped by the gate of the farm.

'Give my love to the old horses,' the driver said, as he always did.

'Thank you,' Callie said, as she always did. She went under the stone arch and walked across the yard going towards the house. Her mother would be starting supper. She would turn from the stove and Callie would know at once from her face whether it was true.

Several horses called to her. Cobbler's Dream in the corner box banged on his door and swung his head with the flashy white blaze up and down to get her attention. She was almost to the corner of the yard where the path came in from the house when Steve backed out of the Weaver's stable, dragging a loaded barrow.

'Hi!' he shouted. 'Aren't you going to see your patient?'

Callie turned slowly round.

'Her back looks much better today. You're doing a good job.'

Callie ran. It was not until she was in the loose box with her head against Miss America's thin thoroughbred neck that she began to cry.

After the Easter holidays started, Callie told her mother that she could not stay at that school.

'I'd better start finding out about boarding schools.'

'We can't afford it.'

'No.' Anna laughed. 'But you could try for a scholarship.'

'I'm not clever enough.'

'We'll see.'

They did not discuss it any more. Why spoil the holidays? The days were roofed with blue sky and whipped cream clouds. The old horses luxuriated in the sun on their dozing backs. Callie rode Cobbler's Dream, and the mule, and Hero the circus horse, and anyone else who was rideable, and she and Steve and Dora jogged up to the higher hills where the turf was patched with rings of white and yellow flowers, like fried eggs.

Miss America's back was healed and they could ride her too. Fleshed out and well fed, she was a pleasant ride, although her thoroughbred stride had been stiffened by pounding on roads, and from the way she chucked up her head, you could guess at the kind of hands that had tugged at her reins.

They rode her in a snaffle, bareback to make sure of not hurting her, and the mare flourished in the warm spring.

'But there's always a fly in the ointment,' Dora said.

The fly was Sidney Hammond, arriving with a lopsided trailer with the tailboard tied with rope, to take back his mare.

'Don't let her go.' Steve and Dora cornered the Colonel in the tack room when he went to get a halter.

'It's his horse. We've done what we set out to do. He's very busy, he says. He's getting a lot of people from town, secretaries and things wanting to go pony trekking at weekends. He needs the mare.'

'She isn't a pony.'

'Dora. Don't *try* to annoy me.' The Colonel did not want Miss America to go either.

Mr Hammond was as smiley and ingratiating as ever, as well he might be, since he hadn't paid a penny for the mare's keep, in spite of all his blessings and promises.

Dora kept out of his sight, in case she might need to put on the pink pants and 'Passion Flowers' disguise again to go and check on Miss America when she was back at the Pinecrest as Beauty Queen. Steve helped Mr Hammond load the mare, making a big fuss about spreading straw on the rotting tailboard in case of splinters.

As the trailer pulled away, he said, 'What a hunk of junk,' loud enough for Mr Hammond to hear, but smiling Sidney merely waved and grinned, and leaned out of the car window to call once again, 'I can never thank you enough, Brigadier!'

'I'll send you a bill!' the Colonel called after him, not loud enough to hear.

'You know he won't,' Slugger grumbled, sweeping up the old manure that Steve had kicked out of the van before he would lead Miss America in. 'You know he's too soft with these folk who could well pay to help out them as can't.'

'Shut up, Slugger,' the Colonel said. 'You know we only ask people to pay what they can afford.'

'And that one could well afford.'

'I said I'd send him a bill.'

'Oh yes, just like he sent in a bill to that old clothes and firewood chap as brought the pony in here for two weeks rest and we had the beggar all winter. Have us all in Queer Street, that lot will. Oh yes, he says. Send in a bill, he says. . . .' Slugger grumbled away, sweeping the gravel before him with short testy jabs.

7

It was Dora's birthday. She had wanted to spend it at the farm, but her mother wanted her at home, so she had to put on her skirt and go down into the town.

Her mother, who was still hoping that she would grow out of horses, although there was no evidence, at seventeen, that she ever would, had assembled a group of 'interesting' people to try to show her the kind of life she was missing.

A girl from an art school, starved and pale, with round glasses like wheel rims and a long dusty dress with a trodden hem. Two serious boys with bushy beards who were teaching problem children to get rid of their problems by screaming and hitting each other. A few grown-ups whose mouths kept on opening and shutting long after Dora had stopped listening.

She was so bored that she ate too much to pass the time, fell asleep on the bus going home, and was carried past the village where she was supposed to change buses.

'Where are we?' She woke with a start as the driver braked round a sharp corner.

He stopped at the next cross-roads and showed her a lane which led to the main road, where she might get another bus back.

It was late afternoon, with twilight settling on the budding hedges in the valley, and damp beginning to rise from the ground through the new spring grass. Dora walked by the side of the road, getting her feet wet. She was not sure where she was, but when she went over a bridge, she thought she might be crossing the sluggish brown river that ran by the

Pinecrest Hotel. If there were no buses on the main road, she would get a lift from the first car that would stop.

'Come back with her throat cut one day, she will,' Slugger Jones always grumbled when Dora turned up from town in a strange car or on the back of a motor-bike.

'There are some weird people about these days,' Anna warned, but Dora said, 'No weirder than me,' and went on hitch-hiking.

She had promised to be back for supper. After that lunch, she could never eat again. But Anna had made a cake. And there would be no 'interesting' people with 'stimulating' talk. Just people who knew each other well, and were sure of being liked.

Behind her in the lane, she heard the clop-clop of a trotting horse, that always stirring sound that brings people to their windows or out to the gate, even if they have their own horses to clop-clop with.

Dora turned and stood still to watch it come by. As the man and horse came into view out of the dusk, she saw that it was Miss America. Dora stepped out into the road and held up her hand like a school crossing patrol man.

The mare stopped of her own accord. She was not so much being ridden, as carrying an unsteady rider, who nearly pitched over her head when she stopped.

'Whoops.' He clung round Miss America's neck and smiled foolishly at Dora, who saw that he was drunk. She also saw that the saddle with which he had so little contact was a heavy broken thing, well down on the mare's bony withers.

Dora saw red. She grabbed the man's arm and pulled him off the horse. He was half-way off anyway.

'Thanks.' He landed on his feet, with the luck of a drunk. 'I was wondering whether to get on the ground or back in the saddle.'

'You shouldn't be *in* that saddle.' Furiously, Dora

37

unbuckled the girth and lifted off the saddle. The sore back had broken open again, raw and bleeding.

Dora swore. 'Here – just a minute—' The man lurched at her, but she went to the side of the road and pitched the dreadful old saddle over a thick hedge into the bushes.

'Now look what you've done!' The man's red face was woeful. 'How am I going to ride this thing home?'

'You're not,' Dora said.

'Have to walk then.' Strengthening himself with a swig from a flask in his breeches pocket, he looped the reins over his arm and started off down the road. The mare was slightly lame.

Dora followed a short distance behind. The man weaved down the lane in the failing light, staggering now and then and propping himself up with a hand on the mare's neck. When he came to the main road, he stood for a while watching the cars go past, turning his head from side to side as if he were at a tennis match.

Dora watched him. Finally he seemed to make up his mind. He took the reins over Miss America's head and tied them very carefully round a signpost. Then he stepped into the road with his arm raised, outlined unsteadily in the lights of a car. The luck of a drunk still held. The car stopped, and he got in and was driven away.

Dora untied the mare and they walked along the grass at the side of the road until they came to the Dog & Whistle, where Dora could telephone for Steve to bring the horse box.

In the farmhouse, Callie greeted her. 'I got you a present. Want to see?'

'Thanks. I got you one too. Want to see?'

'Where?'

38

'In the foaling stable.'

'A new customer!' Callie ran out.

Dora asked Anna, 'Is – er, is the Colonel in a good mood?'

'He was,' Anna said. 'What have you brought home?'

'Miss America,' Dora said. 'Her back has broken down again.'

The Colonel did not say much. He waited to see what would happen. When nothing happened, he telephoned the Pine-crest Hotel.

'Good morning, Brigadier. Nice to hear your voice.'

'I've got your mare.'

'That's good of you.'

'Her back is almost as bad as it was before.'

'That fellow – that stupid drunk – it's all his fault. I tell you, Brigadier, this riding school game is one long headache.'

'What happened?'

'I wish I knew. He came back here with a hangover and a cockeyed story about losing the saddle and tying the horse to a signpost. He'd been back to all the signposts on all the side turnings along the main road, and when the mare wasn't there and wasn't here in the stable, he thought he'd imagined the whole thing, and swore to go on the wagon.'

'Good.' The Colonel waited.

Mr Hammond waited too. Finally he said, 'I thought the mare might have run to you, seeing she was so well kept there before. I'm grateful, Brigadier.'

'You want me to keep her?'

'You know I'm short-handed here.'

'So am I.'

'But your staff is reliable. I work my fingers to the bone, but I have to leave a lot to my boys, and – well, you know what they are these days. You can't trust them with anything. Especially a valuable horse like Beauty.' He would not even stick up for his own family. 'So if you could do me a favour, Brigadier, I'll pay anything you want.'

'You didn't pay the last bill,' the Colonel murmured without moving his lips. He hated talking about money.

'The cheque is in the post.'

Mr Hammond rang off cheerfully, with best wishes to all for the Easter season. The man was incredible. He had no shame at all.

'He's not going to get the mare back though,' the Colonel said. 'But somehow I don't think he'll ask.'

'I worry about his other horses.' Dora frowned. 'I don't see how he ever got a stable licence.'

'Perhaps he didn't,' Steve said. 'Why don't you ask the County Council, Colonel?'

'They'll think I'm suspicious.'

'Well, you are.'

At the County Council, they told him that the Pinecrest's application for a riding-stable licence was on the files, awaiting an inspection.

'Our regular man is off sick. I wonder, Colonel – I know you're a busy man, but you're fully qualified, and I'm sure the hotel wants to get it cleared up before the summer.'

So the Colonel and Steve went back to the Pinecrest Hotel. He refused to take Dora in the sandals and earrings, but he did take Steve in case of trouble.

There was no trouble. He had written authority to inspect the stable. He spent half a day there, with Sidney Hammond following him affably round and thanking him at the end for his time and trouble with a smile like the jaws of a gin trap.

The Colonel turned in an honest and detailed report. It was not his decision whether or not to grant the licence.

8

Since last year, when Cobbler's Dream had captured a thief and saved his own life by clearing the impossible spiked park fence, Steve had begun to jump him again.

The Cobbler had once been a famous juvenile show jumper. When the girl who trained him grew too big, he was bought by a hard-handed child who wanted a vehicle for winning championships, rather than a pony to love. Steve worked for her father. He had to see the marvellous pony making mistakes because of the child. Finally he had to see him blinded in one eye by a blow from a whip. He had taken him away then, and brought him to the farm, and they had both stayed here.

The other eye became half blind, but Cobby had adapted so well that he was almost as surefooted as before, and his fantastic leap over the Manor park fence had proved that he had acquired some kind of sixth sense to judge a jump. He would jump almost anything if you took him slow and let him get the feel of it.

Steve put up some sheep hurdles in one of the fields, and he and Dora made a brush jump with gorse stuck through a ladder. Most of the other horses were too old and stiff to jump, so Dora was teaching the mule Willy, who had no mouth at all, and either rushed his jumps flat out or stopped dead and let Dora jump without him.

Steve and Dora had the afternoon off, so they took the Cobbler and Willy through the woods on the other side of their hill, where there were fallen tree trunks across the rides.

Cobby jumped them all without checking his canter, bunching his muscles, arching his back, smoothly away on his landing stride with his ears pricked for the next jump. Willy jumped the smaller trees. If they did not reach right across the path, he whipped round them with his mouth open, yawing at the bit. If they were too big, he dug in his toes, and Dora had to get off and lead him over. He would jump his front end, stand and stare with the tree trunk under his middle, and then heave his rear end over with a grunt like an old man getting out of the bath.

Near the far edge of the wood, Cobby shortened his stride, trotting with his head high, and turned to the side, listening.

'What does he hear?'

There were people who came to the woods with guns and shot at rabbits and foxes and anything that moved. Sometimes they shot each other.

Steve and Dora both stopped and listened. Only the continual sigh of the breeze moving through the tops of the tall trees.

'I don't hear anything.'

'Cobb does. His hearing is sharper now that he can't see much. So is his nose.'

The chestnut pony had his nostrils squared, as if he were getting a message.

Steve pushed him on, over two more jumps, but he slowed down again, listening.

'There is something. Let's go the way he wants to.'

They rode out of the wood and along the edge of a cornfield. In a grassy lane beyond the hedge, a grey horse was grazing in a patch of clover.

It was a calm horse. It stood still and exchanged blown breaths with Cobby, and then the ritual squeal and striking out. The mule laid back his long ears like a rabbit and said nothing. He distrusted strange horses. When he was turned out with a new one, he would communicate for the first two weeks only with his heels.

The grey horse wore a head collar. It let Steve slip his belt through the noseband, and trotted quietly beside Cobby back to the farm.

The Colonel did not recognize the horse. 'Someone will be worried though,' he said. 'It's a nice-looking horse and well kept.' The grey looked like a hunter, coat clean and silky, whiskers and heels neatly trimmed, tail and mane properly pulled. 'Better ring the police, Steve.'

Sergeant Oddie said at once, 'Oh no! Not that grey again. Look here, I've got the big wedding to worry about, two men off on a drug raid, a three-car crash on the Marston road and some nippers have set fire to the bus shelter. That horse is the last thing I need.'

'It's been out before?'

'Time and again. The neighbours are on my neck about it day and night. Regular wasps' nest, it's stirred up. Here, I'll give you Mrs Jordan's number, and I wish you'd tell her how to build a fence to keep a horse in.'

'But we have,' Mrs Jordan said. 'It's not our fault, or the horse's. Oh dear. I'll come and get him.'

'I'll ride him home, if you could bring me back,' Steve said.

The grey horse looked like a lovely ride, and he was, well schooled, a beautiful mover, quickly responsive, but you could stop him by flexing your wrist.

Steve was surprised when he saw where he came from. The Jordans' house on the edge of a small town had obviously once stood in fields, but new houses had been built close all round, and the fenced paddock was not much bigger than a tennis court. The fence was strong and high enough. The gate looked sound.

'It's they who are doing it,' Mrs Jordan told Steve. 'They used to do it at night, but they're getting bolder now, and they've begun to do it in the daytime if I go out.'

'Who do what?'

'The neighbours. The people in that pink house with gnomes in the garden and plastic flowers in the window-boxes. They open the gate and let David out, then they quickly ring the Police and complain that the horse is loose and trampling on people's gardens.'

'How do you know?'

'Oh, I know all right.' Mrs Jordan was a faded, once beautiful woman, with lines of work and worry round her big sad eyes and her full, drooping mouth. 'When the police were here last time – they were nice enough at first, but now they're getting fed up – I saw that front curtain move, and another time, the woman was standing in the window, blatantly watching and laughing.'

'Why don't you padlock the gate?'

'We have. But she somehow pried the rails loose at night, and then got them back up after she'd chased David out. It's her, not her husband. He's not so bad, but she's a fanatic. She hates horses, because she thinks they're something that rich people have. Rich! She's much better off than us. Her husband is a plumber. But she's the kind of person who can't stand anybody having something she hasn't got, even if she doesn't want it. She wants to buy that piece of land where David's paddock is, and breed chinchillas.'

'Chinchillas!' She looked at Steve with her tragic eyes. 'On what was once our back lawn, where the girls used to have their summer house and swings.'

After they had put the grey horse away in the open shed in the corner of the paddock, Mrs Jordan made Steve go into the house for something to eat before she would drive him home. She seemed lonely, glad of someone to talk to. He sat in a comfortable shabby armchair and listened. He had learned from the Colonel that if you will only shut up and listen, people will tell you things they won't tell to someone who is trying to keep up their end of the conversation.

It was a tragic story. Her husband had been a trainer and show judge. A car crash had killed their younger daughter and left him unable to work for a long time. They had to borrow money on their house and land. Their other daughter Nancy left college and went to work, and Mrs Jordan got a job in an old people's nursing home, but they could not pay the interest on the mortgage. Four acres of their land had been seized, and sold to the builder who had put up all these ugly little houses where the pastures and stables had been.

All the horses had gone, of course, except David, who had belonged to the dead girl.

'How could we part with him? Nancy rides him occasionally, but she has so little time, and she's always so tired. We're all tired, Steve. My husband has a part-time job now, but it doesn't pay much, and he's not well enough even for that. I lie awake night after night wondering what will happen when they take our house in the end and that horrible woman gets David's paddock – our last bit of land – and keeps her wretched chinchillas in prison cages.'

'Death row.' Steve nodded. 'Only one way out.'

'I hate her.'

'So do I,' Steve said with feeling, although he had never seen the woman with the plaster gnomes in her garden.

'Sergeant Oddie rang me up after he talked to you, and said if the horse got out again, we'd have to get rid of him.'

'I thought the sergeant was so busy,' Steve said.

'Not too busy to tell me *that*. And that's what that woman wants.'

46

'Why don't you turn her in?'

'I can't prove it. She's cunning. I've never been able to catch her.'

'Mind if I try?'

'It's not much use.'

'You all go out some night. Make a big noise about driving off in the car, so she knows. But I'll be here. I'll be in the shed with David.'

No need to tell the Colonel. Not that he would mind, but . . . no need to worry him.

'I can't risk any trouble,' he had said. He had his own problems with neighbours. 'We've got to stay on the right side of the law.'

Well, this was the right side, but . . . no need to tell him.

Steve did not tell Dora either, or anyone at the farm.

9

The next evening, after the horses had been bedded down and fed and watered, Steve asked if he could use the truck.

'All right,' the Colonel said. 'What for?'

'I'm going out.'

'Who with?' Dora's rumpled head came over the top of a stable door, where she was rubbing liniment on Dolly's chronic foreleg.

'A girl I know.'

'You don't know any girls.'

'How do you know?'

'You'd tell me.'

Dora rested her chin on the door. Old Doll put her head out beside her and laid back her ears at Steve. She had once been so badly abused by a man that she still only liked women. It was Dolly who had kicked the Colonel in the head.

'You'd be the last person I'd tell.' Steve laughed. 'You'd want to come too, and sit between us and talk all through the film.'

'Are you going to a film?'

'Yes.'

'I want to come too.'

'No.'

'What's her name?'

'Nancy.'

'I don't believe you're going out with a girl,' Dora said, but more doubtfully.

When he drove off, Dora was sitting on the wall by the gate, polishing a snaffle bit and kicking her heels against the

48

bricks. Her face looked closed and sulky, her lower lip stuck out. Steve waved. She did not wave back or look up.

Mr Jordan was a grey, stooped man, with a mouth stiffened by pain of body and heart. Nancy was a bright-cheeked girl with thick bouncing hair and good legs, the kind of girl Steve would have gone to the cinema with if he had been going to the cinema with a girl.

They made the necessary noise about leaving. Racing the engine, slamming the doors, going back for a coat, calling out that they would be late.

'The film starts at eight!' Mrs Jordan called from behind the wheel, to let her neighbours know that they would be away at least two hours.

In the pink house with the window-boxes full of impossible flowers that never bloomed in the spring, nor even in England at all, a shadow moved behind the curtain.

Steve sat in the straw of the open shed and talked to the grey horse and thought about things long gone. Other nights of adventure when you waited, with your nerves on edge and your hair pricking on your scalp. The night when he had stolen Cobby away to safety with sacking wrapped round his hooves.

About nine-thirty, with the family still in the cinema, David raised his head from his hay and swung his small ears forward. Steve listened, holding his breath.

Were there footsteps on the soft ground? Did the night breeze shiver that bush, or was someone behind it? Steve watched, motionless in the dark corner.

David, who liked people, walked out of the shed in a rustle of straw and into the paddock. A thick woman in tight pants was climbing through the fence. She held out her hand as the horse went up to her and gave him something. In the still night, Steve heard his teeth on the sugar. He followed the woman as she moved quickly across the small paddock to the gate.

Steve waited. It was too dark to see much. She had her back to him, but he heard the clink of the chain on the gate. He got up quickly, went silently up behind her and said in her ear, 'Can I help you?'

'Oh my God!' The woman jumped round with a hand on the ample shelf over her heart. As she moved, Steve was almost sure that he saw her fist clench over a piece of metal that could be a key.

'What do you want?' She was breathing fast, and he could see behind her dark fringe tomorrow's imagined headlines chasing each other through her head.

WOMAN FOUND STRANGLED. HOUSEWIFE KILLED IN NEIGHBOUR'S GARDEN. SUBURBAN SLAYING, MYSTERY GROWS.

'What you – what are you doing here?' The woman must be bold to have done as much as she had, but her mouth was twitching now with nerves, because Steve was looming over her threateningly.

'I'm a friend of the family,' he said. 'The horse looked as if he might be headed for colic, so I was watching he didn't lie down. Someone might have slipped him something. People round here have been making trouble, you wouldn't believe it.'

'Oh, I know.' The woman relaxed. 'The poor Jordans, it's dreadful for them, on top of all their bad luck. I try to keep an eye on things for them, when they're not here. That's why I came out, to check on the gate fastening.'

'Oh, I see,' said Steve. 'To check the gate.'

'That's right.' The woman started to move towards her house. 'To check the gate.'

'You keep an eye on things. That's nice.'

'Well,' she said, 'one does what one can. We were all put in this world to help each other, that's what I say.'

'Oh so do I.' With a hand on the neck of the grey horse, Steve watched the woman climb through the paddock fence and go back into her own house, waggling her bottom righteously, like a good neighbour who has done her duty.

'So that's what you ought to do,' Steve told the Jordans.

They looked at each other. 'I'm no hand with electricity.' The father looked baffled.

'I'll do it.'

'She'll see you.' Mrs Jordan glanced towards the pink house. 'She sees everything.'

'I'll do it after dark. There's no moon. She won't try anything on tomorrow after the scare she got tonight. If I use a rubber hammer, I can get the insulators on without making any noise, and I'll put the battery behind the shed so she won't hear it ticking.'

Next day, Steve offered to do Anna's shopping, and bought the battery and thin wire and the insulators while he was in town.

In the evening, when he asked casually for the truck, Dora did not ask him where he was going. She had not allowed herself to ask him about the film last night, which was a good thing because he had forgotten to find out what was on.

At the Jordans he rigged up two strands of electric wire close to the paddock rails where it could not be seen. Then he turned on the battery and waited at the side of the shed.

He chirruped softly. The horse came up to the rail, put out his nose, then jumped back and snorted.

'Sorry, David.' The grey horse stood in the middle of the paddock, looking very offended. 'I had to test it.'

Two nights Steve waited in the straw, with the battery ticking softly on the other side of the shed. He dozed and woke and dozed, but he was sleepy in the daytime, and Dora made embittered remarks about people who stayed out so late with girls that they couldn't do their jobs properly.

Why not tell her and let her watch with him in the shed and share the adventure? Because she kept saying things like, 'When are we going to see this famous Nancy? Not that I care. Or is she too hideous to bring here?' Talking herself out of the adventure.

'She's gorgeous, as a matter of fact,' Steve said, irritated. 'Marvellous legs.' He winked at Slugger.

'Can't go far wrong with that.' Slugger winked at the horse he was grooming. ' "When judgin' a woman *or* a horse, you gotta look at the legs, of course." That's what me grandad used to say.'

'Anyone can have good legs.' Dora's, which were rather muscular and boyish, were covered in torn faded blue jeans, which she refused to let Anna patch, or hem at the bottom.

On the third night, Steve went to bed early – 'What's the matter? She sick of you already?' – and got up again at midnight after everyone was asleep. He stopped the truck before he got to the Jordans', and walked quietly through what was left of their garden and round the side of the house to the shed.

When he whispered, to show the horse he was there, a voice answered him.

'Nancy?'

'I couldn't sleep.' She was lying covered with straw, only her face and hair showing.

'I wanted to do this alone.' Steve came in and sat beside her.

'Why?'

'It was my idea.'

'It's my horse.'

They lay side by side in the straw and talked softly. Nancy told him about the man at work she thought she was in love with. Girls always started to tell you about other men just when you were getting interested.

Steve wriggled his fingers through the straw to find her hand.

'But he's almost old enough to be my father,' Nancy said.

Steve took her hand, and at that moment there was a blood-curdling scream from the other side of the paddock.

David jumped. Steve and Nancy scrambled up. The plump woman in the tight pants was sitting on the ground with her arms wrapped round herself like a straitjacket, rocking backwards and forwards and moaning.

'It can't have been that bad.' Steve and Nancy slid carefully under the fence and went across to her.

'Oh, I'm killed,' the woman moaned. 'Oh, my heart—'

'Just going to check up on the gate, eh?'

She looked up at Steve, her hair, disordered from bed, standing wildly up as if the electricity had gone right through it.

'Yes,' she croaked. 'One does what one can. But there are some people—' she glowered up at Nancy, still rocking and holding herself as if she might fall apart – 'some people who don't know the meaning of the word gratitude.'

After this, Steve did take Nancy to the farm at the weekend, to show her the horses.

The Colonel was delighted with her. He conducted her round himself, hands behind his back, cap over his eyes, very military. Callie was pleased with her because she asked the right questions and said, 'How lucky for Miss to have Callie to look after her,' when they visited Miss America, queening it in the orchard so that the other horses would not disturb the healing wound.

Dora was rather gruff. She took a long look at Nancy's legs, then went off to greet a family of visitors and became very busy giving them a conducted tour of all the horses.

The family, who had only come to see the donkey which had once belonged to their Uncle Fred, kept saying, 'Well, better be getting along,' but Dora dragged them on from horse to horse, so as not to have to talk to Nancy.

Soon after this, Steve got a letter from Mrs Jordan. Their telephone had been cut off because they couldn't pay the bill.

The plump woman and the plumber had put the pink house up for sale and gone away. Two days later – '*If she'd only waited two days, she could have had her revenge in chinchillas*' – Mr Jordan was asked by a friend in Australia to go out and join him on the ranch where he was breeding horses.

'*So we're all going, Steve. A new life. Free passage out if we stay two years, and they can have this poor house and make it into a pub or a Bingo hall or whatever they want. No regrets. Except about David. We sail next week. Please find him a good home and use the sale money for the farm. The best home only. I trust you.*'

David could stay out at night, so the Colonel let Steve bring him to the farm.

'What's *that*?' Dora made a face at the grey as he backed neatly out of the horse box and stood with his fine head up and his mane and tail blowing like an Arab, staring at some of the old horses, who were drawn up in the field, all pointing the same way like sheep, observing him.

'It's the horse we found on the other side of the wood. You know.'

'Nancy's horse.'

'Yes,' Steve said. 'They're—'

'It's too long in the back,' Dora said, 'and I don't like the look of that near hock.'

'They're going to Australia. With Nancy.'

'But other than that, it's the best-looking horse we've ever had here.' Dora grinned. 'Can we ride him?'

'Till we can find the right home.'

'Let's not start looking yet.'

'We've got to work with him a bit,' they told the Colonel. 'He hasn't worked for so long, we'll have to school him before we can show him to anyone.'

And every day when the Colonel, during his morning rounds, asked, 'You got a prospect for that grey?', they said, 'He's still a bit tricky. We want him perfect.'

David already was perfect. They had never had such a marvellous horse to ride. They were not going to let him go in a hurry.

'Got to work with him a bit longer.'

10

Callie had dreaded going back to school, but when the summer term started, Lewis seemed to have been converted by the glories of Easter, because he left Callie alone and did not bully her.

She watched him from a distance. He was strangely quiet. He did not make a dead set for the new, younger ones, as he usually did, twisting their arms to see if they would cry, knocking into them in the cafeteria to make them drop their food.

'School isn't so bad,' Callie told Anna. 'Perhaps I will stay.'

'Take the scholarship exam anyway.' Anna was used to Callie's frequent changes of mind. Tomorrow school might be no good again.

But tomorrow, Callie actually had a conversation with Lewis the Louse.

They were in the library, where you were not supposed to talk, but they were behind a stack of shelves and Mrs Dooley was busy at the far desk.

Lewis had taken down a book and opened it, but he did not seem able to read. Callie was searching for something in an index. She was aware that Lewis was watching her, so she looked up and smiled nervously.

To her amazement, he smiled back, his lower lip hanging on his face like a hammock, his teeth as pointed as his father's, but with gaps from fighting.

'What you do in the holidays then?' he asked.

Callie was so surprised and flummoxed that she could not think of anything.

'Oh – nothing much. I rode. I worked most of the time in the stables. I helped Steve build a gate.'

'Who's Steve?'

'The boy who works at the farm.'

'*Oh*, yeah.' Lewis nodded, remembering.

'He did a marvellous thing.' Callie babbled on, making the most of the chance to get on the right side of the Louse. 'He foiled a woman.'

'Foiled?' Lewis's mouth hung. His vocabulary was not very large.

Callie told him about the woman letting out David and then ringing the police. He listened, his slow dull eyes following the movement of her face, breathing through his mouth like a patient under anaesthetic.

'Who's talking there?' Mrs Dooley came round the end of the bookshelves. Lewis had disappeared. There was only Callie there to take a discipline mark.

Two nights later, the door of the Mongolian horse's loose box was open, and Trotsky wandered across a field of young wheat, eating it as he went and occasionally lying down for a crushing roll.

'Good thing he didn't have shoes on,' the Colonel said nervously to the farmer.

'Good thing I wasn't out there with a gun,' the farmer said grimly.

Trotsky was wily enough to undo a latch if the bolts were not fastened.

'But I know I bolted Trot's door,' Dora said. 'And the bottom bolt too, because he bit me while I was bending down.'

'Someone opened it then,' Steve said. 'Like the Jordans' neighbour.'

Callie kept her mouth shut, which was how she should have kept it behind the library shelves. Was it possible that she had put this idea for new trouble into the Louse's thick head?

He left her alone. She told her mother that she was definitely not going to take the exam. But when Lewis saw she was off her guard, he invited her one day to go with him and buy a chocolate cornet before it was time for her bus.

She went. They never got to the ice-cream van. As soon as they were round the corner from the school, Lewis pulled her into the overgrown garden of an empty house and knocked her backwards into the bushes. She picked herself up and was going to run away, but he grabbed her.

'That's just the beginning.' He stared at her with his horrid revolting slab of face.

'What for?'

'Stopping us getting a licence.'

'What do you mean?'

'Your stepfather. The Sergeant, the Bosun, whatever his daft name is. He done it.'

'It was nothing to do with the Colonel. He only sent the County Council a report on your stable.'

'He wouldn't know one end of a stable from the other.' Lewis was gripping her arm so hard that she would scream if it went on. 'Much less a horse.'

'Let me go!'

'He's got it in for us. Trying to keep an honest man from earning a crust of bread, my Dad says. We've lost a lot of bookings, you know.' His gorilla brow came down threateningly. 'People come to us for the riding.'

'Why don't you clean the place up and apply for another licence?' Callie bit her lip. Her arm was going numb. She would not scream.

'There's nothing wrong with our place,' Lewis growled.

'It's your stepfather, that's who there's something wrong with. We'd ought to put him out of business too. Perhaps we will. Yeah.' He dropped her arm, frowning under the weight of what passed for thoughts. 'Perhaps we will. My Dad says it's a crime to keep them poor old horses alive against their will.'

'It's not against their will!' Callie could have run now, but she stayed to argue, rubbing her arm. 'They're all fit enough to enjoy life. The Colonel says it's wrong to take life from an animal while he can still use it.'

'A crime against Nature.' The Louse was obviously echoing his father. 'Shouldn't be allowed.'

'We save horses! We saved your horse because you were all too cruel and stupid—'

Lewis pulled back his arm and took an open-handed swipe at her, and she ran, ducking through the bushes until she was out on the road where there were people.

When she got home, she kept her sleeve down over her bruised arm and explained her scratches by telling her mother that she had got off the bus half-way up the hill for exercise, and taken a short cut through the brambles.

She told the Colonel that the Pinecrest Hotel had been refused a licence to run a riding stable.

'Thank God,' the Colonel said. 'There is some sense to the Town Hall after all.'

'I'll bet they wish they could put you out of business too.' Callie watched his face to see how he would take that.

'Oh, I don't think so.' In spite of all the cruelty and ignorance he had seen in his work for horses, the Colonel still believed the best of people, right up to the time when he discovered the worst.

'And I've decided,' Callie told Anna and the Colonel – the pain of her arm kept reminding her – 'that I do want to go away to that school.'

'Your name's still on the exam list,' Anna said. 'I didn't keep asking Miss Crombie to take it off every time you changed your mind.'

'Suppose I don't get the scholarship?'

'Miss Crombie thinks you have a very good chance.'

11

One of the disastrous things that people did was to give their small children day-old chicks for Easter. Dear little fluffy yellow Easter chicks. You could buy them in cut-price stores.

Some of them fell out of the paper bags and were stepped on or run over in the crowded street. Some of them were crushed to death by hot little hands soon after they got home. Some died of cold. Some died of the wrong food. Some died of not bothering to live.

The few who survived were either given away when they grew into chickens, or kept in a cellar or a cupboard, or even the bath, until the people got sick of it and gave them away or killed them, or the chickens got sick of it and died. It was a total disaster for all concerned.

This Easter, a town family had staged an even bigger disaster.

Their little daughter was 'mad about' horses, and so when she woke up on Easter morning, the car was standing in the road and there was a horse in the garage.

It was not much of a horse. The family had bought it quite cheaply at a sale. It had a big coffin head, lumps on its legs, a scrubby mane and tail and large flat feet that had not seen a blacksmith for a long time.

'My horsie!' They had bought an old bridle with the horse, and they put it on back to front with the brow band where the throat latch should be and the reins crossed under its neck, and the little girl climbed on, rode away down the middle of the road and fell off before she got to the corner.

She hit her head and was in bed for two weeks, and the horse went back into the garage in disgrace.

Now and then when someone remembered, they fed it a soup can of oats, which it could not chew properly, because it had a long loose tooth hanging at the side of its mouth. It had no hay, because they thought that hay was only for the winter, and no bedding, because they did not know about bedding. There was a small patch of grass behind the garage, and the horse ate that bare, and then licked the ground.

When the little girl was better, she got on the horse again with her friend and the two of them rode round and round on a patch of waste land, clutching the mane and each other and shrieking with joy. Finally, the horse stumbled and fell down, and the children tumbled off, which seemed the easiest way to get down, and a great joke too.

The floor of the garage was concrete and the walls were concrete blocks, sweating a chill damp. When the horse lay down, which it did more often as it grew weaker, it rubbed sores on its elbows and hocks.

If it was lying down when she came home from school, the little girl would get it up by holding the soup can of oats a little way off. When it stood up, she would take the oats away and put on the bridle.

'Work before food, Rusty dear,' she would tell it, and she and her friend would take Rusty to play circus on the piece of waste ground.

She was devoted to the horse. She sang to it. She made daisy chains to hang on its ear. She brushed it with her old hairbrush, but she could not get it very clean, because she did not like the smell of manure, and so she did not clean out the garage, although she told her father she did.

Her father hardly ever went to look at the horse, but he was very proud about it, and told everyone at work how his little girl thought the world of Rusty and it would do your heart good.

The mother did not look at the horse very much, because she was afraid of horses, and said she was allergic to them, which she thought was quite a grand thing to be, and she also did not like the smell that was accumulating in the garage.

But her little girl was happy, and she thought it was a lovely thing for a kiddie to have a faithful pet.

The faithful horse was willing enough to keep going somehow, although he was very thin and lumps of his hair fell out, and he was becoming dehydrated from only having small amounts of water, which the little girl brought him in a seaside toy bucket.

One day when she and her friend were riding him proudly down the road to the pillar box, slapping his ribs to keep him moving, he stopped and lay down in the road with his nose resting on the kerb. All the shrieks and wails and kisses and smacks of the children and the shouts of some masons who were building a wall and the advice of housewives who came out of their houses and flapped their aprons could not get him up.

It happened that the Colonel and Anna were taking a detour across the end of this road to avoid rush hour traffic. They saw the excitement, and turned the car up the street to see what it was.

The Colonel walked through the small crowd and stood for a moment with his hands in his pockets, watching the little girls swarming round the horse like distressed bees, patting it and kissing it and begging it, Rusty dear, to get up. The Colonel looked at the horse and the horse looked at the Colonel, and a message passed between them like old friends.

When the Colonel had got authority to take the horse, he telephoned for Steve to come with the horse box.

'But I don't understand.' The mother had taken the little

girl home and the father was back from work and standing nonplussed in the road, where street lamps were coming on and the masons had knocked off for the day and the housewives and the other children had gone indoors. 'She loved that horse like her own brother. Thought the world of him, it would do your heart good.'

'I'm sorry.' The Colonel was sitting on the kerb in his best suit with the horse's head in his lap. 'But a small child can't be left alone to take care of a horse.'

'But we didn't know!'

'Famous last words,' the Colonel muttered. 'People who don't know anything about horses should stick to goldfish.'

'That's a good idea.' The man began to cheer up. He was glad he was going to be able to garage his car again, anyway. 'I'll get her a bowl of nice fish tomorrow. Take her mind off it. They soon forget, the kiddies.'

He went back to tell his wife and daughter the new idea. The Colonel took off the jacket of his best suit and laid it over the rump of the horse, who lay like a heap of roadmenders' sand in the shadows between the street lamps.

At the Farm, the Colonel pulled out Rusty's loose tooth by rubbing the opposite gum to make that side more sensitive, and then quickly tapping out the tooth with a small hammer.

'Bran mashes now?' Steve let go the bluish tongue, which he had been holding out to the side to keep the horse's mouth open.

'Give him anything he'll eat, if he'll eat.' The Colonel got up from the straw where Rusty was lying. 'He hasn't got much longer.'

'Will he die?' From the doorway, Callie saw the horse through a glittery haze of tears.

The Colonel nodded. That was the message that had passed between him and the horse in the road.

I am dying.

You shall die in peace.

Lewis went back to bullying the younger ones, and Callie kept clear of him. If she could keep out of his way until the end of term, she would be safe and free.

The week before she was to take the scholarship exam, she went early to school for some extra study with Miss Crombie. 'Not that I want to lose you next year, Callie, but I shall be thrilled if you do well.' Miss Crombie flushed and scratched her head with the pencil she wore through her hair like Madam Butterfly. She had a pretty boring life and not much to be thrilled about.

When Callie was in the cloakroom, she heard shouting in the yard outside, and running feet. The bigger boys never came so early, but there was a pack of them, galloping across the empty yard like hounds after a fox. She could not see what they were chasing, but whatever it was had dashed into the bicycle shed and bolted the door.

Whooping and shrieking, the boys attacked the shed with feet and stones and bits of wood. One of them broke a window. It was Lewis, of course, climbing on the bicycle rack and putting in the boot with a crash of glass.

Callie watched, paralysed. She had heard about a girl in New York being stabbed in the street while people hurried past or watched from their windows, and would not do anything to help. Now here she was, just as cowardly herself. *Don't get mixed up. Keep clear.*

Lewis was too big to climb through the window. He and the others went round to attack the shed from the back. As Callie heard the glass of the back window break, the door of the shed burst open and a little spindly boy, legs going like the spokes of a wheel, ran for his life across the yard. The boys were already round the shed and gaining on him as he wrenched open a door and got inside the school.

Help him, Callie. But she could not move. The boys were at the outside door as the little boy rushed into the cloakroom, gasping and wild-eyed.

'They're after me!' He could hardly speak.

Don't get mixed up. Keep clear. 'I can't – this is the girls'—' she began, but the child stammered, 'Save me!' and without thought, she pushed him into her open locker and shut the door.

It locked automatically. It was a tiny space, but the child was tiny, and there were air holes at the top to let out the smell of hockey boots and gym shoes.

Feet clattered on the stone stairs, and Lewis was in the cloakroom with three or four grinning cannibals behind him.

'Well, look who's here.' Lewis began to throw coats and scarves about, looking for the little boy.

'Get out of here.' Callie held herself tense so that the trembling of her body would not reach her voice. 'You're not allowed in here.'

'Who cares?' Lewis began to try the doors of the lockers, pulling out stuff from the open ones, while his mob tore clothes off the hooks and threw shoes and tennis rackets about, just for the mess of it.

'Where's that mucky kid?' Lewis was looking through the air holes of the lockers. What would happen when a pair of terrified eyes met his? What would happen when he saw it was Callie's locker and went at her for the key? It was round her neck on a string. He would probably strangle her.

'What's he done?' If she could just keep them talking, someone would come.

'Croaked to a teacher. Got us in trouble.' A gym shoe, a

purse, a stuffed bear flew out of a locker over his shoulder.

'Why?'

For answer, he tore the photograph of a boy from the back of a door, crumpled it up and threw it in her face.

He was getting near her locker. Her hand went up to the key string at her neck. 'There's no—' she said, 'there's no one—'

'Shut up.' Lewis took hold of Callie's long pigtails, wrapped them round her throat and pulled the ends.

Choking, Callie looked desperately out of the window. Then she saw a miracle, right before her anguished eyes. Big bold Betty Rundle, goal for the hockey team, was rolling in early across the yard. The boys saw her too. Lewis let go of Callie's hair, and they ran. Coughing, Callie pulled the child out of her locker, and dragged him – he could hardly walk from cramp – down the corridor and round a corner before Betty Rundle kicked open the outside door and came whistling down the stairs.

Miss Crombie was angry, puffed in the face. 'What's the point of me getting here early if you can't bother to come early too?' She was never at her best in the morning.

'The bus was late,' Callie said faintly. Her throat still hurt.

'It's for your sake, not mine', Miss Crombie went on without listening. 'Now hurry up and let's go through that French translation before the pagan hordes arrive.'

While she read aloud, misreading some of her own words so that they sounded like mistakes, Callie thought about the little boy as she had left him sitting alone in his empty classroom, sheltering behind an oversize desk as if it was a fortress. After he had told the teacher about his books being thrown in the pond, Lewis had lain in wait for him one morning last

68

week and bent back his fingers behind a bus shelter. That was why the boy came to school early.

'But not early enough for *him*,' he told Callie.

His name was Toby. He was about ten – no one at home remembered his birthday – but undersized, with weak, skinny legs and a large shaggy head on which his ears stuck out like the handles on a porridge bowl. He was a weird-looking child, like a goblin changeling. Callie hoped she would not get mixed up with him again.

'Don't leave me,' he had said, when she put him into his classroom.

'Oh, look. I only hid you to save my own skin.'

'You live up the hill, don't you?' His pointed, big-eyed face was like a marmoset. 'So do I. What bus do you get home?'

When she told him, he said, 'I'll wait after my last class and go with you.'

'Oh, look.' She did not want to get *mixed up* with this child.

'I'd be safe with you, see?' Sitting at the desk that was too big for him, he had nodded confidently, as if Callie was as big as Betty Rundle, and as bold.

He was waiting for her. He waited every day and chattered by her side on the bus. In the morning, he was on the early bus, with his face unwashed and his socks in holes on his dangling legs, his books on the seat to keep a place for her.

He chattered while she was trying to read, telling her things about his home and his cats and his brothers and sisters who were bigger than he was – even the younger one – because he had been ill.

'They gave me up for dead,' he said cheerfully. 'I heard them say so in the hospital.'

The exam was only two days away. Callie swotted all the time.

'Why are you always reading?' Toby asked her when she only grunted at his twentieth question about the horses at the Farm, which fascinated him.

She told him about the scholarship. 'If I get it, I'll be out of this rotten school next term.'

Toby said nothing. This was so unusual that Callie looked at him. Tears stood in his big eyes, and his mouth drooped at the corners.

Why should she feel guilty? It was her life, not his. But she did. Before they got to the top of the hill, she told him he could get off the bus with her and see the horses.

Steve was very nice to Toby. He picked him up so he could see over the half doors. He took him on his shoulder out to the fields and let him open gates and hold them for horses coming through. When Cobbler's Dream came in, he put a saddle and bridle on him and let Toby ride in the jump field.

On the ground, the child was topheavy and misshapen, but on the pony, he did not look odd at all. He sat well by instinct, held the reins the way he was told, and learned the rhythm of rising after Cobby had trotted carefully round a few times on the lunge rein.

'Never seen anyone get it so quick.'

Toby grinned with his mouthful of bad teeth. When Steve lifted him down, he clung to the chestnut pony's neck, went into the stable with him, pressed his big head to his strong chest while he was eating, and had to be prised away by force for Steve to take him home.

Callie went with them. Toby lived in a tumbledown sort of cottage with thin prowling cats and decrepit vegetables and a collection of rubbish and old cooking pots and broken furniture outside, as if there had been a fire.

His mother came out, holding a baby which was dribbling at the mouth and nose. 'Where the hell have you been?' Her voice began to lash at Toby before he had opened the gate, lifting it creaking on its one hinge.

Steve explained. The mother still looked grim, partly because she had not got her teeth in.

'He can come back any time,' Steve said.

'We'll see,' the mother said ungraciously.

Next morning on the bus, Callie was reading history.

'I hope you get bottom marks in everything,' Toby said.

'I'll die if I do.'

'I'll die if you go away,' he said, not in sorrowing self pity; just as a statement of fact.

When the examination came, it was like preparing a horse for a show. There was a special supper the night before. Callie washed her hair and cut her toenails and went to bed with hot milk. Her mother was up early to cook her a big brain-building breakfast, and everyone came from the stables to say good-bye – 'As if I was going to my execution.'

Toby behaved as if she was. 'This is my worst day,' he kept saying. 'This is the worst bloody day I ever had in my whole life.'

When Callie left him at his classroom, where she always had to take him because of Lewis, she said, 'Wish me luck,' but Toby only looked at her as if she were a traitor.

'Good luck!' Miss Crombie patted her on the back outside the examination room. 'I know you can do well.'

And when Callie saw the first paper, she knew she could too.

Waiting to see exam questions is one of the worst times in life, doomed, sick, your brain empty of everything you ever learned. The papers are passed out. You turn them over. Your eye scans quickly down and you see, yes, yes, one after the other, things you know, things you have revised, favourite things – two you never heard of, but there's enough choice without them – and then it is your day.

It was Callie's day. She picked up her pen, squared her elbows, smiled at the invigilator, who did not smile back for fear of cheating, and wrote her name beautifully at the top of the beautiful clean paper. *Question No. 1: Name the 6 wives of Henry VIII and say what you know of each.*

Easy, easy. Katherine of Aragon, Anne Boleyn, Jane Seymour, Anne of Cleves, Katherine Howard, Katherine Parr. She knew them backwards in her sleep.

She began to write: '*Katherine of Aragon, Anne Boleyn, Jane Seymour . . .*'

The image of Toby's face, pinched, pale, grubby, the big marmoset eyes and the pointed chin, lay on the white sheet of paper.

'*I'll die if you go away.*'

Callie sighed, crossed out her first words, and began to write again:

'*Katherine Taragon, Ann Seymour, Marie Antoinette, Katherine the Great, Bloody Mary, Katherine Dubarry.*'

No one could understand it. They called it bad luck, an off day, stage fright. Miss Crombie was upset enough even to call her stupid.

'You *knew* most of those questions. They were tailor-made for you.'

'I lost my head.'

'And lost the scholarship.' Miss Crombie was bitterly disappointed.

'I don't really mind. I never did want to go to boarding school.'

'*I* mind,' Miss Crombie said. 'And I mind for your mother.'

'She didn't really want me to go away.'

13

Toby said, 'I knew you wouldn't get it. But I'm glad you didn't.'

Callie did not know whether to be glad or sorry. She had thrown away her chance – but was it worth it? At school, there was not much she could do to help Toby. It was actually worse for him to be the friend of someone whom Lewis hated as much as he hated Callie.

Once when he tripped Toby up in the corridor, Toby managed to bite him as he scrambled up. The Louse had teeth marks on his hand.

Callie saw them, and jeered. 'He's got rabies, didn't you know? Ooh look – you're foaming!' and ran into the crowd.

Toby came quite often to the Farm to ride. Cobby could be a bouncing, jet-propelled handful when Steve got him on his toes to jump, but he was clever enough to know when to take quiet care of a rider. He had once worked for a paralysed girl, walking by himself into a pit so that she could heave herself from her wheel-chair on to his back.

Riding David, Steve took Toby along the top of the hills, through woods and fields and ferny lanes where he had never been before, because his legs would not carry him far. Colour came to his cheeks and his muscles grew stronger. Even his mother, who never admitted optimism, was forced to say that it might be doing him good.

One evening when Callie brought him back to the Farm, he said he could not ride.

'I hurt my hand.' He had it in the pocket of his droopy shorts which were handed down from someone bigger.

'Let's see.' Steve took out the hand.

'Nothing much.'

Steve gently unwound a blood-soaked handkerchief. The nail of one finger was torn off down to the quick.

'Why didn't you go to the nurse?' Anna asked, when she was cleaning the finger and bandaging it.

'I dunno.' He kept his eyes down.

'Did Lewis do that?' Callie asked.

'Who's Lewis?' asked her mother.

'That boy from Pinecrest. You know. The one who is our enemy because of Miss America, and the stable licence. He's Toby's enemy too.'

'Surely he wouldn't do a thing like that to a little boy?' Like her husband, Anna had an enduring faith in human nature, sometimes ill-founded.

The day when he was chased like a small animal, running for his life into the bicycle shed, had taught Toby not to tell tales to grown-ups. But he told Steve how Lewis had caught him on one of the swings and twisted it, jamming his finger between the chains.

Next day, when Steve had finished the morning work in the stables, he went down the hill to the school.

Callie had told him that some of the big boys went down to the end of the playing fields for a smoke after lunch. Steve hid in the bushes, rubbing his knuckles.

Half a dozen boys came down and lounged about for a while, talking in grunts and guffaws, making grubby jokes about the teachers. Steve recognized the Louse's voice, oozing thick and stupid through his adenoids.

Steve crouched, then suddenly leaped out and grappled with him. Surprised, Lewis went down, and they rolled over and over, punching and kicking and scratching and hurting each other in any way they could.

As Steve had expected, the other boys were too yellow to

74

join in. They watched for a while, circling the desperate fight like dogs. Then when Lewis began to scream as Steve was on top of him rubbing his face into the ground, they ran off.

Cursing, his face smeared with earth and blood, Lewis somehow scrambled up. Before he could get away, Steve caught him with a fist on the side of the jaw and the Louse went down like a felled tree.

Steve wiped his face on his sleeve, rubbed off his hands on the grass and ran them over his curly hair. He found a piece of paper in his pocket, and left a scribbled note tucked behind the ear of the snoring boy.

'You want more of the same? Try starting anything else with the little kids.'

14

Nothing happened for a while. The Louse was away from school for the rest of the week. Steve had a scratched face and a lot of bruises and Callie got up very early, did all his stables for him and brought him a mug of tea in bed.

The grey stable cat had three kittens. They were keeping the prettiest one with the Elizabethan ruff of white fur round its face, and a home had been found for the other two at a village grocery whose storeroom needed the protection of this famous family of mousers.

On Sunday evening, Steve put the kittens in a canvas shoulder bag and rode Cobby to the village, trotting along the side of the road in the gathering dusk.

The grocery people insisted on giving him a snack – he was the kind of boy whom women instinctively fed, not to fatten him, but to mother him – and it was almost dark by the time he started for home.

Dark, light, sunlight, grey shadows, it didn't make much difference to the Cobbler with his half sight, especially on a road he knew so well.

He trotted steadily, ears constantly moving, alertly forward, swivelling back, one forward and one back, because he depended so much on his hearing.

Steve rode half dreaming, the empty bag swinging at his hip. He knew the feel of the pony so well that it was almost like the movement of his own body. He sat relaxed, with a loose rein, not bothering to rise to the smooth trot, fancying himself a cowhand, legs stuck out in chaps, shoulders slack, single-footing through the desert sagebrush behind a herd of lowing cattle, going leisurely to the water-hole.

The motor-bike came out of nowhere, with no light. It threw itself at them round a corner and roared by so close that Steve saw the rider's face in the instant before Cobby reared, slipped on the road and came down hard, with Steve underneath.

His leg was pinned under the saddle. The pony struggled, and at last the weight of him lifted and he was up. Steve did not even try to get up. He did not try to move his leg. He was cold and sweating at the same time, with lead in his stomach and a sick spinning head, and he knew that something was badly broken.

He raised his head to try and look at his leg, lying with the foot at a strange angle, then quickly dropped his head on the ground and kept it there until the blood came singing back into his ears and he knew that he would not faint.

In books when a rider lies hurt on the ground, his faithful horse lowers its head, nosing him gently, and he whispers into its ear, 'Go home!'

In life, things don't work out like that. Cobbler's Dream was a few yards away at the side of the road, his foot through the reins, tearing at the long grass as if he had not had a decent meal for weeks.

Steve whistled to him. He moved on, contentedly grazing. It was almost dark now. Steve could barely see the rounded outline of his quarters, moving steadily away.

No cars came by. Steve's leg had been shocked numb at first, but now feeling was coming back, and with it pain. If a car did not stop soon, he would have to start screaming. If the Louse's big brother came back on the motor-bike to see how much damage he had done, he would have to shout to him for help.

Someone must help. Anyone. Help me. 'Cobby!' he shouted, his face in the long grass.

'Who's there?' A high, nervous voice, some way down the road.

'Help!'

A small dog yapped. Feet on the road. Then they stopped – 'Help!' – came on again. Then a hysterical tongue was licking at his face and Steve grabbed the little dog tightly, in a sweat of panic that it would touch his leg.

'What's happened?' A woman walked round and stood in front of him, staring down, her hand in her mouth. She looked in a panic too.

'I've broken my leg.'

The woman gasped and knelt down.

'Don't touch it!' Steve shrieked. She pulled back her hands and got up.

'I'll run back and get help. I live quite near. You stay there,' she added unnecessarily and ran, feet fading down the road, the dog yapping and yipping as if something marvellous had happened.

Steve closed his eyes and began to groan.

He was in a small hospital in the town where the Jordans had lived among the harassing new neighbours. His leg was in plaster to the thigh. It was very uncomfortable, and 'Yes, it does hurt,' he answered to the question that everybody asked.

The Colonel was furious. He was usually easygoing, a peace-maker; but after what Steve told him, he wanted to steam right down to the Pinecrest Hotel and tell soapy Sidney Hammond what he thought of his rotten, vicious, ugly son Todd.

'No, don't.' Steve closed his eyes. It still made his head ache if anyone raised their voice. 'It was an accident.'

'That's not what you told me when you came out of the anaesthetic. You said it was deliberate. He came at you without lights and practically knocked the pony over. He probably did knock him over.'

'He slipped.'

'What difference?' The Colonel picked up his cap and stick. 'I'm going to tell that two-faced swine—'

'Then he'll tell you what I – what I – oh hell. What I did.'

'What did you do?' The Colonel's voice dropped with a sigh from indignation to resigned patience.

'It was a revenge thing. I'd beaten up his younger brother. You know,' he added hopefully, as if he could persuade the Colonel that he had already heard about the fight, and had not minded.

'I thought you weren't going to get into any more fights, Steve.'

'I can't now.' Steve closed his eyes again and lay like a corpse in a coffin. The Colonel put a hand on his forehead and went away.

15

Steve came back from the hospital with his leg still cocooned in the long heavy plaster, scrawled over with messages from the nurses.

'Behave yourself – Cathy.'

'Good luck from Rosalita.'

'Mary Ellen – don't come back.'

'Love always Susie' and a heart with an arrow.

He could move about slowly with crutches. He spent one day sitting in the garden with his radio and various dogs and cats who were glad to find someone sitting still, and Anna bringing him things to eat and drink.

'This is the life,' he told her, but the next day he was out at the stables, trying to do his work again.

'Here, let me.' Dora ran up when she saw him at the outside tap.

'Go away. I am going to be the only man on crutches ever to carry a full bucket of water.'

He settled the crutches under his arms, bent down with difficulty, tried to pick up the bucket and grab the bar of the crutch with the same hand, and lurched forward in a flood of spilled water as Dora caught him just in time.

'Careful.' She propped him up against Ginger's stable. Her face was grave with anxiety, so she quickly smiled. 'That's expensive plaster, you know.'

Gradually Steve found out what he could do. He could carry a feed bucket, hung round his neck on a piece of bailing wire. Then he had to get into a loose box, move the horse out of his way with his shoulder or his voice, prop a crutch against the wall by the manger, unhook the bucket from his neck without the horse getting its nose in and strangling him, and tip the feed into the manger before the greedy horse knocked the bottom of the bucket and scattered the whole lot into its bedding.

He could sweep a bit, and do some grooming, leaning against a quiet horse. He cleaned all the tack, which there hardly ever was time for, and blacked the harness that Cobby wore to pull the blue cart out to the fields. But there was not much more he could do except sit on the old mounting block made out of a milestone (CLXVI miles to Tyburn) and play the guitar to Dora and Callie.

The Shetlands and the donkey had gone back to the children's camp for the summer, and one of the very old horses had died, but five skeletons had come in from the stable of a man who had skipped the country to avoid arrest, and abandoned them. Dora and the Colonel and Slugger had more than they could do.

Steve's plaster would not come off for at least a month, the doctor had said after the last X-ray. So the Colonel rang up the Employment Office and asked for a temporary stable hand.

'I mean a real one. I'd rather have nobody than a damfool girl who gets her big toenail trodden off, or a long-haired layabout who shouts at the horses and goes to sleep in the hay with a lighted cigarette.'

After a few days, Mac turned up. He came in a fairly decent car, but terrible old clothes, a burly man with shaggy hair and a grizzle of growing beard, some age past forty.

'I'm looking for work.' He came rather shyly into the yard. 'They told me to come here.'

'Know anything about horses?'

'Not much.'

'Like 'em?'

'I guess so.' He was American.

'Worked with them before?'

A pause. '*Uh*-huh. But I can learn.'

'References?'

The man smiled and shrugged his shoulders. Under the hair, he had a weathered face, craggy, with the kind of thoughtful, clear-sighted eyes made for scanning far horizons, or searching a face. The Colonel liked the look of him and took him on.

In his dirty old trousers and his yellow-grey sweater that had once been white, pulled out of shape, with loops of thick wool hanging, Mac went straight to work helping with the evening feeds.

There was a storm coming up. You could see it far down the valley, rolling blackly towards the hills, so all the horses were brought in.

Mac pitched hay and carried water buckets, doing what he was told, not asking any questions, not answering any about himself, quiet with the horses, though he seemed to know nothing about them. When Dora said, 'Two on that side need water – the grey and the roan. Know what a roan is?' he thought for a moment, then smiled. 'Sorry.'

When he smiled, his broad tanned cheekbones lifted and his eyes narrowed to a grey glint.

'It's a sort of reddish speckled—' Dora looked at him sharply. 'I've seen you somewhere before.'

Mac shook his head. He had hay seeds in his hair and beard. 'Only in your dreams.'

'What do you think of him?' Dora asked Slugger Jones, as he was leaving for his cottage across the road.

'What do I think? she asks. I seen 'em come, I seen 'em go. Mostly I seen 'em go.'

'I hope Mac stays.'

'Call me Mac, he says, coming out of nowhere. I seen 'em come, I seen 'em go,' Slugger grumbled to no one in particular, clicked his knotted fingers for his terrier and ambled through the archway.

When the work was done, Dora took Mac round to all the loose boxes and told him the names and stories of the horses.

'Cobbler's Dream.' Everyone started with Cobbler's Dream in the corner box. He was so striking, with his bright white blaze, his head always over the door, watching, demanding attention, chewing his hay now, and dribbling it into the yard. Mac picked up the bunch of hay and gave it back to him. Cobby turned his head to observe him with his good eye.

'He was hit in the head,' Dora said. 'Spoiled, stinking brat with a whip. He used to be a champion show jumper. Still could be, even though he can't see much. But we don't go to shows.'

'Why not?'

'We're not good enough. We couldn't afford the clothes anyway. And – oh, I don't know. A horse doesn't mind showing off, but having to perform perfectly, dead to order, our idea not his . . .'

'Maybe he likes it.'

'How do we know?' Dora looked up at him. 'We say a horse loves to jump because he gets all excited, but perhaps he's only nervous. Look at this one – Wonderboy. He belonged to Callie's father, who died. He loved to race, they said, but how do we *know*?'

Mac went 'Hm' into his beard. Dora wondered if she was being a bore.

'I'd love to know what Spot thought about the circus.' She showed Mac the broad-backed apaloosa. 'Three fat ladies in silver wigs and spangled tights danced on him at once, the

Colonel says, though I don't know how he knows, because he won't go to the circus. Anna, his wife, took Callie once and they saw Hero.' She took him across the yard to the brown, ewe-necked horse that Callie had saved. 'His rider was forcing him to lie down, and pulling his head so far round that he couldn't, and then beating him when he didn't. So Callie stole him.'

'How did she get away with that?'

Mac seemed interested. Perhaps he – perhaps he was a thief too? He would tell nothing about himself. On the run? Incognito? The beard looked fairly new and the car was too good for the clothes. If he had stolen that, he'd better get it away from the road.

She showed him the four newcomers – the fifth had had to be destroyed yesterday – the pitiful thin horses which had been abandoned, tied by the head and helplessly starving.

'The owner was some sort of underworld gambling type, who had bought this big house and the horses to make himself look respectable in the neighbourhood. He left in a hurry, he—'

She stopped dead, staring at Mac. What if he—? The thought was into her head and out again in a fraction of a second. She laughed.

'What's so funny?' Mac was frowning at the black horse with the wound on its bony head, shoulders hunched in the awful sweater.

'Fantastic things one thinks.'

'Such as?'

Dora always said what she was thinking. 'I thought for a second, what if you were that man?'

'What would you do?'

'Kill you, I suppose. The halter on this horse was so tight that it was embedded in the flesh. The vet had to cut it out under anaesthetic. Even if it heals, he'll have a dent in his head for ever, like a fossil. All the horses had halter sores. They had nothing to eat. They had chewed all the wood within reach. The one we put down yesterday had started to bite at her own chest.'

'It's unbelievable,' Mac said.

'It's true.'

Dora showed him Fanny, with an empty socket where a drunken gipsy had knocked out her eye, and Ranger and Prince, whose mouths had been cut to bits by the gangs of 'Night Riders', with wire for a bridle. She showed him Pussycat, who had broken down on her way from Scotland to London with a petition for the Queen, the brewery horse and the old police horse and ugly Ginger, who used to have a milk round before the dairy went motorized.

'They were going to put him down, but all the ladies in one street clubbed together and bought him. They call him Peregrine. They think he's beautiful. Do you?'

'I wouldn't know one horse from another,' Mac said.

Heavy drops began to fall out of the sky like lead pellets. The sky blacked over at great speed, like the end of the world. Dora shook back her short hair and stuck out for her underlip to catch the rain. Mac pulled up the collar of his bulky sweater and lowered his beard into it.

Anna ran out, with a coat over her head. 'Come on in!' she called. 'Come in and have some supper,' she told Mac.

'Thanks,' he said. 'I'll get something. I have to go find a room.'

'You can stay here.'

'Thanks.' He backed away. 'I'll be O.K..'

The rain suddenly came down like a waterfall. He ran, splashing to his car.

Anna ran with Dora back to the house.

'What's he afraid of?'

'I don't know,' Dora said. 'I don't think we'll see him again.'

16

He was back in the morning.

He worked steadily and well. He came on time. He left late if there were extra things to do. He became part of the Farm.

After a while, he gave up his lodgings and came to live in the little room behind the tack room.

There was room for him at the farmhouse, or across the road with Slugger Jones and his wife, but he preferred the stuffy little room, which was built into one side of the stone arch, and smelled of leather and horse nuts and his pipe tobacco, and the soups and stews and beans he cooked up on a small stove.

Anna would gladly have fed him, but he wanted to be alone. He was nervous among a lot of people. When visitors came, he got busy in the barn or out in the fields. Sometimes he talked to Steve or Dora or Callie, telling very little about himself, and that little different each time.

He said he had been in gaol, been in the Army, been at sea, been to Australia, lost everything in a flood, lived under the ice in the Antarctic for two years. He threw out bizarre bits of information as if he did not expect to be believed, and nobody believed him.

He still said he knew nothing about horses, but he was naturally good with them, and seemed to like being with them better than people. The Colonel thought he might have been a ranch hand once. There were days when he walked like a cowboy, and when it rained he wore an old hat he found in the barn, tipped over his eyes like a ten-gallon Stetson.

Besides the car, he did not seem to own much. He had very few clothes, a few paperback books, but no photographs. No pictures at all of anybody who belonged to him.

'Haven't you ever been married?' Callie asked him. She and Toby were the only ones who were allowed to come into his room. When the evenings were cool, he sometimes lit a fire in the smoky fireplace and cooked something marvellous in a black iron pot – beans and sausages and molasses and onions and hot pepper ketchup with beer poured in on top. It was much better than supper at the house. They sat on the floor and ate out of the pot.

'Like in the Wild West,' Toby said. 'Was you ever out West, Mac?'

'Listen kid, I been everywhere.' He always said something like that, to stop a question.

'What was it like?'

'Like everything else – loused up.' He always said something like that too.

While they were eating the marvellous beans, he would drink whisky out of a tin mug, and afterwards he would lie down on the low sagging bed and go to sleep. He slept for hours. They had never known a man sleep so much.

Lancelot, an ancient rickety skewbald who had been saved from the fate of being shipped abroad for slaughter, was the oldest horse in the stable. The Colonel judged him about thirty. When Dora or Steve showed him to visitors, they always added a few years to make the people gasp and give him extra sugar. 'Ah, the poor old thing!'

'What's poor about him?' This always disgusted Slugger. 'Life of Riley, he's got. Nothing to do but eat and sleep and make a big mess in his manger.'

You always had to look in Lancelot's corner manger before you tipped in his feed. His front end was fairly strong, but like most old horses, he was getting weak in the loins, so he sat on his wooden manger.

One night the manger went.

Steve, lying stiffly in bed in his uncomfortable plaster cast, heard a splintering crash from the stable. It sounded as if a tree had fallen through the roof.

By the time he had lifted his heavy leg to the floor and groped for his crutches under the bed, the upstairs corridor of the farmhouse was full of running feet. When he got out to the stables they were all there – the Colonel, Anna, Dora and Callie, pulling and pushing at Lancelot who was sitting on the floor like a dog, with his brown and white tail fanned out among the wreckage of his manger.

They finally got him to his feet, where he stood trembling like an old man with ague.

'Once more down like that, and he won't get up,' the Colonel said. 'I'll get Mac to fix a bar across the corner. He can sit on that.'

'Where is Mac?' Steve was leaning on his crutches in the doorway, hating to be only a spectator.

'Fast asleep.' Callie had looked through his cobwebby window. 'The whole place could burn down before he'd know it.'

The surgeon at the local hospital was worried about Steve's last X-rays. The leg did not seem to be mending properly, and he wanted Steve to go to London for a specialist's advice about another operation.

'Over my dead body,' Steve said. 'I'm not going through *that* again.'

'You want to limp for the rest of your life, like me?' the Colonel asked.

'Doesn't seem to bother you.'

'And stiffen up and have to stop riding?' The Colonel had been marvellous in his military days, riding for the Army in international shows, working one year with an Olympic team.

'That damn Toad.' When Steve thought about Todd Hammond and what he had done, he burned with rage, and the palms of his hands sweated with the desire to take him by his stringy throat. 'I should have crippled his lousy little brother. I will too when I get my leg back.'

'I'll drive you to London,' the Colonel said.

Anna went with them, and Callie begged to miss two days of school, so that she could go too.

School was a farce anyway. She had studied so hard for the scholarship exam that the muscles of her mind could not cope with revising for end-of-term exams.

Miss Crombie was very disappointed in her. 'You've gone off,' she said, as if Callie were sour milk.

'What'll I do for two days without you?' Toby put on his pathetic face, eyes very large, mouth drooping, those big bat ears sticking out at right angles.

'Dora is going to take you for a ride.'

Dora was going to ride with him over to the park of the deserted Manor house to show him the famous spiked iron fence which Cobbler's Dream had once so heroically jumped. They started off that evening as the others were leaving for London.

Steve hugged Cobby round his strong arched neck and said good-bye to him, as he always did before he went anywhere. He got into the back of the car with Callie, stowing his clumsy leg away with difficulty, wincing.

Dora and Toby rode out through the archway, Toby with

his head up and his back straight, short legs very correct, his small triangular face split by the smile that would not leave it until he scrambled down at the end of the ride.

'Take care of the Cobbler, Tobe!' Steve leaned out of the car window.

'He's supposed to take care of Toby,' Dora said. 'You care more about that horse than anyone.'

'Why not? He cares more about *me* than anyone else does.'

'Fishing.' Callie pulled Steve back inside, the Colonel crunched his gears in a way almost impossible to do with this car, and they drove away.

Mac was going to drive his car to the park of the Manor house.

'If you'd only learn to ride,' Dora said, 'you could come with us.'

'I'd be too scared.'

'You could ride Willy. Anyone can ride a mule.'

'Except me.'

He followed them slowly in the car along the switchback road at the top of the hill, past the racecourse where some men were staking out enclosures for the point-to-point meeting, and then he went ahead to open the cattle hurdles across the Manor drive so that they could ride in the park.

Because he was watching, Dora showed off a bit with David: slow canters and figure-of-eights with a flying change of lead, turns on the forehand and what she thought was a turn on the quarters. David was well schooled, but he needed a lot of leg and a lot of flexible collection. His figure-of-eights were fast and wide and he was not always on the right lead, but Mac would not know that.

'You see?' Dora pulled the grey horse up in front of Mac. 'It's easy. Isn't he a great horse?'

'Except that he don't always change leads in back as well as in front.'

'How do you know?' He wasn't supposed to have seen that. 'I thought you didn't know anything about riding.'

'Oh, I don't.' Mac had his head under Toby's saddle flap, tightening the girth. 'I guess I read it in a book. I read where it said you should use a lot more outside leg.'

'Well, you read it *wrong*.' Dora pulled David round. Steve was always telling her she did not use enough leg, but she was not going to hear it from Mac, who didn't know what he was talking about.

She took Toby down to the bottom slope of the park where the terrible fence stuck out above the brambled undergrowth, a ditch on the take off, a drop on the other side into the road.

The leader of the Night Riders, trying to escape capture, had ridden Cobby at this impossible jump, not caring if he impaled the pony on the rusty spikes.

Toby and Mac looked at the wicked fence with reverence.

'I could jump that, I bet,' Toby swaggered, but without conviction.

Mac said, 'You'd be crazy to try.'

They went back through the gate to the other side of the fence, where Cobby's rider had fallen and been caught unconscious, with the side of his face split open.

'On that very patch of stones,' Dora said. 'If you look, you can probably still find some teeth.'

Toby got off immediately to look. They let him search for a few minutes, scrabbling among the stones like a miniature grave robber, but it was getting late, so Mac lifted him on to the pony and they went home.

After seeing the jump, which had become a famous legend and was known among local people as Cobbler's Leap, Toby was prouder of the pony than ever. Dora let him unsaddle him and feed him by himself, and he stayed in the loose box, brushing and fussing and trying to whistle through his teeth like Slugger, while Dora and Mac finished the other horses.

When Dora looked over the door, Cobby was still eating.

'How much did you give him? He should be done by now.'

'Just a tiny bit extra.' Toby measured a small gap with the thumb and finger of his birdlike hand. 'Because he was so good.' At home, Toby did not get enough to eat, so to him, feeding was loving.

'Not too much, I hope.' Dora did not go in to check. Toby raised his arms and she lifted him easily over the half-door and carried him out to the car because he was tired.

Cobby went on eating.

17

When they came back from the cottage, Dora felt she had to ask Mac, 'Do you want to come up to the house?' It seemed odd for her to be alone there with all the food, and Mac alone in his little room with perhaps bread and cheese, which was sometimes all he had.

'*Uh*-huh,' he said, and she wished she hadn't asked him. 'I'm going to have a drink and go to bed. I'm bushed. You want a shot of Scotch?'

Dora said, 'No, I hate it,' and felt childish. It would have been more sophisticated to try and drink it.

Her mother had always insisted, 'Have a glass of wine. Learn to drink at home.' Last time Dora went home, her father gave her a glass of water that turned out to be vodka. Dora had been sick.

She went to bed early too, and saw Mac's light go out as she passed the staircase window.

She was woken out of her first deep sleep by a noise from the stables. Banging and thumping, hooves against wood. She sat up. Better go out. What was the good of Mac sleeping out there if he never heard the horses? Poor old Lancelot would have sat all night in the ruins of his manger before Mac woke.

Dora pulled a sweater over her pyjamas and trod into her frayed gym shoes. When she ran out of the back door and down the path, she saw that the lights were on in one block of the stables.

Mac was in Cobby's corner box. The pony was down and groaning, swinging his head about, kicking out at the wall.

'Colic.' Dora went quickly inside.

'Yeah. We've got to get him up.' Mac had a halter on the pony and was tugging at his head. 'Come on, boy – hup, hup! Come on – get up there! Here Dora, you pull this end, I'll try and heave behind.'

They struggled, pushing and pulling, but the distressed pony was as heavy as the great brewery horse.

'I thought you never woke,' Dora panted.

'Couldn't sleep. My past catching up on me. Good thing. If this jughead don't get up, he'll twist his gut and we'll lose him. Try the broom.'

Without questioning why Mac seemed all of a sudden to know what to do, Dora ran for a broom and poked Cobby in the side with the bristle end, trying to shift him. The pony groaned and swung his head round, bumping his nose against his distended stomach.

'Yes, *I know*,' Dora gasped. 'I know what's wrong.' She jabbed hard and the pony snapped at the broom, drawing back his nose from his bared teeth. 'If anything happens to you, Steve will – oh Cobby, get *up*!'

'Move over.' Mac pulled back his foot to kick the pony in the ribs.

'No!' Dora kicked Mac herself. 'Don't you know his stomach is full of gas? Don't you know *anything*?'

'Not much,' Mac said mildly. He went out of the box.

All right, she had kicked him. He wasn't much use anyway. She went on tugging at the rope in a hopeless kind of frenzy. Cobby would die. Steve would come back and Dora would tell him about Toby and the feed. Her fault, her fault. She began to scream at the pony, half sobbing.

'Here, let's try something else in his ear besides yelling.'

Mac was in the box, crouching in the straw beside Cobby's head, which was held out rigid, his jaw set against the tug of the halter rope.

'Hold him like that – tight.' Mac had a tin mug in his hand. He caught hold of Cobby's ear and quickly poured something into it. In a moment, Cobby was up, struggling and staggering, tossing his head and agitating his ear, furious, distressed, distended – but standing up.

'Warm coffee.' Mac emptied the mug into the bedding. 'Learned that from an old horse thief out in Nevada.'

For the rest of the night, they took turns walking Cobby in the yard. He was no better. They had to keep him moving. When Dora telephoned the vet, his wife said he was out with a foaling mare. He would come as soon as he could. No idea how long.

They had tried everything. Colic drench. Liquid paraffin. Huge dose of aspirin in Coca Cola, most of which went down Dora's sleeves as she held up the pony's head. When he would not walk, she went behind him with a broom. He was still in pain, nipping, cow kicking, swinging his head about like a club. He would lie down if they let him.

'Will he die?' Dora had accepted that Mac really did know what he was doing.

'Maybe.'

'We can't – oh Mac, *do* something!'

'Try one more thing.' He gave her the rope and ran across the yard to his room. When he came out, he had one of his flat pint bottles of whisky wrapped round with sticking plaster.

'Hang on to him. Don't want to lose any of this.' They backed Cobby into a corner, Dora got hold of his tongue, and Mac poured all the whisky down his throat.

18

When Steve came back, Cobby was his old self. The whisky had begun to shift the painful blockage in his intestines almost at once.

'Mac saved his life.' Dora said. 'Why did he pretend to know nothing about horses?'

'Perhaps he was a groom, and got sacked for drinking.'

After the heroic night, Dora tried to get the lonely man to talk to her.

'If you can talk about things, they aren't half so bad,' she said.

'They aren't bad,' Mac said. 'Go away Dora, there's a good kid, and leave me alone.'

'At least come for a ride. Do you good. I don't believe any more that you can't ride.'

'I don't want good done to me. I want to be let alone.'

'I came to see if you wanted to go to the cinema.'

'You joking?'

'Why?'

'I already told you. I hate the movies.'

'There's an old Cosmo Spence film on. He's good.'

'Big deal.'

Dora went to the cinema with Callie and they sat through a rather dated film made several years ago, about a Centurion of ancient Rome who rode thousands of miles bareback, looking for his girl friend who was carried off by barbarian hordes. As usual in a Cosmo Spence film, the horse part was the best. He rode a big creamy Arab and performed incredible feats of horsemanship.

'He does all the riding,' Callie whispered to Dora in the dark. 'No stunt man.'

'How do you know?'

'I read it in a magazine. That's how he got famous. After all, he's not that good at acting. You don't need to be if you look like that, the magazine said.'

'You don't need to be if you can ride like that.' Dora watched the screen enviously.

The last point-to-point of the season was late this year, because there had been epidemics of coughing in several stables.

Part of the course was over Mr Beckett's land. He went wild if one of the Colonel's horses was on his property, but the races were different. He got paid, and they didn't go over his vegetables or his seedling fir trees.

At one point, the course ran past the Farm's bottom pasture. You could sit on the fence and get a grandstand view of the horses coming over the brushwood jump at the top of the hill, galloping down to make the turn at the flag, then slowing through the plough to the stone wall, and on to the turf again and out of sight behind the wood. After the second time round, you could run up the hill, through the hedges where the first two jumps were, and into the crowd along the main part of the course to see the finish.

It rained all day. It always did. This course was known as The Bog. But everyone at the Farm went to the races, except Mac, who had begun to drive off somewhere in his free time instead of staying in his room and sleeping.

He had been gone every afternoon last week. They thought he had a girl friend, but no one knew who or where, and no one asked him.

After the second race, Callie and the Colonel stayed at the top of the hill to see the next lot of horses come into the paddock. None of them were special, except a big bay who walked with his groom as if he owned the ring of turf, catching at his snaffle, tail swinging, splendid muscles moving under his shining hide.

'That horse of Dixon's looks well,' the Colonel said. 'I think I'll put something on him.'

'Don't waste your money, Brigadier.'

He turned and saw smiling Sidney Hammond at his elbow, all his teeth on show, a sporty black and white check cap pulled over one eye to make him look like a shrewd judge of horse-flesh.

'That liver chestnut there. That's the one.'

'That weed? It couldn't run water.'

'Make no mistake, Brigadier.' Mr Hammond winked with the eye that was not covered by the check cap. 'You've got to know the inside story on these nags.'

'I do, with a lot of them,' the Colonel started to say, but Mr Hammond had taken his race card and was marking horses in other races that 'couldn't lose'.

To get away from him, they left before the jockeys came into the paddock. As they went towards the line of bookies under their dripping coloured umbrellas, Callie said, 'If he did know anything, he'd give you all the duds.'

'He seems friendly enough.'

'Make no mistake, Brigadier.' Callie looked up at him and winked. 'He'd put you out of business, if he could. The Louse said so, and I believe it.'

They went back to the pasture fence and watched the big field of horses come over the thick brush fence in a bunch, riders leaning back for the drop on the slope of the hill.

Blue with white cross, red and yellow spots, orange with green sleeves and cap. The colourful thunder of them was gone too quickly, crowding round the flag and spattering away through the sticky plough.

'Dixon's horse is going well.' The Colonel had his field glasses up. 'Anyone else have anything on him?'

No one answered. They were all staring after the horses.

'I said, "Anyone—".' The horses disappeared over the wall and behind the wood. The Colonel lowered his glasses and looked round. 'What's the matter?'

'Didn't you see?' Callie spoke at last. 'That man on the weedy liver chestnut, with the gold jacket and blue cap?'

'It fell back there, through the plough. I knew in the paddock, it—'

'But didn't you see? It was Mac.'

When the field came round the second time, Mac was far behind, the liver chestnut black with sweat, nostrils wide and scarlet. It heaved itself through the brush rather than jumped, landed with its head low, and was held together cleverly by Mac's hands and balance.

When he got to the plough, he pulled up and turned the horse. He rode slowly back, reins loose, slumped in the tiny racing saddle in the gold jacket that was too tight for him, the blue silk-covered helmet clamping down his thick hair, the chin strap round his beard. He looked more like a trick motor-cyclist than a jockey.

'Hi there,' he said, as he came nearer.

'Good race,' the Colonel said politely, 'as far as it went.'

'He's not half fit, but this friend of mine had a good sale for him if he ran well. Broke his collar bone last week and couldn't ride, so he asked me to help out. Some help.'

'He's not a stayer,' the Colonel said, 'but you got him farther than most people could.'

Mac laughed. 'I was practically carrying him.'

They were having an ordinary horsey conversation as if nothing strange had happened.

99

With his tacky old raincoat over his muddy borrowed silks and boots, Mac came up to the house for a long hot bath. He stayed for supper, but left before the end of the meal. He did not say any more about the race, and no one asked him, although they were bursting with the need to ask him many things.

When he had gone, the Colonel said, 'You know, he does look slightly familiar, under all that face foliage. He rides like an old hand. Perhaps he's a trainer, who got ruled off for dope or something.'

'I think he's had some tragedy.' Anna said, 'and has come here to forget.'

'Perhaps he's a murderer,' Dora suggested.

'A spy,' said Steve, and Callie said, 'Perhaps he fell out of a train and lost his memory.'

Mac did his work. What difference did it make?

Except that now that they knew he could ride, he started to ride David. He worked with him every day, schooling him in the jump field, while Dora and Callie and Steve watched and marvelled at what he could do with the grey horse.

'It will add a hundred pounds to his price.' The Colonel was delighted. 'I'm glad I waited to sell him.' Though he would have sold David long ago if Steve and Dora had let him. 'I'm going to start talking about him to some of the dressage people. We should get a really good price for him.'

'Couldn't we possibly . . .' Mac was giving Dora some lessons and David was beginning to go well for her too.

'I need the money,' the Colonel said, 'for these other horses who need us.'

'. . . just for the summer?'

'The barn roof has got to be repaired. I can't afford to keep him.'

19

The Colonel was always hard up. The Home of Rest for Horses was run mostly on gifts of money. Even the people who paid something to keep their old horses here did not pay enough. Sidney Hammond had not paid a penny for Miss America, who was still at the Farm and growing quite fat and leisurely on a life of good grass and no work, a big welt of scar tissue still disfiguring her back.

The price of feed and hay and bedding went up every year. Repairs were expensive. All the gutters needed replacing; they dripped rivulets down hairy old heads stuck out into the rain. The new barn roof would cost far more than the sale of David would bring.

The Colonel would soon have to talk to the Finance Committee. He hated to do that as much as they hated having to hear him.

And so when the continuity girl walked into the yard one day and asked the Colonel if he would ride in the Battle of Marston Moor for a historical film they were shooting locally, the Colonel could have cried, because of the money she offered.

He laughed instead. 'Me? Ride down the side of a gravel pit and jump a stream with a wounded man across my saddle? Good God, no. It would kill me.'

'But I heard you were the finest rider round here. Olympic team and all that.'

'Oh, I could ride a bit in my day.' The Colonel screwed up the side of his face, as he did when he was embarrassed into modesty. 'But that's long gone. Damn knee's too stiff. Look at it.' He bent his lame leg as far as it would go. 'Not much more movement in it than that boy.' He nodded at Steve on his crutches, playing hopscotch in the yard with Callie.

The plaster cast was slightly bent at the knee, so that he could sit. He had found that he could sit on Cobbler's Dream, with the plaster leg stuck out with no stirrup. Since the London specialist had said that he thought it would mend without another operation, Steve was taking more chances with it.

'Oh hell.' The continuity girl was small and dark, with a lively manner and bright black eyes. She looked Italian, but her name was Joan Jones. 'I'm sorry.'

'So am I,' said the Colonel. 'I could have paid half my next winter's hay bill.'

'And we could have finished our outdoor shooting this week. We've been on location too long already. We've got to get the battle scenes done before the weather breaks.'

'Marston Moor?'

'Sixteen forty-four.' Callie had hopped over to listen.

'First defeat of the Royalists,' Joan Jones said, to show she also knew a thing or two. 'Michael Fox, who plays Prince Rupert of the Rhine, he's in command of King Charles' men, and when they're routed by Cromwell and that lot, there's no one to rescue this wounded Cavalier, so Rupert does this great bit on the horse to save him.'

'And breaks his own neck,' the Colonel said.

'No.' Callie had studied the Civil War for the scholarship exam. 'Rupert lived for years after they cut off Charles the First's head.'

'You should have told the stunt man that,' Joan Jones said. 'The first time we tried it, he fell off and cracked two ribs and dropped the Cavalier into the water.'

'You didn't tell me you'd tried it,' the Colonel said.

'I wasn't going to until you said you'd do it. We've got just the right place, over the other side of the valley, that marvellous stretch of bleak moorland, and the sudden sheer drop into the quarry. It looks twice as high and steep from where we've got the camera.'

Mac had been working with David in the field behind the stables. He came round the side of the barn, the horse walking relaxed and limber, the man moving easily to David's long swinging stride.

As he came into the yard, one of the puppies ran at him from nowhere, yapping under his feet. David shied violently, and whipped round to bolt off with his head up.

Mac hardly moved in the saddle, just shifted his weight slightly back and somehow controlled the horse and turned him quietly round without appearing to do anything.

'My God.' The continuity girl was standing in the yard, staring at him with her mouth open and her black eyes astonished. 'Cosmo Spence.'

'What? That's one of my staff,' the Colonel said. 'Mac – bring the horse over here.'

'He's the living spit of Cosmo Spence. Same build. The eyes. The lazy, insolent way he sits a horse. Take off the hair and beard and I'd have sworn . . .'

'I've doubled for him,' Mac said, 'in my movie days. I was supposed to look like him, but I think that's an insult to me.'

'He did all his own stunts,' Joan Jones said.

'Says who? He had a good publicity man.' Mac grinned, his teeth very white through the grizzled beard. 'I done a lot of riding for him, back in the States.'

'Was it *you*,' Callie said, 'in *Angel on Horseback*, where the Centurion jumped right over that cart with the oxen and through the tent and out the other side?'

'Yup.'

'And in *Calgary Stampede*, where he was the only one who

could ride the black horse? And in *Blue Ribbon*, where he's jumping against the clock and the flashbulb goes off and the horse crashes through the barrier?' Callie had seen nearly all the Cosmo Spence films.

'Uh-huh. I cracked my ankle doing that, and they had to lift me on and off.'

'Listen,' the continuity girl said excitedly, 'you want to make some big money?'

Mac shook his head. He was not interested in money. He would not even let the Colonel pay him overtime when he worked in the evening, painting doors.

'Pity.' She turned away. 'The Colonel could have used that money, even if you couldn't.'

'What would I have to do?'

'One day's work.' She whipped round at once. 'Ride for Michael Fox. Prince Rupert of the Rhine at the Battle of Marston Moor. Long curly hair and a suit of armour and those floppy boots. The Mad Cavalier, they called him.'

'Michael Fox, that jerk.' Sitting on David, Mac spat on the ground, a bad habit he had picked up in his Western days. 'He couldn't play a Cavalier, sane *or* crazy. Why give a part like that to a guy who can't ride a bicycle, let alone a horse? Why didn't you get Cosmo?'

'Didn't you hear? He had a breakdown. Very bad. His wife walked out on him, and he was drinking. He's washed up, I'm afraid.'

'You are Cosmo Spence, aren't you?' Steve and Dora and Callie had forced their way into Mac's room with a bowl of Anna's chicken soup – rice and celery and onions and big chunks of chicken. You could almost eat it with a fork. They came in quickly before he could stop them, and stood with their backs to the door so that he could not open it and throw them out.

'What do you think?'

'I knew all along,' Callie tried, then shook her head. 'No, I didn't. But when we saw that film, it bothered me all the time. He looked familiar, Cosmo did. I mean, more than just from other films.'

'If I was Cosmo Spence,' Dora said, 'I'd want everyone to know it.'

'That's just it.' He – Mac – Cosmo – sat on the edge of his bed and ate the soup out of the bowl, with the spoon handle sticking up into the side of his beard. 'Too many people *did* know. And they get sick of you.'

' "All these new kids coming up." My agent used to call me every day, long distance, collect, Hollywood to New York – wherever I was. "You got to get a new image. You've got to get another big part or you'll be finished." '

He put the bowl down on the floor, wiped his mouth on a dirty towel and threw it into a corner. 'Television. That stupid Western series with the fat guy and the little black kid, and I'd done three movies in a row that were all stinkers. I was so goddam tired. My wife stayed in New York. She never came on location with me. I rang her every day. I was lonely. I had all those phoney friends, but no one really but Elsa, after our – well, we had a little girl, but she died.'

No one said anything. He had never talked before. Now it seemed as if he could not stop.

'It wasn't the babysitter's fault.' He ran his strong hands through his beard and his thick hair, and dropped them, slapping the edge of the bed. 'We went to a party. She suffocated in her crib. I never went to any more parties after that. I'd never liked them anyway. Horses were the only thing. I had ten one time when I lived in Wyoming. That was – oh,

I don't know – one time when Elsa left me. She always came back after a bit, and we'd start over.

'Then I came over here to talk about a part my agent wanted me to do – lousy part, jolly coaching days, in capes and beaver hats, I'd have looked like hell – and Elsa wrote she'd gone to Mexico for a divorce. I cracked up. All shot to pieces. Nervous breakdown, you know?'

He looked up at them. Standing by the door, they nodded, although they did not know what it must be like to have the very fibres of your being snap, so that you could not cope with yourself, or anyone else.

'Every time I had to talk to anyone, I cried. Hotel clerk, taxi driver – God damnedst thing you ever saw. They were going to put me in a clinic. I ducked off, got on a train to somewhere, got me – room – I didn't even know what town I was in – hid from everybody and let my hair and beard grow, and didn't surface until I was flat broke.'

'Was that when you came here?' Dora asked.

'Yeah. I'd gone to the Employment Office to get work as a builder's labourer, or something, but someone said "Horses", so I scooted straight up here. Glad I did.' He grinned at them.

'Has it – I mean – has it helped?'

'You bet. I think I'm beginning to be real again. I think I'm beginning to be real for the first time in years.'

'Mr Spence, would you mind,' Callie asked politely, 'if we went on calling you Mac?'

He laughed. 'Finest thing I ever heard.'

20

When Mac saw the gravel quarry that the film director wanted him to ride down, carrying a limp man, and when he saw the common grey horse he was to ride, he said, 'Nothing doing. Not on that clumsy screw.'

'The stunt man took him down O.K.'

'And fell off into the stream, man. They told me.'

'It's the best horse we've got. It's trained.'

'I got one back home is better trained. I got one will go anywhere with me, *and* stay up on four feet.'

'Bring it over tomorrow, and we'll retake the close-ups with Michael.'

The Colonel said No. 'Not David. It sounds too tricky. Never mind about the money. It's not worth the risk.'

'There's no risk. I've had him down banks steeper than that. He's as surefooted as a cat. And the stream – I wouldn't have gone near it on that plug they produced, but David isn't scared of water. He'll jump big, and he'll jump clean.'

'Carrying a man across the saddle?'

'It's a little guy. I've seen him. And the armour is made of aloominum. Light as a feather.'

'I don't know.' The Colonel chewed at the skin round his nails. 'It's too far to ride over there anyway, and Steve can't drive.'

'Mac can drive the horse box,' Steve said. 'I want to take the Cobbler.'

'What for?'

'They need some more Cavaliers in retreat. Duke of Newcastle's Yorkshire White-Coats.'

'With a broken leg in plaster.'

'I'll have armour and a big boot over it. They used to ride with their legs stuck out anyway. I get eleven pounds. I'll put it in the collection box.'

'Don't bribe me.'

But the Colonel eventually agreed to let Mac take David, if they wrapped his legs. They took the ankle boots that old Flame used to wear because she knocked her fetlocks with the opposite hoof, and the wardrobe people painted them grey to look like bits of armour.

David also wore an armoured breastplate, jointed armour over his mane, like the back of a shrimp, and another piece over his forehead. The bridle and reins were of wide coloured leather, studded with bright metal. When he stood on the high ground at the top of the quarry, with his head up and his long tail blowing, he did look like a seventeenth-century battle charger. Mac, in armour and boots, with a glossy wig, his moustache curled and his beard greased into a point, looked like a Cavalier.

'But he still looks like Cosmo Spence.' Joan Jones was in the group by the cameras.

'In his better days,' someone said. 'Poor old Cosmo. He's had it completely, I hear.'

'I heard he was dead,' the cameraman said.

The wounded Cavalier, a resigned young man with a chestnut wig and a Vandyke beard, lay on the lip of the quarry, his helmet gone, his face carefully bloodied with panchromatic make-up. The cameras were placed so that as Mac galloped across them, it would not show that he was not Michael Fox, who had already climbed awkwardly on David for a close-up of the start of the heroic ride. Mac was on the horse now, nudging him with his legs and holding him in lightly, to keep him on his toes.

'Action!'

Standing on the roof of the horse box in the road, Callie and Dora and Toby watched Mac wheel David, as Michael Fox had done, make him come up a bit in front, then trample, then off at a hand gallop that would look faster when they ran the film.

Behind him rode a group of Cromwell's Ironsides. The wounded boy lay like a dead doll on the edge of the quarry. The steep drop below him was the only way of escape.

Mac brought David to a stop with all four feet together at what would look like the very edge of the quarry. He vaulted off, heaved the young man on to the front of the saddle, jumped on behind him, and glancing back at his grim pursuers, he pushed David over the edge and slid him down sitting back on his quarters.

They jumped down the last part where the slope levelled out. The stream at the bottom had firm banks, and with his arm round the boy, Mac gave David three strides and he was over, just as he had said, big and clean, and galloping off over the moor to where a scattered band of White-Coats waited at the foot of the low hills.

On the crest of the hill, in silhouette, a boy on a chestnut pony waved a plumed hat to cheer him on, his leg in the plaster cast stuck out on the side away from the camera

Long afterwards, when the film was finally released, Dora and Callie saw it every day for a week.

David was superb, although you couldn't see much of Mac, because when Michael Fox found out it was Cosmo Spence, he made them cut out the bits of film that showed his face.

But on the skyline, Cobbler's Dream was unmistakable, with his head up to the wind and his long mane streaming from his crested neck. On his back, the young Cavalier stood slightly askew in one stirrup, and waved his plumed hat against the sky to cheer on Prince Rupert of the Rhine.

21

It was something to tell at school.

'Our horses are in a film,' Callie said, to anyone who would listen. She did not usually have much to say at school. It was safer to keep quiet, so that nobody could find out what your real self was like, and attack it.

'Our horses are in a film,' she told Rosa Duff, who sat next to her.

'Go on,' Rosa said.

'It's called *The Mad Cavalier*. You'll have to see it.'

'Is it a horror film?'

'No.'

'Oh.'

Toby, who had been born chattering, and had never learned to keep his mouth shut, even when he was teased, boasted to the younger ones.

'My horse was in a film.'

'Your horse. You ain't got a horse.'

'I have then. I ride it.'

'It ain't yours.'

'How do you know?'

'Because I know it ain't.'

'Well, that's all you know then, because it is.'

The arguments scuffled back and forth, as they did every day among the small boys. Toby's story of the film was submerged in a turmoil of arms and legs.

'Break it up, break it up.' Two or three big boys lounged across the playground, pushing through the smaller ones. If you did not nip out of the way, you got shoved aside or knocked down.

'Toby's a film star!' One of the small boys jumped up and down like a frog, pointing at Toby, trying to get on the right side of Lewis Hammond by jeering.

'I ain't said—'

'Better not say nothing.' Lewis pushed his face close up and wiped his horrible nose back and forth across Toby's button nose so hard it made his eyes water.

The Louse swaggered on.

The frog boy was still jumping up and down inanely, jabbing a finger at Toby.

'Toby is a li-ar,' he sang. 'Where is Toby's fa-ther?'

Toby's father was in prison, but he did not think they knew that.

'Shut up!' he screamed, his eyes still watering, from rage as well as pain. 'You think you're so big, but we got a famous film star at our place, so stuff *that*.'

He was at the Farm so much that it was 'our place', just as the horses were 'our horses'.

'Go on.' The boy stood still.

'Who is it then?' The others, who had been running after the Louse and Co., throwing gravel as near as they dared, turned and came back.

'Cosmo Spence.'

'Who's he?'

'Never heard of him.'

'Been dead for years.'

'I'm sorry, I forgot.' Toby told Mac about letting the secret out at school.

'I told you not to tell anyone.'

'Oh, it's all right,' Toby said cheerfully. 'Most of them had never heard of you and the others thought you were dead.'

Instead of cheering him, this upset Mac more than the letting out of his secret.

'You see,' he said. 'I am finished. They don't know me any more, the kids.'

'I thought you didn't want to be known.'

'Only if *I* choose. Not if they choose.'

He was gloomy for the rest of the afternoon, muttering about being all washed up, and giving the best years of his life, and nobody caring.

But towards evening, there was a tremendous noise in the road outside. Three cars pulled up together, and a crowd of screaming women rushed into the yard. 'Where is he? Where is he?'

The schoolchildren had told their mothers, and they had all come looking for Cosmo Spence, idol of their youth.

'Cosmo!' They rushed at him like a pack of yapping beagles.

Dora looked at Mac, and saw that he was terrified. He was pale and shaking, unable to move. She pushed him into a stable and bolted the door.

His fans were streaming through the archway. Dora had been washing down the yard. The hose was still running. She grabbed it, twisted the nozzle to a full jet and turned it on the women.

Their giggling shrilled to screams. They ran, skittering over the cobbles, while Dora stood in front of the stable door where Mac crouched, holding the hose like a fireman, flushing out one woman who had ducked behind a wheelbarrow, and chasing her out after the others, through the arch and into the cars.

'Thanks, pal.' Mac stood up and peered cautiously over the door.

'You still want to be known?'

'No, sir. It brought it all back. The shakes. Geez, I'd be a nervous wreck if I ever had to go to a première again. They tear your guts out. It's terrifying. They eat you alive.'

'Like vampires,' Dora said.

'Yeah. They suck your blood.'

Next morning, they found him in his room, packing the few clothes and possessions that he owned.

'I hate to let you down,' he told the Colonel, 'but after yesterday, I can't stay here.'

'Where are you going?'

'Back to the States, I guess.'

'To Hollywood?'

'No, sir. Being here at the Farm has taught me a hell of a lot. It's shown me the way I want to live. I'm going to get me a ranch somewhere and start a place like this for old horses in the States. Get a couple of good kids to work with me—'

'I'll come,' Callie said.

'Maybe later.' He smiled at her with his very white teeth which had been straightened and capped in his film star days. 'I'll be there a long time, honey. Just another old horse put out to grass.'

22

In the summer holidays, Callie worked harder than she ever did at school, but it did not seem like work. It seemed like the real purpose of living.

With the horses mostly in the fields, there was not so much stable work to do, but summer was a time for repairs and painting and mending fences and trimming hedges and restoring the land. With the money Mac gave him from the film, the Colonel was able to buy a small tractor to plough up part of the pasture, and harrow and re-seed.

In the long evenings, Steve and Dora and Callie rode on the fine springy turf along the top of the hills, or went down to the river, bare-back, and barefoot in shorts. They rode the horses into the water, then tied them up to graze in the lush meadow, while they had supper on the midge-misted bank.

One evening, the Colonel came into the kitchen, where Dora was starting to make sandwiches.

'If you're going riding,' he said, 'don't take David. A chap is coming over to try him.'

'Are you really going to sell him?'

'Dora, I must. I can't have a fit young horse taking up room here. We'll be crowded for the winter as it is, with more coming in.' He went on through into the office.

Dora put down the knife in disgust, threw the bread back into the bin and gave the end of the ham to the dog that was sitting behind her, as a dog or cat always did when anyone worked at the counter.

She and Steve and Callie stayed at home to view this interloper, whom they were prepared to hate.

He was a quiet young man in well-cut breeches and decent boots, with a country face and not much to say. He stood at the door of the loose box and looked at David for a long time without making any comment.

The Colonel did the same. They both chewed a piece of hay. Then the young man went up to David and patted him casually on the neck and murmured to him. He ran his hand down his legs, and picked up a foot, then came back to stand by the Colonel, and they both looked at the horse again.

Horse-trading is a strange, slow, closed-mouthed business. As an old sportsman once wrote:

The way of a man with a maid be strange,
But nothing compared
To the way of a man with a horse
When buying or selling the same.

'Throw a saddle on him?' the young man said at last.

'If you like,' the Colonel said, as if the young man had not come especially to ride David. 'Steve?'

Steve took his time. He went slowly on his crutches, although he was by now quite nippy on them, and carried the saddle back on his head. He brought the worst saddle, and had to be sent back for another. He took a long time tacking up, moving the buckles of the cheekstraps up and down and ending in the same hole, since it was David's bridle and already fitted him. The young man watched. Another unwritten law of horse trading is that you don't help to get the horse ready, even when the groom has a broken leg.

'Go easy with him,' Steve said, as he held the grey horse for him to mount. 'He's very jumpy.'

'Shies a bit, does he?' The young man sat sideways, adjusting a stirrup leather.

'No,' said the Colonel, and Steve said, 'Yes, he shies a lot. He's a very nervous horse.'

He showed him where he could try David, and disappeared. He could not bear to watch.

The young man rode quietly for a while in the schooling ring, hopped over a few jumps, then trotted down the lane alongside the hedge to the big field where he could gallop.

When he was nearly at the gate, Steve suddenly started up the tractor with an explosive roar behind the hedge. David shied violently – any horse would – shot off with his head up, jumped the high gate with feet to spare and galloped off before the young man could collect him.

'That's the end of *him*,' Steve said to Dora behind the hedge.

They worked with the tractor for a while, and when they came back to the house, the Colonel said, 'Chap's coming back for David tomorrow. He's very pleased. He thinks he can make him into an Event horse, when he's worked up his dressage and his jumping.'

They stared. 'Can he handle him?'

The Colonel smiled. 'He should. He was runner-up in the Pony Club Combined Training Finals two years ago. Bad luck, Steve.'

Bad luck because the horse was sold, or because the trick didn't work, or both? With the Colonel, you were never quite sure how much he knew.

At the beginning of August, two girls in a red Mini were driving by and saw the sign on the gate and came in to visit the horses. They were secretaries from London, and they were on their holiday.

'At least, we *were*,' they told Anna, who greeted them, as

everyone else was in the hay field. 'But it's all been ruined this year.'

In answer to an advertisement in a magazine, they had booked rooms at the Pinecrest Hotel.

'*Ride every day,*' they had been promised. '*Fine mounts. Beautiful countryside.*'

'When we got there,' the fair plump one was round all over, with round eyes and round pink cheeks like polished apples, 'the stable was almost empty. Just two skinny old horses, but Jane and I wouldn't ride those poor things.'

'The people were quite nice, but we wouldn't stay. It was the horses we'd come for. They wouldn't give us our money back.' Jane was the dark one with glasses. 'We tried to protest, though Lily and I are no good at doing that, but they showed us a piece in small print at the bottom of their letter.'

She fished in her shoulder bag and showed Anna the letter, which warned in a fine print whisper, '*Deposit not refundable under any circumstances.*'

'Anyway,' Lily said. 'It's too late to get in anywhere else where there's horses. On the way home, we saw your sign and thought we'd just come in. It's the nearest we'll ever get to a horse this summer.'

When Anna had showed them the horses in the orchard and the top field, Lily and Jane helped her to carry cold tea and buns down to the far hay field. Cobbler's Dream was in the shade of a hedge with the cart, and they fell on him with affectionate cries and gentle caresses. They were frustrated horse lovers, who had always lived in the city and could only pat police horses and watch the Lifeguards. While the workers drank tea and rested, they seized hay forks and began to turn the windrows, with more energy than skill.

Anna talked to the Colonel, and then she said to Lily and Jane, 'Why don't you spend your two weeks here? You can have a room with Mrs Jones across the road. Steve won't have his plaster off for another week or two, so you can help us in return for a free holiday. If you'd like to.'

'If we'd like to!' They dropped their forks, prongs up, the way amateurs did, and rushed at her.

23

They were not much use, because they did not know much, but they were sweet and amiable girls, and kept saying that it was the happiest holiday they ever had.

They were never out of bed in time to do the morning feeds. They overturned wheelbarrows full of manure in the middle of the yard. They put horses into the wrong stables. They went barefoot and got their toes trodden on. They ran the lawn mower without oil. They left potatoes on the stove to boil dry. Lily dropped the wire cutters down behind bales of hay. Jane dropped her glasses into the pond and could hardly see. They left a gate unchained, and the Weaver, who was always chewing on things, flipped up the fastener and let himself and Stroller out into Mr Beckett's clover.

Fortunately, Lily and Jane were out for a late moonlight walk with Slugger's terrier. They could never bear to go to bed before midnight. That was why they could never get up.

The little fox terrier squeezed through a hedge and set up a frenzy of barking, which began to be answered by dogs from all round and far away, until it seemed that the whole hillside was awake.

When the terrier would not shut up or come back through the hedge, Lily and Jane ran down the road to the gate and found the Weaver and his friend gorging themselves on the ripe clover.

The girls sat on the gate in the moonlight and thought how nice it was to see the dear old horses enjoying such a succulent meal.

The terrier was still barking, and so were all the other dogs.

An upstairs light went on in Beckett's farmhouse, and then a downstairs light.

'I say,' Lily said to Jane, 'if this field doesn't belong to the Colonel, perhaps we'd better try and move the horses.'

Jane had a belt. They tried to get it round the Weaver's neck, but he always moved just a few steps away. They got it round Stroller, and tugged and entreated and slapped him gently on his broad rump, but his huge feet were planted firmly in the clover and he would not budge.

The belt broke. While Lily and Jane stood and watched the horses and talked about what they should do, they heard Slugger call to his dog from the other end of the field. The dog went to him, and when he saw the horses, he came wheezing up through the field.

'What's this, what's this. Come up, you old fool. Get out of it.'

Although the girls had not been able to get a hand on the Weaver, Slugger went easily up to him, grabbed a handful of his mane and yanked him off towards the gate.

'If them fool women would get behind that dray horse and throw a sod at him, he'd follow,' he grumbled.

'It seems a shame when he's having such a good feed,' Lily said.

'Good feed? They never heard of grass staggers?' Slugger asked the moon disgustedly.

He got the horses back into their own field before Mr Beckett came down the lane in his Land Rover, with his two big dogs in the back, still barking. He saw the trampled clover and the hoof marks and started walking towards the Farm.

'It was our fault,' the girls told Slugger. 'We'll talk to him.'

'Good luck to *them*.' Slugger whistled his dog and hobbled off towards his cottage.

'We're so sorry.' They ran panting up to Mr Beckett.

'It was dreadful of us.'

'We forgot to chain the gate, you see.'

'It won't happen again.'

'Wasn't it lucky they didn't get grass stumbles?'

'Grass staggers, Lily.'

'They did love your clover though. It's a beautiful crop,' Lily said, as graciously as the Queen Mother congratulating a cottager on his tomatoes.

Mr Beckett, with Wellingtons and a raincoat over his pyjamas, stood scratching his bristly grey head as they bombarded him with friendly apologies. He did not know what to say. Even his dogs had stopped barking.

'So please don't be angry, because we're dreadfully sorry we woke you up, but everything is all right now and there's nothing to worry about.'

'I told the Colonel, if his horses got on my land again—'

'Oh, but look. They haven't done any harm. The clover will all spring up again.'

'—I'd shoot 'em.'

'Oh, you can't have meant that, surely.' Lily beamed at him with her polished cheeks, and Jane asked him to come back to the cottage for a cup of tea.

'I've not seen you two before, have I?' Mr Beckett looked at them suspiciously. 'Are you related to the people here, or what?'

'Oh no, we work at the stables. Grooms, we are.'

'We take care of the horses.'

'Oh my,' Mr Beckett said. 'The Colonel must be hard up for labour.'

He went back to his Land Rover, cursed at the sleeping dogs and drove off.

Lily and Jane passionately wanted to ride, but when Dora let them try with the mule, Lily got on facing backwards, and then Willy headed Jane straight back into his stable and almost knocked her brains out on the doorway.

'Oh Willy, that wasn't very nice.' Lily led him out again.

'How could you have ridden every day at Pinecrest if you didn't know how?' Dora asked.

'That was why we wanted to ride every day, silly. We were going to learn. Turn him, Jane! Don't let him run back again. Pull the left strap, same as a bicycle.'

Dora let them fool about for a while with Willy. The long-suffering mule either stood like a rock with one girl on his back and the other dancing backwards in front of him, holding out a lump of sugar, or made sharp rushes for his closed stable door, the feed shed, the hay barn, and finally out through the archway.

Jane shrieked like a train whistle. A man and a boy coming in from the road grabbed the reins and brought the mule back into the yard.

'Going to a fire?' The man laughed at Jane, showing all his teeth.

The lanky boy, with pimples and long greasy hair, stared insolently, sucking his teeth and looking Jane up and down.

'I was going out for a ride, thank you.' Jane dismounted with what would have been dignity if her knees had not buckled at contact with the ground, so that she had to clutch at the man's arm.

'Whoa there, Missy,' he said.

She peered at him shortsightedly. 'I know you, don't I?'

'Should do.' It was Sidney Hammond, proprietor of the Pinecrest Hotel.

'Well, er – excuse me. I've got to go.' Lily had run to the house. Jane left Todd Hammond holding the mule and followed her. Dora had disappeared too when she saw who it was, in case they recognized her as the girl with the pink slacks and Passion Flowers.

She sent the Colonel out to them.

'A pleasure, Brigadier,' Sidney said, pleasantly enough, though his teeth were gritted, rather than grinning. 'I see you've got two of my young ladies up here. I didn't know you'd gone into the hotel business.'

'Who—? Oh them. They're working for me. They had a bit of bad luck, they – oh yes.' The Colonel remembered.

'Two rooms for two weeks.' Mr Hammond said. 'Plus all meals, not to mention what that kind will spend at the bar once they're in holiday mood. That's quite a little loss to me, you will agree.'

'They wanted horses,' the Colonel said. 'It's not my fault.'

'And yet my memory tells me – correct me if I'm wrong – that not too long ago, you gave yourself a little tour of my stables.'

'Oh, that.'

'Yes, that.'

'It was nothing to do with me,' the Colonel protested, but Sidney Hammond held up his hand.

'Please, my dear Brigadier, we'll let bygones be bygones. I'll not hear another word.'

Which was a good thing, since the Colonel was quite embarrassed, and did not have another word to say.

Willy relieved the tension by snapping at Todd, who hit him on the muzzle. The mule spun round and kicked out, as the Toad jumped out of the way.

'You've got to be careful with mules.' The Colonel took hold of Willy.

'Is that why you let those silly girls ride him?' Sidney Hammond asked. 'I hope you've got good Third Party Insurance, Brigadier, ha, ha.'

Miss America was in her stable because of midday flies, and

Dora, played by Gillian Blake

Steve, played by Steve Hodson

Slugger, played by Arthur English

The mare and foal at Follyfoot

Dora

Slugger

Ron Stryker, played by Christian Rodszka

Dora with Steve and Slugger

Steve

Dora

Ron Stryker

Follyfoot Farm

Dora and Steve

The Follyfoot foal

Steve and Dora

Steve and Dora

when the Colonel had unsaddled Willy, he found Mr Hammond and Todd looking at her.

'My mare looks a treat.' He was smiling Sidney again. 'I must say you've done a fine job with her.'

'Thank you.'

'I came to tell you I'll be bringing my trailer up for her tomorrow.'

'I thought you – I thought you'd given up your stable.'

'In a business way, yes. With the money we spent on those horses, we couldn't make it pay,' said slippery Sidney, as if they had never had the conversation about the riding stable licence only five minutes ago. 'But we still keep a few favourites for our own use. My boys are great riders. Beauty Queen will get plenty of work, don't worry about that.'

'That back of hers won't stand any work at all,' the Colonel said, 'the way the scar tissue has lumped up. You put a saddle on it, it will break down again.'

'Oh, I *know*. We just want her as a pet, and I'm going to lead my little grand-daughter about on her. "Grandpa," she says. "Take me for a wide." Of course, she thinks it's riding, though all she does is sit there while I lead her round the path and her Granny snaps her picture.'

It was a beautiful image, except that the Colonel was almost sure he had not got a grand-daughter.

'It came to me what he was going to do,' he said later at supper. 'He was planning to get some horses in again, and get round the licence difficulty by raising the price of rooms to include riding, so that he wouldn't actually be charging for the hire of a horse.'

'Very clever,' Steve said.

'He is cunning. I wish he wasn't so affable with it. I always find myself quite liking him, although I know he's a rat.'

'Rat, Toad, Louse. You should call the exterminators.'

'I told him he could have the mare—'

'Oh *no*!'

'—when he paid the bill. She's been here quite a time. If I charge full boarding fees, he can't possibly pay.'

Everyone applauded him, and Lily said, 'Colonel dear, you *are* clever!' as if there might have been some doubt.

24

Towards the end of their holiday at the Farm, Lily and Jane
got restless, and wanted to go into town to dance.

'Dora, you come. Do you good.'

'I can't dance.'

'You can stand in the crowd and twitch,' Jane said. 'That's
all there's room for.'

'It's not my style.'

'Perhaps it ought to be,' Anna said. 'Sometimes I worry
about whether this kind of life is right for a young girl.'

'You sound like my mother,' Dora said.

'Thank you. Is that a compliment?'

'No.'

The three girls went off on the bus, but they never got to
the dance place, or even into town. On the way, they passed
a fairground, and it looked so inviting, with coloured lights
and blaring music, that they spent the evening there instead.

Dora went on the big roundabout three or four times. It
was strange. She could ride a real horse at the Farm almost
any day, and yet she could not resist the fascination of sitting
astride the cool wooden painted horse, up and down and
round and round, all four legs impossibly prancing, nostrils
flared, teeth bared, the twisted barley sugar brass pole to lay
your cheek against, the crowd and the trodden grass and the
upturned faces spinning faster and faster into a blur, the blare
and tootle and thump and clash of the pipe organ, swelling
and fading and swelling again as you came round past the
bosomy figurehead ladies, the painted signs: 'Longest Ride at
the Fair', 'Oh Boy!', 'Yes! It's the Galloping Horses!'

When Dora got off, Jane, shooting at random without her glasses, had won a large yellow rabbit at the rifle booth. 'Something for our money at last.'

'What can you do with it?'

'What can you *do* with it?'

What did you have to do with an enormous yellow nylon fur rabbit except keep it on your bed until you got sick of it and stuck it on top of the cupboard to collect dust?

There was another, much smaller roundabout at the end of the fairground, among the 'Kiddies' Rides'. Feeble cars on tracks, with steering wheels which the kiddies turned zealously and thought they were driving. Little boats that floated endlessly round a doughnut-shaped tank of dirty water, while a strong dreamy boy stood in the hole of the doughnut and turned a crank to keep them moving.

The merry-go-round was not turned by a dreamy boy. Instead of painted horses, there were four live ponies, each with a breastplate attached to a bar which turned on the hub as they pottered slowly round and round.

It was not exactly cruel, and yet it was not exactly what a pony ought to be doing.

Dora and Lily and Jane watched for a while. A big man with a simple face and a wobbly paunch lifted the children into the saddles. They rode round a small circle, the bigger ones jiggling and bouncing, or sitting tight, lost in a dream that they were galloping, the tiny ones petrified, staring at their proud mothers all the way round, begging silently to be lifted down.

The ponies were Shetlands with trailing tails, quite well kept. Although Dora and Lily and Jane watched critically, with the narrowed eyes of experts, they could find no cruelty to complain of, except possibly to small children.

But Dora said on principle, as they turned away, 'The ponies hate it.'

'Oh no.' The paunchy man turned round, with a wriggling child in his arms. 'They like it.'

'How do you know?'

Someone in the crowd giggled.

'When I put the harness on, each one walks to his place and stands to be hitched up. Don't you, love?' The pony hardly came up to where his waist would be if he had one. He could have bent over it, if he could have bent, and touched the ground on the other side.

He put the child gently into the saddle, whistled, and the ponies moved forward, little hoofs the size of coffee mugs pockmarking the soft ground. When he whistled again they stopped, and the children were lifted down.

'Not much of a ride for five pence,' Jane said, since there was nothing else to complain about.

The man turned his mild face round to her and said, 'Quite enough for my little ponies.'

The fair was closing when they left. They were waiting at the bus stop, when Jane suddenly cried out, 'My rabbit!' She had left it at the fair, near the pony-go-round where she had put it down to pat one of the Shetlands.

'Come back with me.' She dragged at Dora's arm.

'We'll miss the bus.'

'Anna will come for us. She said she would if we phoned.'

The bright fairground illuminations were out. There were only a few working lamps where people were cleaning up or shuttering the booths, and windows and doorways of trailers spilled patches of light on to the trampled ground.

The yellow rabbit was not where Jane had left it.

'I could have told you.'

'They probably put it back in the rifle booth for tomorrow.'

'I'm going to look. I'd know it anywhere.'

'It's all shut up.' Lily began to walk back.

'My rabbit.'

Going to the gate, they passed a small open-sided tent where the four Shetlands were tied in stalls with canvas partitions.

Lily ran in out of the darkness, and put her hand on a pony without speaking to it. The pony jumped, pulled back, broke its thin rope and made off, ducking and swerving in fright as the three girls tried to catch it.

It knocked over some crates, tripped over a guy rope, skittered round the ticket booth and out into the road, hard little hoofs pattering, with Dora and Lily after it. Jane had fallen over the crates and the rope too and was some way behind.

It was a fairly busy road. The cars were not going fast, but they were coming steadily in both directions. The pony ran along the side of the road, then swerved across the middle. For a moment, it was caught in headlights, outlined all round like a haloed donkey in a Christmas crèche, and then it disappeared in a scream of brakes.

The car skidded, slid into a car coming the other way, and was rammed from behind, just as the first car was hit in the back. The crashing and screeching of brakes and the tinkling of glass seemed to go on for ever.

When Dora and Lily ran up, there were five cars already involved in the crash, and one more just skidding up to bash headlights into tail lights. Screech. Crash. Pause. Tinkle. Car doors opened everywhere and the road was full of people.

'It was the pony,' the first driver kept shouting, waving his arms about.

'What pony?' No one could see a pony. Dora and Lily were on hands and knees looking for it under the car.

They thought it must be dead, but Jane, limping along with her knees grazed and her ankle bruised, met the pony going home head on. She grabbed it by the broken rope and yelled to the others, 'I've got it! I've got the pony!'

If she had not done that, the girls might have been able to slip away and let the people in the cars, none of whom was hurt, argue about hallucinations and bad lighting and blind spots in the road. As it was, the police got the whole story, and the newspaper also got the whole story, slightly wrong.

'RESCUE EFFORT ENDS IN SIX CAR CRASH'

After they explained to the police, Lily and Jane had talked to a newspaper reporter, thinking he was a detective, because he wore a belted trenchcoat with a cape on the shoulders, like old television films.

'We were sorry for the ponies,' they had said. They added, 'But then we saw that the man was good to them,' but the breakdown lorry arrived with a deafening siren as they said that, and the story that came out in the paper sounded as if they had deliberately let the pony loose.

The Colonel went to the owner of the pony and also to the newspaper, to set the story straight, but he got several letters from the kind of people who may never write so much as a Christmas card, but are always moved to write a letter when one of Our Dumb Friends is involved.

Some of the letters were cranky. Some were sentimental. One had a twenty-five pence postal order in it 'to buy the little fellow a bag of carrots.' One was a poison pen letter, unsigned.

'Why can't you people mind your own business?' it said. 'Not that your business is anything to boast of, keeping those wretched animals alive that should have been put out of their misery long ago ... Trying to stop a man from earning an honest crust of bread ... Should be stopped yourselves ... We know your sort and what we know we don't like.'

'What are they talking about – "crust of bread"?' The Colonel looked up. 'Who could have written a thing like that?'

'The man at the roundabout?' Jane suggested.

'Not with that gentle face,' Dora said. 'And the writing is too good.'

'The writing ... Jane,' the Colonel said, 'go and get me that letter you had from the Pinecrest Hotel. The one that Sidney Hammond wrote.'

The handwriting was the same.

25

In September, when the fruit pickers came to the valley, they brought two ponies up to the Farm for their annual holiday. The Colonel would always take in working horses and ponies for a few weeks of rest. The owners paid what they could, or nothing if they couldn't.

Sometimes, about this time of year, a costermonger's pony or a gipsy horse would be brought in 'for a rest', and the owners would then disappear, so that the horse would be sure of good food and shelter for the winter. They would come back all smiles in the spring, with gifts of firewood and vegetables, and probably be back the next autumn to try the same thing again.

The Shetlands and the donkey were back from the children's camp, and Steve would soon go to fetch the nurseryman's Welsh pony who came every year. His plaster was off now, and the leg mended. He brought a piece of the cast back after they took it off at the hospital, and they buried it at the spot where the motor-bike had ditched him, and Callie drove in a stake, as if it was through the Toad's heart.

An old man wandered vaguely into the yard one day, clutching the newspaper story about Dora and Lily and Jane and the fairground pony.

'I seen about this place in the papers,' he said. 'Touched my heart. I wish I could give you people something for the wonderful work you do, but I'm not a rich man.'

'Who is?' The Colonel had Ranger's foot in his lap, trimming the hoof.

'Got my pension, that's about all it is, and my chickens and goats, just about keeps me going.'

He had watery blue eyes and wispy grey hair over a pink scalp. 'I got an old mare. Hard-working old girl. I'd give anything to give her a bit of a reward for all the years she's given me.' He sighed and shook his head at his turned-up boots, then raised his eyes to see how the Colonel was taking it.

'I'm sure you would.' The Colonel put down Ranger's hind foot and moved round to the other side.

'I seen in the paper that they can come here for a rest.' The old man followed him round, shaky but determined. 'So I came up to ask whether my old girl—'

'I'm awfully sorry.' The Colonel kept his head down, because he hated having to refuse anyone. 'I'm full up at the moment.'

'She can stay out in all weathers. She'd be no trouble to you. I just thought, if I could get her on to some good grass for a month or so, it would mean the world to her.' He paused, and watched the Colonel working skilfully on Ranger's hoof. 'She's earned her rest, mister.'

'Oh, all right.' The Colonel put down the hoof and stood up, slipping the curved knife into the pocket of his leather apron. 'But only for a month. We've got too many for the winter already. Just a month, all right?'

'God bless you, sir.' The old man's eyes swam with emotion. 'And all who work with you.'

But in spite of his shaky hands and his moist, emotional eyes, he turned out to be a pretty shrewd old man. In a neighbour's truck, he brought the mare, and also her treasured companion, a nanny goat in milk, so that the Colonel should have some return for his kindness.

'Who's going to milk it?'

'Not me.'

'Count me out.'

'I'm too busy.'

'I don't know how.'

It turned out that the only person who would milk the goat was Toby, and he managed it very well, sitting on a stool with the three legs cut down to make it the right height, and the goat working on her cud like chewing gum. She was crabby with everyone else but him. He milked her twice a day before and after school.

'Who wants to drink goat's milk?'

'Not me.'

'I hate it.'

'Anna can make cheese with it.'

'I don't know how.'

So Toby took the milk home to his mother, and she gave it to her sickly new baby, who began to thrive.

The goat was out in the fields all day with the mare, making rushes if the other horses came close. The dusty black mare was getting on in years, with battered legs and a long bony head with flecks of white round the eyes like spectacles. Her name was Specs. She had been in the old man's yard for years. She was reasonably fat, but she tore into the meadow grass like a fanatic. After two weeks, someone discovered that she was in foal.

'The old game,' the Colonel said. 'Sneak them in here to have it. But he's not going to get away with it.'

When the old man did not turn up at the end of the month, the Colonel went to the town where he lived and drove round for two hours looking for the address the old man had given him. There was no such address. No one had ever heard of the old man, or his mare, or his goats and chickens, or even his neighbour with the truck.

'He'll be back in the spring,' the Colonel said when he came home, 'for his mare and foal. The old devil.'

But Callie and Toby were thrilled, and so were Steve and Dora. They had not had a foal at the Farm since the Colonel had rescued the mare at Westerham Fair.

Callie took extra care of Specs. The vet said it was a first foal, and she was a bit old for it, so Callie brought her in every night and gave her extra food and vitamins, and came out in her nightdress long after she had gone to bed to shut the top door of the stable if the night turned cold.

They kept her in the separate foaling stable behind the barn, since she seemed to be getting pretty near her time.

'Will you wake me?' She made the Colonel promise to call her if the foal was being born. She had a private fantasy that the old man would never come back, and they would be able to keep the foal. She would call it Folly. Follyfoot, after the Farm. She would handle it and play with it right from the start, so that it would always like people.

'Don't worry,' she murmured into the mare's long furry ear. 'Callie's here.'

The old lady rested on her scarred and weary legs, with her grizzled head low and her bottom lip hanging, ratty eyelashes down over her spectacled eyes. She was not beautiful, but she was content. Her sides bulged like a cow. The Colonel thought it would be any time now, and Callie would hardly risk going to sleep.

On the bus to and from school, Callie and Toby talked endlessly about the foal, planning its future like doting parents. New babies in Toby's family had always been more of a burden than an excitement, but this one was different. He and

Callie could hardly exist through the school day until they could rush back to the farm.

Callie started to ring her mother up half-way through the morning to ask, 'Any news?' Once, at break, she was in the call box at the end of the staff corridor, and she turned and saw a squashed white triangle of nose flattened outside the glass, where the Louse was staring at her. When he took his face away, it left a wet smear.

Callie held the receiver and kept on pretending to talk long after her mother had rung off. But the buzzer went for class, and she had to hang up and come out of the box. Lewis fell into step beside her, quickening his pace as she quickened hers.

'Talk to your boy friend?' he asked.

'It was my mother.'

A teacher was passing. Lewis put his hands in his pockets, to look like two friends strolling. 'Everything all right at home?'

'Yes.' Callie did not dare to say, Mind your own business. 'We're expecting a foal,' she said nervously, because they were turning into an empty corridor and it was safer to keep him talking. 'At least, Specs is. That's what we call her, because she's got white hair round her eyes, like spectacles.' She laughed uneasily.

Lewis did not say anything. When they reached a corner, he suddenly peeled off like a fighter plane and was gone. He did not seem so vicious this term. Perhaps he was growing out of it at last. Perhaps it was going to be a lucky year.

26

Two nights later, the telephone rang. Everyone in the house woke and sat up. It was two o'clock in the morning. The ringing in the hall sounded loudly through the still house, like disaster.

It was Mr Beckett.

'This is it, Colonel.' He was sputtering with rage. 'The horse was all over one corner of my winter wheat, and then right through my seedling fir trees, galloping as if the devil himself was behind. I took a pot shot at it. Said I would, didn't I? No, I didn't hit it, but I tell you, Colonel, I almost wish I had.'

It was Specs. The door of the foaling stable was wide open. Her hoofmarks led through the orchard and the open gateway, across the lane and on to Beckett's land.

The Colonel got into the car to go round to the other side of Beckett's farm. Steve and Dora and Callie were starting out on foot through the orchard when Steve stopped.

'Let's ride,' he said. 'If they chased her, she may be miles away.'

When they came out of the house, they had all heard the motorbike, screeching along the road into the downhill curve. They did not see the riders, but they were all sure who it was.

They took Cobby and Hero, and Dora rode the mule. It was a dark night. No moon, and a damp mist hanging over the ground, and on the trees like veils. They could not follow the mare's tracks.

They rode round the edges of Beckett's arable land, and

along a cart track between his cow pastures. Ahead of them, they saw the Colonel's lights on the road and went to join him.

'Better go home,' he said. 'We'll try in the morning.'

They went back into the fields, but they did not go home. They kept riding about in circles, farther afield, covering the land. If Specs heard or smelled the horses, she might come to them.

When the first line of light began to creep along the edge of the far hills, they were all exhausted, and the mule was falling into every rut and over every stone, even those that were not there. Callie was cold and Hero was bored. Every time they made a turn away from home, he would fight to turn back. Steve and the Cobbler rode ahead, picking their way between the low bushes scattered over a fallow field. They were a long way from home. Callie was not even sure where they were.

Halfway across the field, Cobby suddenly raised his head, his small pointed ears tightly forward. He stopped. Steve pushed him on, but he stopped again, head up, all his senses alert.

'He's heard something,' said Steve, 'or got a scent.'

'Probably a field of oats,' Dora said.

'Let's see where he'll go.'

Steve dropped the reins and sent him forward. Cobby broke into a jog. They went through a gap in the hedge and over a stubble field. At the far end, a plank bridge took them over a deep dry ditch. The mule hesitated, distrusting the bridge. Dora slapped him with the flat of her hand, and he was just scrambling across when Cobby stopped again and backed, almost knocking Willy into the ditch.

He switched off to the side, and as they followed the edge of the ditch, they saw the dark shape of the mare.

Callie held the horses, while Steve and Dora jumped down

139

to Specs. The foal had been born. It had been born still wrapped in the thin sac of membrane which had protected it for so long, floating inside its mother. Jammed in the ditch, weak and exhausted, the mare could not turn and rip the sac with her teeth, and the foal was suffocating, drowning in the fluid.

'Just in time.'

Steve freed the small wet head. They could not tell if it was alive or dead. Dora had once seen a man fished out of the river and saved by mouth-to-mouth breathing. She took the foal's head and breathed steadily into its nose, until its lungs moved and the foal began to breathe life of its own.

When they showed her her wet black colt, poor old Specs was too weak to lick it. She bumped it with her grey whiskery nose, and then dropped back her head.

Her eyes were glazed and dull. She looked as if she would die.

Steve rode across the field, and followed the road to the nearest house, where he astonished a sleeping family with a demand for blankets for a dying mare and her new-born foal.

When it was light, the Colonel came with a break-down lorry and a canvas sling. Somehow they got Specs out of the ditch and on to her feet. The Colonel and Steve and the two men from the garage pulled and pushed and half carried her up the ramp into the horse box. Callie sat on the floor in front with her arms round the struggling, long-legged foal.

As soon as he was in the stable with his mother, he pushed his face against the exhausted mare and tried to suck, but there was no milk for him.

The vet came three times that day, and gave Specs injections, but she had been infected from the difficult birth, and in the evening, he said, 'She hasn't got much chance. You'd better try and find a foster mother.'

'We're going to raise him by hand.' Callie pulled the colt away from his mother and pushed the bottle of milk into his soft mouth.

Slugger's wife had found a feeding bottle that had been used for one of her grandchildren, and they fed the colt with milk from the old man's goat. It had to be fed little and often, the way a mare feeds her foal, wandering away from it before it can take too much.

'Never rear it,' Slugger droned. 'You know what they say: Lose a mare, lose a foal.'

'What about cows? They take the calf away at once and feed it by hand, don't they?'

The Colonel borrowed a special calf feeding pail from Mr Beckett, who had calmed down when they explained that last night was not their fault, but the colt much preferred Slugger's grandchild's bottle.

He was always hungry. It seemed to be always time to feed him. At almost any hour of the day or night, you could find the Colonel or Anna or Steve or Dora or Callie or Toby tipping the bottle of goat's milk down to the soft, demanding nose, the long legs braced, tail quivering, blue eyes bulging with greed. They took it in turn to set their alarm clocks and go down in the night to the stable where Specs lay in the straw, licking anxiously at her foal, her white-rimmed eyes full of the trouble she could not understand. The fever had gone into her feet, and she would not stand.

But the colt would not give up. He was full of life and bounce, and he gave his mother no peace.

'Shouldn't we take him away from her?' Dora was trying to get Specs to eat, holding the food in her hand. The mare would nibble a bit, then turn her head away. 'She isn't getting any better.'

'But she's alive.' The Colonel would never give up his stubborn hope of life for his animals. 'She's alive because she's got a colt. Take him away, and you take away her will to hang on.'

The colt was called Folly, as Callie had planned. Cobbler's Folly, Steve called him, since it was Cobbler's Dream who had found him.

Callie hated being away from him at school.

'Had your foal yet?' Lewis asked quite affably.

'Yes. A colt.'

He raised his thick eyebrows, which met in the middle of his nose, so that his whole brow furrowed when he moved them.

'Mother and child doing well?'

He lowered the brows. With those dull eyes and that hanging mouth, you could not tell how much he was hiding. It *must* have been him and the Toad who chased our poor Specs. But there was no way to prove it.

'The colt is lovely,' Callie said. 'But the poor old mother nearly died.'

'Oh well,' said the Louse. 'We all come to it.'

Callie did not tell him that because the lovely colt had kept bothering Specs to get up and feed him, the milk had begun to come at last, and the fever left her. She did not tell him about the miracle. He would not understand things like that.

Some time after that, Lewis stopped coming to school.

Steve had to go back to the hospital for a final X-ray. While he was there, one of the nurses, the one who had written, 'Love always Susie' on his plaster cast, gave him some interesting news.

142

Two patients had come in with food poisoning, which was traced to a tin of contaminated meat found on the rubbish heap at the Pinecrest Hotel, where they were staying.

The hotel had been closed down and the owners had gone away.

The old man came back in the spring. When they told him about Specs, he nodded and sucked his loose false teeth and did not say anything.

Specs and her colt belonged to him, of course. Callie went sadly out to the field. Folly left the other horses and came to her at once. He still liked people best, because they had first cared for him.

He put his inquiring nose into her hand. She let him lick the salt of her skin, and then flung her arms round his neck and wept into his growing mane. The colt put his head down to graze, to get rid of her, and moved away.

When Steve came to the gate, Callie was sitting in the grass, tearing daisies to pieces.

'Stop sulking,' he said. 'He's gone.'

Callie looked up and saw Steve through a mist of sun and tears.

'The old man has moved into his daughter's flat. We're keeping Specs and Folly.'

Dora at Follyfoot

I

When Dora went into the stable yard after lunch, Slugger was sweeping.

'What's wrong, Slugger?'

Slugger Jones, a man of habit indoors or outdoors, always slept after Sunday lunch, and never swept the yard until after the evening feeds. Especially on a Sunday when visitors might come and scatter toffee papers, and cigarettes hastily stamped out when they saw Steve's notice:

'EVERYTHING AT FOLLYFOOT BURNS,
INCLUDING MY TEMPER.'

He had originally written, 'The Colonel's temper,' but had blacked that out and put 'my'.

'What's wrong, she wants to know.' Slugger swept towards Dora's feet, and over them. 'Man doing a bit of honest work and she wants to know what's wrong.'

Dora looked over Willy's half-door and made a face at the mule, who dozed with head down and ears lopped out from wall to wall. She felt like riding, but there was nothing much here that wasn't lame, stiff, blind, ancient, or pensioned off from work for the rest of its life. That was the only snag about a Home of Rest for Horses. Dora and Steve were always trying to sneak in a horse that was fit enough to ride.

Dora put a bridle on Willy and the old Army saddle that was the only one that fitted him, since his back had been permanently moulded by his days as an Army mule. When she brought him out, Slugger was leaning into the water trough to pull out the stopper.

'Where are you going?' His voice was a muffled echo inside the trough.

'Into the woods. I'm still trying to teach Willy to jump logs.'

'I wouldn't go there. Not in the woods I wouldn't, no.'

'Why?' What did he expect? Murderers? Madmen? The shadowed rides through the beechwoods were calm and safe as a cathedral.

'Ask a silly question, you get a silly answer.' Slugger was scrubbing a brush round the sides of the trough. 'You might miss someone.

'What do you – oh Slugger, was that what the telephone was? The Colonel?'

The Colonel, who owned Follyfoot Farm, had been in hospital for nearly two months. He was coming home at last.

Dora climbed on to the mule, slapped him down the shoulder with the reins because his armoured sides were impervious to legs, and rode out of the yard and down the road to be the first to greet the car.

At the crossroads, she stopped and let Willy eat grass while she lolled in the uncomfortable saddle and drifted into her fantasy world where she was brave in adventures and always knew the right things to say.

She heard the sports car on the hill. Even with Anna driving, the gearbox still made that unmistakable racket from losing battles with the Colonel. When the car stopped and he looked out with his lopsided smile, Dora hardly knew him. His face was thin and pale, his eyes and teeth too big. His hand on the edge of the car door was bony and white. He was still biting round his nails, but they were clean. At Follyfoot, nobody's nails were ever competely clean, finger or toe.

'Hullo, Dora.'

'Hullo.' She pulled up Willy's head, not knowing what to

say. 'Are you all right?' Well, he must be, or he wouldn't come home. 'Did it hurt?' Operations always hurt. 'I'm glad you—' Willy suddenly dropped his head and pulled her forward on to his bristly mane.

The Colonel laughed his old laugh that ended in a cough. Anna moved the car forward. Dora kicked Willy into his awkward canter and followed them home on the grass at the side of the road.

Callie, the Colonel's stepdaughter, was at the gate to open it, with his yellow mongrel dog in ecstasies, tail beating its sides. Slugger was in Wonderboy's loose box, pretending not to be excited. He came out with his terrible old woollen cap tipped over his faded blue eyes, and the Colonel laid an arm across his shoulders.

'Good to be back, Slugger.'

'How's it gone then?'

'No picnic.'

'Teach you to stay away from that foul pipe.'

'It was the old war wound. The doctors say it was nothing to do with smoking.'

'That's what *they* say. I burned that old pipe.'

Anna wanted the Colonel to rest in the house, but he had to go all round the stables first, leaning on his stick, lamer than usual, and then out to the fields where some of the horses were grazing in the sweet spring day.

Fanny the one-eyed gipsy horse trotted up to him. The Weaver lifted his head with his cracked trumpet call, and then went back to chewing the fence rail, weaving hypnotically from foot to foot. Lancelot, the oldest horse at the Farm, perhaps in the world, mumbled at the grass with his long yellow teeth and looked at the Colonel through his rickety

149

back legs. Stoller the brewery horse plodded up and nosed into his jacket for sugar.

'He remembers which pocket.'

The Colonel had gone into and out of hospital wearing the patched tweed jacket with the poacher's pockets wide enough for a horses' nose.

In the jump field, Callie was lungeing the yearling colt, Folly.

'Shaping up quite nicely.' The Colonel watched with his horsy look, eyes narrowed, a piece of hay in his mouth. Horses are always chewing grass or hay, and people who live with them catch the habit.

'What do you mean?' Callie bent as if she were going to pick up and throw a piece of earth, to make the colt trot out, head up, long legs straight, tail sailing. 'He's perfect!'

The Colonel laughed. 'Nothing changes, thank God. Where's Steve?'

'I think he's out with the horse box,' Dora said casually.

'What for?'

'Oh—' She stuck a piece of hay into her mouth too. 'To bring in a horse.'

'I thought the stable was full.'

'Well it is,' Dora said. 'But we found this horse, you see. The junk man died, and the old lady, she tried to keep it in the back garden, tied to the clothes line, and it's all thin and mangy like a worn old carpet, and so we . . .'

'And so they thought it was just what we needed to keep us busy in our spare time,' Slugger grumbled, leaning on the gate.

The Colonel laughed. 'Nothing changes.'

2

A few days after he came home from the hospital, the Colonel took Steve into his study for a long talk, and later he called in Dora.

He was sitting in the leather armchair with his feet on the fender in front of a bright fire. It was a good day, but he felt the cold more than he used to.

No one had used this room while he was away. It was so unnaturally tidy and clean that Dora stopped in the doorway to take off her boots.

'Come in, come in, there's a hell of a draught.'

She padded in her socks over the carpet that was as thin and worn as the old horse they had just rescued from the widow's clothes line. Its name was Flypaper, because it attracted flies. Dora was treating its motheaten patches with Slugger's salad oil.

'Sit down, Dora.'

She sat on the stool at the other side of the fireplace. The Colonel's hand wandered to the desk where his chewed pipe used to be, groped for a moment, then came back to his pocket and took out a paper bag.

'Have a peppermint.' He held the bag out to Dora and took one himself. 'Poor substitute for tobacco.' He stuck it in his lined cheek. 'But I'm trying.'

'Are you really all right?' The others pretended that he was the picture of health, but Dora always said what she thought. 'You look terrible.'

'Thanks.' He shifted the peppermint to the other cheek. 'I'd rather hear that than people telling me I look wonderful when I feel like death. It's going to be a long pull, I'm afraid. I've got to go abroad for a bit, Dora. Down to the South where it's warm and dry and there's nothing to do.' He made a face. 'I'd much rather be slogging round here in the rain and mud with the horses.'

'Don't worry about them,' Dora said quickly. 'We can manage.'

'Can you? I've been wondering if I ought to get someone in to run this place.'

'Oh no!' Dora stood up, her face stubborn. 'I couldn't work for anyone else.'

'What about Steve?'

'He's only a boy. I wouldn't let him boss me about.'

'All right,' the Colonel said. 'Give it a try as your own boss. I think you can cope, between you. If you get into a muddle with bills, my accountant will help you. Just be careful with money. Don't buy any horses. If you get a really needy case, of course take it in. Slugger will gripe, but fit it in somewhere. But no buying. Remember that Shire horse – the one you and Steve found at the Fair, and you sold the bicycle to get it?'

'And then found he was stolen anyway, and I had to give him back to the farmer.' Dora smiled, remembering the fat, sloppy horse with the curly moustache. 'Yes, I remember. It wasn't Steve. It was that boy Ron Stryker, and *he'd* stolen the bicycle.'

'That was when I fired him. Useless layabout. I never should have hired him. But you take what you can get these days. If you need any help—'

'We won't.'

'There's this chap I know. Bernard Fox. The one who has the big stable over the other side of the racecourse.'

'Where you can eat your dinner off the yard?' Dora had once sneaked a look round the grand Fox stables. 'It doesn't even smell of horse.'

'Well, we can't all manage that, Dora.'

As she stood with her arm on the mantelpiece among the Colonel's photographs and trophies and the silver model of his famous grey jumper, the fire brought out the stable essence of Dora's clothes.

'But Bernard says he'll be glad to help any time you need him.'

'We won't.'

'He may look in at the Farm some time. Be reasonably polite, will you?'

'I always am.'

'You do try.' The Colonel reached out and took her hand and squeezed it. 'Go ahead with the work then, Dora. It's all yours.'

When she went out, Steve was grooming a horse in the corner box. His head came over the door when he heard her feet on the cinder path.

'What did he say?' He had been waiting for her to come out of the house.

'He's got to go away.'

'I know.'

'He said about being careful with money. Not buying horses, and all that. What did he say to you?'

'That too, and – well, I'm more or less in charge.'

'Funny,' Dora said. 'That's what he said to me.'

'Who is in charge here?'

The woman who stormed into the yard was red in the face under a plastic rain bonnet. 'One of your ponies was out last night and walked all over my pansy bed.'

'The black and white beggar?' Slugger knew that Jock the
Shetland was a magician pony who could squeeze through
hedges and between fence rails, and undo bolts with his teeth.

'I didn't see the beastly thing.' She glared at Slugger from
under the rain bonnet. 'Only its nasty little hoof marks, all
over my pansy bed.'

'Spoil many plants?' Slugger asked.

'I haven't put any in yet. But that's not the point. I want
something done.'

'I could send the boy up to rake over the bed,' Slugger said,
and the red-faced woman pounced.

'Are you in charge?'

'Oh dear me, no. In charge, she says. Oh no, lady.'
Slugger faded.

'Who *is* in charge here?'

'Not me.' Steve put on a dopey face.

'Not me.' Dora backed away.

But that evening when some visitors with children were
going round the loose boxes, exclaiming and sighing and
mooning over the old horses, the father asked Dora, 'Where's
the boss then?' and she heard herself answering, 'Here. It's
me.'

Then when she was with the children in the donkey's
stable, lifting them on to his back, she heard the father say
Steve, 'Bit young, that girl, to run this place.'

And heard Steve laugh. 'She doesn't, actually. I do.'

3

Callie had refused to go abroad with her mother and the Colonel. She made the excuse of school.

'But there's only a few more weeks,' Anna said. 'You could join us at the villa then. You can swim down there, and sail and play tennis, and there are lots of young people your age.'

'I don't need young people my age. I need horses. And they need me.'

It was true. Callie was needed at Follyfoot. Steve and Dora and Slugger all worked extra hours, but the stable was full, and this was the time of year to mend fences and gates, to lime some of the fields, and prune dead branches out of trees and touch up peeling paint. Soon it would be time to get in the first crop of hay.

Dora sat up late at the Colonel's desk, falling asleep over bills and letters. Steve had taken over all the hoof care and the treatments for the unsound horses that the Colonel used to do. Slugger, who did the cooking as well as a thousand outside jobs, had not had a day off for weeks.

His sister came up to the Farm in her husband's dry cleaning van to see if he was dead.

'Sorry to disappoint you, Ada.' Slugger set down a loaded wheelbarrow.

'An old man like you.' His sister clicked her loose teeth. 'You'll collapse on this job.'

'Then I'll be at the right place, won't I? They can put me out to grass with the old horses.'

Callie got up early to help in the stables before she caught the bus to school, and did mucking out instead of homework in the evenings.

Her teacher sent a note home. Dora answered it, signing herself 'Guardian', but the teacher threatened trouble if things did not improve, so Callie stayed away from school, to avoid the trouble.

An extremely polite man came to the Farm one afternoon and found Callie in the feed shed with a brush and a big pail of whitewash. She gave him an overall and another brush, and they worked together for the rest of the afternoon, and Slugger made tea for him before he left.

'Nice of him to help.' Steve came up from the bottom field with Dolly and the cart full of planks and saws and hammers. 'Friend of yours, Callie?'

'He was the attendance officer.'

Callie had to go back to school for the rest of the term, and she had to do her homework, to stop them writing to her mother and the Colonel.

There were two reasons why no one must write that sort of letter to Anna and the Colonel. *One:* Not to worry them. *Two:* If he thought Steve and Dora couldn't cope, the Colonel might bring in a manager to run Follyfoot. Or write to his friend Bernard Fox.

The Farm was sloppier than usual. The horses were content, but there was no time to do everything. The manure pile had not been spread, and was growing out alarmingly from the side of the barn. Straw was not stacked away in the Dutch barn. The horse box was still covered in mud from its last trip across a field. They did not want the grand stable keeper coming round with burnished boots and foxy face to match his name.

He did come. He came one morning when Steve and Dora were doing what Ron Stryker used to call 'taking five minutes'.

They were stretched out in the sun on two bales of straw, with Steve's radio going, and the brown mare Pussycat, who was wandering loose in the yard to pick up dropped hay, thoughtfully licking the sole of his shoe.

'Good morning, good morning.' He strode briskly into the yard, burnished Bernie Fox in tall polished boots and sharply cut breeches, cap over his eyes, crisp ginger moustache at the ready. 'I hope I'm not interrupting your work.'

Steve jumped up and banged off the radio on a supersonic howl. Dora scrambled upright, pulling straw out of her hair. Old Puss leered with her lower lip hanging, and shambled stiffly away.

'Fox is the name. Bernard Fox. Good friend of the Colonel's. He asked me to keep an eye on things, so I thought I'd just look in as I was passing by.'

'How – how nice of you.' Steve said nothing. Boys never did, in a pinch. So Dora produced a few cracked words. 'Would you like to see round?'

Bernard Fox had already seen quite a lot in the few moments he had been in the yard. Straw bales in the corner instead of stacked away. A fork left in a loaded wheelbarrow. Muddy heads looking over doors, with burrs in their forelocks. Pussycat licking the door of the feed shed, the nearest she could get to oats.

'Better shut the yard gate while she's loose,' Mr Fox said.

'She never wanders away,' Dora told him.

'You can't assume anything with horses. They're unpredictable.'

'She knows when she's well off. She's gone far enough in her old life. A man was riding her from Scotland to London with a petition for the Queen. After a week, Puss lay down by the side of the road and wouldn't go any farther, so the man had to go on by train, and when he got to London, the Queen was in Australia.'

Dora thought Bernard Fox would be interested, but he only said, 'I'd still like to see you shut the gate.'

He did not exactly order (he'd better not). He just stood there in the superb boots, with his foxy head cocked, confident of being obeyed.

Dora stamped off, muttering and growling. The gate had dropped, because the hinge was loose. With her back to Bernard Fox, she tried to latch it without him noticing that she had to lift it.

'Need some longer screws in that hinge, don't you?' he called out breezily.

He had several other breezy suggestions.

'Better get that muck pile shifted.' He looked round the side of the barn. 'Danger of spontaneous combustion. It's hot enough for mushrooms already, I see.'

'We're growing them to eat,' Steve invented. 'Organic gardening.'

They could not keep him out of the tack room. Cobwebs. Mildewed leather. A bridle with a grass-stained bit hanging on the cleaning hook, as if that were enough to clean it.

'Colonel forgotten his Army training?'

'Of course not.' Dora was not going to have him criticizing the Colonel. 'We've had no time to clean tack. Haven't got time to ride anyway.'

'And nothing much to sit on.' Bernard Fox's cold ginger eye took in the few dusty old saddles, which were all they had.

'Bit risky.' He looked into the loose box where Stroller was keeping company with Prince, who had been turned out of his stable for Flypaper, whose mange might be catching.

'They get on all right.'

'Start a kicking match sooner or later. Why don't you turn 'em out?'

'It's going to rain.' Steve looked up at the low sky, which

might let down water on Bernard's burnish at any moment. 'Stroller is rheumatic and Prince is coughing.'

'So will Stroller be, if you leave them together. Isn't there an isolation box?'

'Yes, the foaling stable. But Lancelot's in that.'

'Who's Lancelot?'

'The oldest horse in the world,' Dora said proudly.

Bernard Fox looked glumly over the door. Lancelot, with a rack full of hay, was eating his bedding. He was the only horse who could manage to have both a pot belly and sticking out ribs. His wispy tail was scratched thin at the top. He had rubbed away half his mane under his favourite oak tree branch. His long teeth stuck out beyond his slack lips and his neck curved the wrong way, like a camel.

Bernard Fox looked at him for a long time, orange eyebrows raised, mouth pursed under the trim moustache. Lancelot looked back at him, his sparse lashes dropping over his clouded eyes.

'Ought to have been put down long ago.'

'The Colonel doesn't believe in taking life.' Dora thought he couldn't know the Colonel very well, or he would be aware of that. 'Unless a horse is suffering.'

'I'm suffering just looking at him.'

'Lancelot is very content—' Dora began but he had walked off to look over the gate of the jump field, where Folly and a few other horses were grazing. The gate was tied with a halter rope. One of the jumps was wrecked from Dora's efforts with the mule.

'Nice colt.' Even Bernard Fox could not find fault with Folly. 'Who's working with him?'

'Callie is beginning with the lunge and long reins. She's the Colonel's stepdaughter.'

'You'll be sending him to a trainer though?'

'I don't see why. Callie does very well, for her age.'

'How old is she?'

'Twelve.'

'I see.'

He asked, 'How did the horse box get so filthy?' (Going over a ploughed field to rescue a fallen calf), and, 'When are you going to get that stand of hay cut?' (When we get time), and as he was crossing the yard to leave, 'What is *that*?'

It was Slugger, coming out of the back door in his long cooking apron and his woollen cap, waving and shouting, 'I did it! A loaf of bread – it rose! Come and get it before it falls down!'

'Would you like some home-made bread and butter?' Dora asked politely. Bernard Fox was so narrow and trim he did not look as if he got enough of things like that.

'Thanks, but I must get on. I've got an appointment. Big thoroughbred breeder from America.' (Who cared?) 'I've stayed longer than I should.' (Too true.) 'But I promised the Colonel I'd help, and I'm a man of my word.' (Too bad.) 'And help is what you youngsters need.'

Dora and Steve hated to be called youngsters. They were doing a grown-up job with grown-up responsibilities. They were paid. They were independent. They had both left home, more or less for good.

'We're all right.'

Instinctively they stood side by side, arms touching. They had fought and argued and annoyed each other many times since they were left on their own, but they were very close now, scenting the Fox as enemy.

'You need another stable hand.'

'We've got Slugger. And Callie.'

'Slugger is the one with the bread, I take it. And Callie is the twelve-year-old? I'll make some inquiries tomorrow and see if I can get hold of someone efficient. I'm sure the Colonel will agree.'

'Not to someone who treats horses like horses,' Dora said. Hard to explain what she meant – the caring, the understanding, the sharing of life between animal and man. Impossible to explain to Bernard Fox.

'Better than treating them like inmates of a cosy old folks' home,' he said. 'Good day to you, Miss Dorothy. Steven.' His hand went politely to his cap. Steve and Dora clicked heels and saluted, and Bernard turned on his burnished boots without a smile.

Dora's heels did not click very well. A puppy had eaten one of her shoes, and she was barefoot. As he passed her, Bernard Fox said out of the side of his mouth, 'You're asking for tetanus.'

4

Bernard Fox, a man of his word, as he said, cabled for the Colonel's permission, and found a new stablehand within a few days.

It was a girl who used to work for him.

'Always these mucky girls,' Slugger and Steve grumbled to each other. 'Nothing but girls. Remember those two – Lily and Jane – used to squeal all the time and get their toes trodden on? Why can't we get a man round here? Nothing but sloppy, useless girls.'

Dora went on brushing mud off the white parts of the Appaloosa horse Spot (he never got mud on his brown patches where it wouldn't show), and pretended not to hear.

'If this new one wears tight purple pants and dangly earrings and calls me Daddy-O, I'm packing it in,' Slugger said.

'I'll go with you,' said Steve, 'if she paints her eyes like dart boards and wants to darn my socks.'

'He said "efficient".' Dora hung an arm over Spot's door to bang the mud out of the curry comb. 'He didn't say insane.'

Phyllis Weatherby, the efficient stablegirl, was coming in two days' time. They pretended not to care, but they did work extra hard to spruce the place up so that she would know that this was how things were done at Follyfoot.

She was not on the afternoon bus with Callie.

'Relax, everybody.' Callie ran into the yard and spun her ugly school hat into a tree. 'Perhaps she won't come at all.'

Slugger went into the house to take off his boots and put his feet up. Steve and Dora settled down to play cards in the barn. Callie changed her hated school uniform for her beloved bleached jeans and took Folly for a walk to the village, showing him the world.

She was back quite soon in a car she had flagged down for a lift.

'He got away!' She panted into the barn. 'A car backfired and I couldn't hold him. He went off down the High Street with the rope trailing, knocked over a couple of bikes, went across the main road – cars swerving and screeching, it was awful – through a hedge and off across the fields, I've no idea where he's gone!' She sat down on a bale of hay, scattering the playing cards, and burst into tears.

'I'll get the truck. Dora, you take Hero and follow the colt. You can't miss those little tracks.'

Dora put a bridle on Hero, tried to vault on to him bareback, failed three times, and climbed on from the milestone mounting block. Steve was backing the truck out of the shed when Slugger ran shouting out of the house in his socks and his old indestructive Army vest.

'Folly's loose!'

Dora turned back. 'He's across the main road. That's where we're going.'

'He may be headed home. Mrs Ripley at the Three Horseshoes saw him run through her yard, going like smoke, she said on the phone.'

Callie got into the truck. 'Hurry, Steve.'

'Better wait, if he's headed home.' Slugger put his hands on the door.

'How do we *know*?' Callie was anguished.

'Tearing round the roads won't help.'

'We've got to do something – let go!' She tried to pry his fingers from the edge of the door. She thumped them. She even bent down and bit the horny knuckles.

Slugger paid no more heed than if she were a fly. He had turned his head away to listen.

'Let go,' Callie pleaded. 'Oh hurry, Steve!'

But Steve had heard what Slugger had heard, and jumped out.

Specs, Folly's mother who had long ago seemed to forget the colt was hers, had heard it too. Her shaggy head was over the door, ears pricked, eyes staring out of the white circles round them. Her head swung up and she called, deep and throaty, as she had not called since Folly was a skittery foal straying too far from her in the field.

Other heads were coming out in a chorus of neighs, whinnies, grunts, and a donkey's ear-shattering bray. And then from beyond the hayfield at the bottom of the hill came the faint answer, high and shrill, unmistakably Folly.

Dora and Hero were off down the grass track, scrambling over the low bar in the gateway and down the side of the hay field to open the bottom gate for him. They came back together, Folly bounding and teasing, knocking up against Hero's stiff, steady trot, galloping off in a circle, snatching at the tall hay, running ahead with his tail up and his head down to buck and squeal.

At the bar, he stopped and sniffed. As Hero began to step carefully over, he took a flying leap and landed in front of him. Hero stumbled. Dora fell off. Hero recovered and trotted back to the yard without her.

At this moment, a car stopped in the road and a tall girl in the sort of raincoat you see in photographs of sporting events walked in.

Hero was wandering loose with one foot through his reins. Callie, with tear stains on her face, was chasing Folly round the yard, trying to grab the flying rope. Slugger was hobbling after her in his socks and khaki vest, swearing at the cobbles. Dora trailed in with mud on her behind.

'With all the practice you've had, you ought to be able to

fall off on to your feet.' Steve laughed at her, and Dora wiped a muddy hand in his hair.

'Excuse me,' said the girl in the raincoat, 'is this Follyfoot Farm?'

'Foyft Fahm,' she said. She droned in her nose without opening her mouth, as if she couldn't spare the words.

She was no girl either, when you saw her close. Dry and leathery, she would never see thirty again, nor even thirty-five, the kind of woman who has stuck with horses because she can't get a man.

'Right,' she said, when she had introduced herself as Phlis Wethby. 'Right, let's get hold of that little clod.'

'I can't—' Callie was still breathlessly playing Tag, Folly's favourite game. Phyllis Weatherby strode over, and as Callie grabbed and he flicked away, she was there to catch him on the other side.

'Get'm off guard, right?'

Most of her sentences began and ended in 'right'.

'Right,' she'd say, 'we'll get the mucking out finished and this lot turned out and these other nags groomed before we break for lunch, right? Steve, you take the end stables and Dorothy can start down that side. Right Slugger, there's all those cobwebs should have been got down from the beams years ago.'

'We keep 'em to catch flies.'

'Nonsense. Asking for coughs. Use the old birch broom, right?'

Dora followed Steve into the shed where the barrows and forks were kept.

'Right,' she droned between closed lips, 'you know what I think? She's come here to be boss, right?'

'Wrong.' Steve set his jaw.

But Phyllis Weatherby was hard to resist, because, like Bernard Fox, she expected to be obeyed, which hypnotized you into obeying. Or she would tell you to do something you were just going to do anyway, so it put you under orders. She was hard to ridicule, because she had no sense of humour and couldn't tell the difference beween a joke and an insult. When Slugger was driven to mutter, 'Oh, knock it off, you silly old cow,' she slapped poor Trotsky on his bony triangular rump and said, 'Right, he does look more like a cow than a horse.'

When Dora said, 'Right Phyllis, it's your turn to load the muck cart, right?' she answered, 'Right, you can take my turn while I soak that pony's leg, right Dorothy?'

'The name is Dora, if you haven't washed your ears lately.'

'Short for Dorothy. Right.'

But she did her share of the work, you had to give her that.

Rejecting the comfortable, shabby farmhouse because there were spiders in the bath and mice in the larder, she had taken a room at the Cross Keys Hotel in the village. But she was back at the Farm before anyone was up, throwing pebbles at the bedroom windows and clashing buckets fit to wake the dead, which Slugger sometimes wished he was when he woke and found that the nightmare of Phyllis Weatherby was true.

She brought her lunch from the hotel, because she couldn't get her tight-fisted lips round Slugger's doorstep sandwiches. She ate quickly, and jostled the others out of their usual hour of lazing in the sun, gossiping, dozing, reading, swilling mugs of the strong sugary tea which Phyllis prophesied would rot all their teeth.

This annoyed Slugger so much that one day he took out his teeth in his red bandana handkerchief and opened his mouth and said, 'Look Phyll, it did.'

'You were right, right?' Dora grinned.

'All right, back to the mines.' Phyllis Weatherby dusted crumbs off her strong capable hands and stood up. 'Fooling about won't get the work done.'

She chivvied the old horses as much as the people who looked after them. Hero must be schooled, though he was long past it. The Weaver must wear a cribbing collar to break him of his habit of crib biting with his long yellow teeth on his manger or door (it didn't). Even Lancelot's senile dreams were disturbed. He did not care to go out in damp weather. You could open his door and he would just stand there, swinging his head like a hammer and watching the rain.

'Right, get a move on.' Phyllis pushed him towards the door with her shoulder. Though she was thin, she was sinewy and tough. 'Get out and get some exercise.'

'He's too stiff,' Dora said.

'If he's not sound, he shouldn't be kept alive.'

'That's what Bernard Fox said. Why does everyone want to put down poor old Lance?'

'If Mr Fox said it, it's right. He is a master horseman.'

'If you were the oldest horse in the world,' Dora laid her head against Lancelot's neck as he sagged at the edge of the orchard, too bored to eat grass, 'you wouldn't want a master horseman. You'd want a friend.'

'Well, he can't have it both ways,' Phyllis said offensively. 'He must either shape up or be put down.'

'That's not the point of Follyfoot,' Dora said into Lancelot's straggly mane.

'Right. I can see that.' Phyllis Weatherby began to shake up bedding, hissing to herself as if she were a horse.

How were they going to get rid of her?

5

Quite a lot of their time was spent discussing how this could be done without trouble. Phyllis Weatherby was in touch with Bernard Fox. He would hear from her about trouble, and report it to the Colonel.

How were they going to get rid of her?

One Sunday when Steve had gone to see his mother, and Callie and Dora wanted to try and make a dress, Phyllis insisted on taking them to a horse show to see what riding was.

'We know what riding is,' Callie objected. 'We just don't happen to have anything much to ride.'

'If some of these old horses had been kept working,' said Phyllis, to whom a horse was a vehicle, 'they wouldn't have stiffened up, right?'

The show was quite large and smart, with a lot of teenage girls on expensive horses with jockey caps tipped over their noses and a blasé air of having seen it all before. Which they had, because they had been going to shows ever since their ambitious mothers stuck them on a pedigree Shetland in the Leading Rein class before they could walk.

They all rode beautifully and their horses were perfectly trained. Phyllis Weatherby thought this should be inspiring, but Dora and Callie found it rather depressing.

'Push-button ponies,' Callie said, to cover her jealousy of the splendid well-schooled ponies trotting round the ring in the Under 12.2 Hands class. 'What's the fun of that?'

'More fun than something that either won't go or runs

away.' Phyllis stood at the rails with a know-all face, wearing jodhpurs to look like an exhibitor.

'If you're referring to the day Willie wouldn't move and Stroller took Steve into the pond—' Dora began, but Phyllis was laughing at something in the ring, high in her nose, an unusual sound. She didn't laugh much, and when she did, it was at, not with people.

'Look at that,' she jeered. 'If that's a push-button pony, someone's pushing the wrong button, right?'

Out among the show ponies and the snobby little girls with hard eyes, someone had mistakenly sent a long-legged boy, topheavy on a tiny dun Shetland. His feet were almost on the ground. When they cantered, he had to lean back to keep his balance. The little pony was slower than the others. They passed it or bumped into it, the snobby little girls swearing at it from the sides of their mouths without losing their smug, professional faces. One of them flicked at the Shetland with a whip as she went by. It swerved, the boy lost his balance, and his jockey cap, which was too big for him, tipped over his eyes.

He pushed it back vaguely and cantered on. He was a thin, dreamy-looking boy, apparently unaware that he was a spectacle.

'Somebody ought to tell him.' Dora could hardly look. 'It's not fair.'

'Let him make an ass of himself.' Phyllis Weatherby laughed in her nose again. 'Serves him right.'

'I meant not fair to the pony. He's much too big for it.'

'A Shetland can carry twelve stone.' Phyllis and Dora had got into the habit of always arguing. Either of them would say black was white to contradict the other.

The rosettes were awarded. Four smug faces rode out of the ring, and ten disgruntled ones, plus the dreamy boy who did not seem to have noticed defeat. Outside the gate, his parents, plump and tweedy, received him and the pony with hugs and lumps of sugar, and the father took several pictures, getting in the way of the next class going into the ring.

'Let's go and tell them,' Callie urged Dora.

'Mind your own business,' Phyllis said. But when she was watching the next class, with comments to show she knew a thing or two: 'Snappy little roan ... pulls like a train ... overflexed, etc., etc.,' they slipped away.

Walking over to the horse box lines, Dora asked Callie, 'What shall we say?'

'He's too big for the pony. It's cruel.'

'But they look as if they were just stupid, not cruel.'

'Stupidity is cruelty.' Callie echoed the Colonel. 'People who don't know anything about horses shouldn't be allowed to keep them.'

But this was one of the most difficult things about being in the business of animal rescue. Easy to attack deliberately cruel owners who beat or starved their horses, or drove old crocks into the ground. Much harder to tell kind, sentimental fools that their 'pet' was suffering through their ignorance.

It was too late anyway to tell the plump tweed-suited people anything. Among the smartly painted horse boxes and trailers was a red minibus. As Dora and Callie came up, they saw it move away, the father driving, the mother beside him in her mauve tweed hat to match her suit, and the dreamy boy in the back with the dun pony.

They must have lifted it in, and it was small enough to stand between the seats, like a dog.

'Let's follow them.'

Phyllis had come after Dora and Callie to see what they were up to. She behaved like their keeper, in or out of the stables.

'Want a laugh?' They pointed to the minibus turning out

of the gates of the showground. 'Guess what's in that?'
'What?'

'Get the car and we'll show you. Let's follow them.'

They caught up with the red bus. The dun pony's head was sticking out of the back window, so Phyllis had her laugh. She passed the bus, hooted, then slowed down to let it pass her, so she could get another laugh. The boy's face was alongside the pony's, his fair hair blowing with its mane. Callie waved at him and grinned, so that he would not think they were making fun of him, and he waved back.

In a suburban road of neat houses with trimmed lawns and clipped hedges, the red bus stopped at a white stucco house called The Firs, and turned up the drive. Phyllis slowed for a last look.

'I'm going to tell them now.' Dora turned the handle of the car door.

'You can't do that.' Phyllis moved forward as the door opened. Dora and Callie fell out, and she drove away without them. Leaning back to pull the door shut, she shouted, 'All right, walk home, right?'

They picked themselves up from the drive, picked gravel out of the palms of their hands and followed the bus.

6

There was a sign on the side of the red minibus, 'J. R. Bunker Ltd. Builders and Decorators.'

'We saw your pony at the show,' Dora said. 'Can we have another look at it?'

'Help yourself.' Mr Bunker was headed for the house. 'Mind she doesn't bite.'

The dun pony had been put into a garden shed, which she shared with flower pots and spades and more dangerous things like scythes and empty bottles. There was no window and no half door. She stooped in the dark, and when Dora opened the door, she nipped out under her arm and off into the garden.

Callie ran to catch her.

'Don't worry,' Mrs Bunker said. 'She always does that. My little lawn mower, I call her.'

Callie was tugging at the pony's mane, but she could not move her, nor get her head up from the turf.

'She'll only come if you hold sugar in front of her,' Mrs Bunker said. 'Or an ice-cream cornet. She loves chocolate ices, anything sweet. That's why we call her Lollipop.'

'Is it good for her?' A question was more tactful than a statement.

'Good heavens, I don't know.' Mrs Bunker turned on Dora round amber eyes like glass beads without much behind them. 'But I'm so fond of dumb animals, you see, I can't deny them what they want.'

'That's not being kind,' Dora said bluntly, her tactfulness

used up. 'That's being foolish. Did you give your son every-thing he wanted when he was a baby?'

'Yes, of course.' The round eyes were surprised at the question. 'He's our only child, you see.'

The dreamy boy was sitting on a wall, kicking the heels of his riding boots and humming to himself. His pony had not been fed or watered. His saddle was on the ground where he had dropped it. His bridle hung upside down on the branch of a tree.

'He's too big for Lollipop.' Callie had her belt round the neck of the dun pony, whose ears did not reach her shoulder.

'I know, isn't it absurd? But all the children round here go to the shows, so Jim does too, though he never wins, because the judges are crooked. The whole thing is rigged.'

'It's because he's too big for the pony,' Callie repeated.

'Should we get another one?'

'Oh no!' Dora burst out. 'I mean, you'd have to build a proper stable, wouldn't you, and find out how to take care of it. There's a lot more to keeping a horse than sugar and chocolate cornets.'

'We didn't know.' Mrs Bunker twisted her plump ringed hands. 'Everyone seems to have a pony. We didn't know it was all that difficult. How do you girls know so much?'

'We work at Follyfoot Farm,' Dora said. 'The Home of Rest for Horses.'

Mrs Bunker's eyes misted over at once. Always a bad sign when people began to blubber at the mere idea of an old horse. 'Ah the dear patient beasts. I read a piece in the papers about the horse you rescued with the broken jaw. I couldn't do that kind of work. I'm too sensitive. I can't stand suffering.'

'You're making Lollipop suffer,' Callie said.

Mrs Bunker's hands went to her mouth. 'Oh, but we didn't know. We didn't know.'

'Famous last words,' Dora muttered.

'Perhaps we should get rid of her – send her to the auction sales.'

'I wouldn't. You don't know who'll buy her. Find her a good home.'

'It would break Jim's heart.'

'No, it wouldn't Mum, honest.' The boy, who had not spoken a word so far, slid down from the wall and came over. 'I don't care whether I ride or not, honest I don't.'

'Oh, but you *do*! Everybody rides. The Maxwell children ride, and the Browns, and all Sir Arthur's kiddies up at the Manor. All the children round here have ponies, and all those who don't wish they had.'

'They can have Lollipop then.' Jim kicked a stone along the path, went after it and kicked it again, scuffing the toe of his riding boot, trying to kick it into a drain.

'We could look for a home for her,' Callie said.

'But I'd be so sad. How could I face those trusting eyes?'

'We could have her at the Farm till we—'

Dora trod on Callie's toe. 'No more horses, the Colonel said,' she hissed.

'He said not to *buy* any.' Callie turned back to Mrs Bunker. 'Till we find a good home.'

Mrs Bunker went to ask her husband, who for all his proud photographing seemed glad to have Lollipop off his hands. He came out at once and put her into the bus before they could change their minds. Callie and Dora sat at the back with the pony. Jim did not come. He sat on one of the gate-posts with a magazine, waved to Lollipop and went back at once to the magazine.

Half-way up the hill, a light truck came up behind them. Dora and the pony happened to look out of the window together, and the truck swerved and nearly went into a tree. It was Steve.

He recovered and passed them, tapping his head to show

they were mad. At the gate of the Farm, he opened the door of the bus, and the pony hopped neatly down.

'What the – ?'

'Just for a short time,' Dora told him in the soothing voice she used on the Colonel.

'We agreed not to take in anything unless we both—'

'Case of desperate need,' Dora whispered. 'Extreme brutality.'

Steve scratched his head. The amiable parents in the minibus did not look like extreme brutes.

Phyllis Weatherby was waiting too, in the entrance to the stable yard.

'How *dare* you!' She was red in the face, trying to shout through closed lips. 'How dare you!'

'These nice young people are going to find a home for dear little Lollipop.' Mrs Bunker leaned out of the bus window, all smiles and beads.

'Not here, they aren't,' Phyllis Weatherby said rudely.

Mr Bunker, fearing a hitch, put the bus into gear and moved off before Phyllis could put the pony back in.

'Wait!' she called, and ran after them in her classy corduroys, knock-kneed instead of bow-legged, which she should be at her age if she was really as horsy as she said. 'Come back!'

The bus gathered speed. She stopped and shook her fist. Mrs Bunker pretended she thought she was waving, and waved back gaily out of the window.

Phyllis Weatherby was so angry, she was almost in tears, Dora was almost sorry for her.

'I *told* you not to interfere with that pony. I *told* you!'

'So what?'

'You're not the boss.' Steve had to be on Dora's side, against Phyllis.

'Mr Fox said—'

'Mr Fox, Mr Fox. He's not the boss either.'

'I'm going to tell him.'

'Tell away.' Steve laughed. If he had not been bigger than Phyllis, she would have hit him.

'Where are you going with that pony?' She picked on Callie, who was smaller. 'There's no stable room, and if you put it out, the others will kick its stupid head in.'

'I'm not going to.' Callie was walking the little pony like a dog on a lead.

'Take it back,' Phyllis Weatherby ordered. 'It's a long walk but serve you right. Take it back.'

She stormed into Flypaper's stable and began ferociously mucking out, swearing at the amiable horse to 'Move over! Get up, damn you!' Flypaper stood by the end wall and looked at her with hurt, astonished eyes.

Callie tied the pony to a stake on what had been a lawn by the house when anyone had time to keep a lawn.

Dora went to get her jacket out of Phyllis Weatherby's car. Steve called her urgently to help with Lancelot, who had sagged down to roll and couldn't get up, and she ran, leaving the car door open.

This is what they pieced together afterwards:

Callie was famous for rotten knots. Lollipop, who was a clever little pony, must have untied the rope with her teeth, wandered away and got into the car, reminded of her own minibus. When Phyllis left, still blindly furious, she banged shut the door and did not find out until she slammed on the brakes at the Cross Keys Hotel and a soft nose bumped the back of her neck, that she had a tiny pony sitting on the floor of her car.

'Carried on alarming,' the hotel manager told Dora on the telephone. 'She turns the pony loose, goes straight upstairs and packs her bags and takes off. "Send the bill to the Farm," she says.'

'Oh Lord.'

'It's not so much that, since I trust the Colonel. But the pony is in my wife's kitchen garden. She's holding it off her lettuce seedlings with a rake.'

Dora went on her bicycle to fetch Lollipop, and led her home, trotting by the back wheel. A car with a silver thoroughbred on the radiator slowed alongside.

'Phyllis Weatherby stopped by my place on her way home,' Bernard Fox said. 'Had some trouble?'

'Oh no, no trouble at all.' Dora wobbled. It is hard to ride a bicycle slowly and talk to someone in a car without bashing into it or falling off, especially when you are leading a pony.

'Phyllis was very upset.'

'She was tired. Working too hard.'

'Some strange story about someone putting a horse in her car . . .'

'There you are, you see. Hallucinations from overwork.'

'It will be hard to find another worker like that.'

'Don't bother.' Dora put the hand with the leading rein on the handlebar and steadied herself with her other hand on his car. 'We've got someone.'

'Have you really?'

Dora nodded. Not quite as big a lie without speech.

'I'll stop in and have a chat with them.'

'They're not there yet. They should be coming in a few days.'

'If they don't, I'll find you someone else.'

Dora let go the car as he drove on, wobbled sideways, and the Shetland pony bit her in the ankle.

7

They sat up late that evening, laughing about Lollipop in the back seat, and worrying about Bernard Fox.

'If we don't find another stablehand,' Dora was lying on the floor with the Colonel's yellow mongrel, 'burnished Bernie will.'

'And it could be worse than Phyllis.'

'Impossible.' Slugger had disliked Phyllis from the first day, when she told him to put his hands under the tap before he went to work in the stable. *'Before!'* He was still stewing over it.

' "Carrying germs of disease," she says. So I says to her, "If there's any disease round here, it's in your head".'

'You didn't,' Callie said.

'I should have. The next one we get, I'm going to tell 'em first day who's boss here.'

'Who is?'

'Me.' Slugger thumped his chest into a hacking cough.

'Who *are* we going to get? The Colonel tried all the agencies when Ron Stryker left, and there wasn't anyone who knew one end of a horse from the other.'

'Easy,' Slugger said. 'One end bites and the other kicks.'

'We'll have to try.' Steve tipped back his chair. 'Oh lord.' He let it down with a crash. *'Suppose Bernard Fox persuades Phyllis to come back?'*

'She was in love with him,' Callie said sombrely. 'The master horseman.'

With no Phyllis Weatherby to clash buckets and throw stones at windows, they all slept late. Callie missed the bus for school, so Steve took her down in the truck and went on into Town to go round the employment agencies.

Dora went out to start feeds. She whistled her way round the stables, glad to be on her own, although there was so much work to do. It was easier to start a day by yourself, and work your way gradually into sharing it with other people.

Horses, that was different. It was biologically impossible for a horse to get on your nerves. They were always glad to see you, each one greeting you in its own way. Wonderboy with a high neigh. Ginger with a low whinny. The Weaver with a hoof tattoo on his door. Stroller nodding his head up and down. Hero standing diagonally across his box with his nose in the manger to make sure you knew where to put the feed.

Prince, who would never trust people again, stood at the back of his box, flicking his ears. Dora spoke to him and went in quietly. He was still nervous, even with months of gentle handling, after his terrible experience at the brutal hands of the Night Riders. His mouth was permanently ruined by the crude wire bit. Dora was tipping the soft mash of bran and crushed oats and molasses into the manger when a shattering roar made the horse jump, and tread on her toe.

It is the hardest thing in the world to get a horse off your toe. Pushing her shoulder against his, Dora finally managed to get Prince off her poor big toe, which was already permanently bruised and blue, the trademark of a horse keeper.

She limped angrily out to see who was insane enough to ride a motorcycle into a farm full of horses.

She might have known. Strolling across the yard, lighting a cigarette and throwing down the burning match, his long red hair tangled on the shoulders of a fringed purple jacket—

'Ron. Ron Stryker. I might have known.'

'Missed me, eh? Knew you would. So I took pity on you and come back to work.'

'The Colonel's not here.'

'Oh, he'll be glad. Always liked me, did the Colonel.'

'Is that why he fired you?'

'Just a temporary misunderstanding, my dear.' Ron held out his hands as if to shake Dora's hand, then quickly grabbed her arm and kissed her.

Dora hated being kissed. Or did she? She was never quite sure. But she knew she hated being kissed by Ron Stryker. She wiped the back of her hand across her mouth, and Ron picked up the bucket and went into the feed shed and began to measure out oats and horse nuts, just as if he had never been away.

Dora went to tell Slugger.

'How are we going to get rid of him?'

'Why try?' Slugger had lost many battles with this cocky, tricky boy. 'If we've got to have another stablehand, you know what they say: Better the devil you know . . . Find out where he's been working, and we'll send for references.'

'Well, I'll tell you.' Ron leaned on a pitchfork, and slid his eyes sideways in the way Dora knew so well when he was thinking up a good fable. 'I been working for these blokes, name of Nicholson, see? Lovely people. Very classy. Head groom, I was.'

'Come off it, Ron.'

'Well, I mean, until we had the spot of trouble.'

'Get the sack again?'

'No dear, I resigned. We parted like gentlemen, Mr Nicholson and me.'

'Then he won't mind if Steve or I write for a reference?'

'Well, of course he won't *mind*.' Ron's eyes slid off in the other direction. 'But why bother? The Colonel knows me. Why waste a stamp?'

When Slugger came out and saw the shaggy red head appear over a stable door, he said, 'I thought it couldn't be worse than Phyllis Weatherby, but it is.'

'Kind of you to say so.' Ron grinned with his chin on the door like a puppet.

'Steve phoned,' Slugger told Dora. 'The truck packed up in Middlesbrough, and he's leaving it at a garage there. He never got to Town. I told him our troubles was over now that Superman was back on the job, so he said for Ron to go and fetch him home on the back of the bike.'

'There, you see.' Ron came out of the stable, wiping his hands on his tight jeans. 'You do need me. How do, General?'

He shook hands with Slugger, and Slugger yelled and pulled his hand away from the trick crusher handshake.

8

Dora wrote to the Colonel, and he wrote back, with a sigh in his handwriting:

'All right. Keep Ron Stryker if you can stand him. At least he knows the job. Anna says lock away the silver. P.S. What happened to the girl Bernard Fox found?'

'Better answer that bit right away,' Steve said, 'before he hears from Bernie.'

'You answer.'

'You'll make it sound better.'

Steve hated writing letters. His childhood had been a strange one, with no love and not much schooling. So Dora banged out a story on the typewriter in the study.

It began: *'There was this little tiny pony, you see ...'* and ended up: *'I know it was bad luck on poor old Phyllis, but we laughed till we fell down and you would have too.'*

Steve offered to fetch Ron's trunk and his guitar and his stereo set and his transistor and his cowboy boots and his collection of comic papers from the Nicholsons where he had lived.

'The truck won't be ready till next week, but we can take the horse box. More room for all the loot you've probably knocked off. Come on, Ron.'

'I haven't the time to come with you.' Ron picked up a broom and started to sweep.

'Parted like gentlemen.' Dora laughed. 'Are you scared Mr Nicholson will shoot you on sight?'

'Lovely people.' Ron did not answer awkward questions. 'Salt of the earth.'

Dora went with Steve in the front of the horse box, following the directions Ron had written:

'Left at the boozer, fork right past that crummy place where they make pies out of dead cats, over the cross roads where the bus crashed and they had to cut the people out with a blow torch, straight through that town where the bloke murdered his wife, right at the boozer, left at the next boozer, and down Suicide Hill, you can't miss it.'

The Lovely People turned out to be horse dealers. It was a huge stable with about fifty horses in loose boxes, stalls and fenced yards, the sort of come-and-go place where horseflesh is just that – flesh, not soul – and represents only money.

Mrs Nicholson was in the large tack room, bullying two girls who were cleaning bridles. She was a beefy woman with muscles like a man and cropped grey hair round a shiny red face.

'Ronald Stryker!' She let out a bellow that set the curb chains jingling. 'I told that rotten little creep if he didn't get out of the country, I'd set the police on him.'

'What did he do?' Dora asked.

'It was what he didn't do,' Mrs Nicholson said darkly. 'Such as work. Keeping his fingers off other people's property. Following orders. Watching his mouth. Want any more?'

'We just came for his things.'

'You'll have to ask my husband.' Mrs Nicholson picked up two heavy saddles together and slung them with ease on to a high rack. 'I threw the junk out of the staff cottage and he put it somewhere. Out in the rain, I hope.'

Mr Nicholson was roughly the same shape as his wife, and

the same colour, and made the same kind of loud noises.

'Stryker!' His veined red face grew purple. His bull neck swelled over the collar of his ratcatcher shirt. 'You friends of his?'

Dora nodded. Ron was right. Waste of a stamp to write for a reference.

'Bad luck on you. His stuff is in the shed out there with the tractor. If he hadn't sent for it, I was going to put it on the dustcart tomorrow.'

They found the tin trunk (heavy as lead, what on earth was in it?) and the guitar and the transistor and stereo and a strange garment like a military greatcoat from the First War with holes where the buttons and badges used to be. They put it all into one side of the horse box, and were shutting up the ramp when a familiar red minibus pulled up in front of the long stable building.

Mrs Bunker waved to Steve and Dora, then dropped her hand uncertainly. 'I do know you, don't I? Oh yes, of course. Lollipop. How is the darling pony?'

'Eating,' Dora said. 'A nice family came to see her yesterday. They may take her.'

'It will break Jim's heart.'

'No, it won't, Mum,' he reminded her.

'Oh no, of course, because you'll have your new pet. We're here to look at a larger pony.' Mrs Bunker was dressed too smartly, everything matching, not quite right for the country.

'I thought you were giving up horses,' Dora said.

'We were, but people were quite surprised to hear that Jim didn't ride any more. I met Mrs Hatch who runs the Pony Club camp, and when she heard that Jim wouldn't be camping this year, she was quite disappointed. Then Mr Bunker was up to look at the roof at Broadlands. You know, that huge old place where poor Mr Wheeler lives by himself since he lost his wife. My husband does all his work. And the old gentleman asks him, "How's Lollipop?" He takes such an interest in the young people. When he heard she was too small for Jim, he supposed we'd get something larger. So when Mr Bunker went up to supervise his men who are building the squash court up at the Manor, Sir Arthur told him this would be the best place to look.'

'But you've got no stable.' Dora's heart sank. A Shetland in that cluttered shed was bad enough. A large pony would be disaster.

'Oh yes. Mr Bunker has put up one of those nice pre-fabs.'

Dora's heart sank lower. They might acquire a large pony and a nice pre-fab stable, but where were they going to get sense?

'Where's Jim?' Mr Bunker, who was also dressed rather too smartly, came out of the stables brushing hay off the trousers of his unsuitable suit.

His wife looked round. 'He's wandered off somewhere.'

'Well, you come along, Marion. They have several fine animals here, and the daughter is going to show them. Why don't you come with us?' he asked Steve and Dora, 'since you know more than we do.'

He looked down and picked another piece of hay off his suit. Mrs Bunker was easy to understand. Foolish. Mr Bunker was more complicated. Hard to tell how shrewd he was, or whether he was laughing at you.

Steve and Dora put a piece of hay in their mouths and followed him through the stables to a schooling ring on the other side, where a girl the same shape as the Nicholsons, but smaller, was leading out a nervy black pony.

She had a hard-boiled face and a tough, professional manner. She mounted, adjusted her stirrups, checked the girth, muttered to the restless pony, and looked at her father for instructions.

'Trot him out a bit, Chip.' He leaned on the rail with his cap over his eyes and his legs crossed. 'Chip off the old block, she is.' He watched her trot the black pony smoothly round the track, perfectly flexed, stepping out. 'Extend the trot!' Chip obeyed, without appearing to move her legs or hands. 'It's all there under you,' Mr Nicholson said to the Bunkers, who hadn't a clue what he meant. 'You can't fault him. Right, Chip - walk. Then canter him a figure eight. All his orders were bellowed, as if Chip were deaf or at the other end of a football field.

The showy black pony made impeccable figure-of-eights, cantering very slow and supple, performing a flying change of leads without breaking the rhythm.

'Win anywhere with that one,' Mr Nicholson said. 'Always in the money.'

Chip had stopped in front of them, as if they were judges at a horse show, the black pony standing out well, head up, ears forward. Mrs Bunker's amber eyes grew dreamy, imagining Jim in that saddle with the red rosette on his bridle.

Dora read her thoughts. 'But Jim could never ride that pony,' she said tactlessly, and realized that the thin pale boy had materialized at her side. 'Or could you, Jim?'

'I don't know.' He was a very negative boy, half in the world, half in his own dream world.

'Looks quiet enough to me,' his father said.

'That's because that girl knows how to ride it.'

'So will young Jim, He's taking lessons,' Mrs Bunker said. 'Sir Arthur suggested it, and told us the best instructor to go to.'

'But does he really want a show pony?'

On the other side of Dora, Steve nudged her and muttered, 'Shut up. It's their business.'

'That pony's hotter than it looks. The child will get killed.'

'No, I won't,' Jim said placidly.

'You like the pony, young man?' Mr Nicholson looked down at him from under his cap.

Jim shrugged his shoulders.

'He likes it,' the mother said. 'What's its name?'

'What's his name, Chip?' The dealer did not know the names of horses who passed through his hands, without looking at his records.

'Dark Song.'

'Oh, that's a lovely name.' Mrs Bunker's eyes shone. 'I think we should buy it, James.'

'How much?'

In the etiquette of horse trading, it was much too soon to mention money. Mr Nicholson cleared his throat and re-crossed his legs the other way. 'I'll make you a price.'

'How much?' repeated Mr Bunker, forging on like one of his own bulldozers.

'Five hundred to *you*.'

'Too much.'

'It's a steal.' Mr Nicholson looked outraged, trying to embarrass the Bunkers. 'He's worth far more than that, but I like to send my customers away happy. Then they come back.'

'Oh, we wouldn't come back, I don't think,' Mrs Bunker said. 'If we bought that pretty pony, we wouldn't need another.'

'It's too much.' Her husband was coming out of this more strongly than she was. 'Show us something else.'

Chip, who had been sitting impassively in the saddle, staring straight ahead, raised one sandy eyebrow and rode out of the ring.

She came back with a chunky little chestnut, white socks, white blaze, picking up his feet, very showy. She trotted and cantered him, and when her father shouted, 'Pop him over some fences!' she and the pony soared over jumps of blood-curdling height without either of them turning a hair.

'Do you think Jim could learn to ride like that?' Mrs Bunker's eyes were again dreaming of her son, sailing over fences in an arena where the crowd roared.

'On that pony, he could,' said Mr Nicholson (child murderer). 'Quiet as a baby. Anyone could ride him.'

'He was pulling all the way.' Dora had to say it.

'Mouth like velvet.' Mr Nicholson shot her a look. 'You could ride him to church.' He had all the horse trading clichés. 'What do you say, young man?' He clapped a heavy hand on Jim's narrow shoulder.

Jim shifted a sweet to the other side of his mouth. 'I don't really care for jumping, thank you,' he said politely.

'O.K., Chip. Get that bay pony out here.'

A stable boy was standing by the gate of the ring, holding a pony which was probably the one they had planned to sell to the Bunkers. The other two were window dressing. It was a plain but pleasant looking bright bay. It moved rather lifelessly with Chip, who looked bored, hopped neatly enough over two small jumps, stopped, stood still.

'Perfect picture of a child's hunter,' Mr Nicholson said, though it did not look as if it had enough energy to keep up with hounds for long. 'Tailor-made for you. Willing and wise. Safe as a rock. Look at him stand. Grow barnacles, that one would, before he'd move on without command.'

'You think that's the one we should buy?' Mrs Bunker asked naïvely.

'If you ask my advice, Madam, I'll give it to you,' Mr Nicholson said, as if he did not dish out advice all day long whether anyone asked for it or not. 'You'll not find a pony of this quality, if you—'

'How much?' Mr Bunker interrupted.

The dealer named a price that was less than the black or the chestnut, but far too much for this rather ordinary pony, whose quality, if he had any, was not in his looks.

But Mrs Bunker was prodding her husband with a finger in a white glove and hissing, 'Let's!'

'You like it, son?'

'He loves it,' Jim's mother said. 'What's its name?'

'What's its name, Chip?'

The girl shrugged. She got off and led the pony away, as if she were sick of riding it.

'His name is Barney,' Jim said, more positively than usual.

'Why, dear?'

'Grow barnacles, he said.' Jim only listened to scraps of conversation. 'Barnacle Bill.'

'What do you think?' Mrs Bunker asked Steve and Dora.

'There's something not quite right about him.' Mr Nicholson had not moved away, so Dora had to say it in front of him.

'You should get him vetted,' Steve said. 'He looks a bit off.'

'The vet's just seen him,' Mr Nicholson cut in. 'Touch of shipping fever. We've only had him down from Scotland a few days. They always get a touch of that, didn't you know?'

'No,' Steve said, meaning: They don't always get shipping fever; but Mr Nicholson took it to mean that he didn't know, and said tartly, 'You kids don't know everything.'

'Will he fit in the bus?' Mrs Bunker asked.

'Hardly, Madam.' How could he sell a perfectly good pony – any pony – to people who so obviously knew nothing? 'But I'll tell you what I'll do for you. I'll get one of my men to hitch up the trailer and run him over to your place this afternoon, so your boy—'

'How much extra?'

Mr Nicholson named a figure that was roughly twice the fair price for transporting a horse that distance. Then his thick hands clenched and the cords of his neck stood out as Dora told the Bunkers cheerfully, 'We've got our horse box here, and we have to go right by your place. We'll bring him.'

There *was* something a little funny about the pony. Something about the expression of his eye – what was it?'

He was very stubborn. When Chip led him up to the horse box, he stopped dead at the foot of the ramp, with his head stuck out and his jaw set against the pull of the halter rope. Mr Nicholson picked up a handful of gravel and threw it. He shouted, he hit the pony with a whip, he tried to pull it in with a long rope round the quarters. He finally hit it with a short plank of wood and called it an obstinate swine. Chip flung the halter rope over the pony's neck and went away.

Mrs Bunker began to wring her hands. Jim had wandered away. Steve, who had been standing watching with his hands in his pockets, said, 'Can I try?'

'He's all yours.' Mr Nicholson walked off, so unfortunately he didn't see Steve speak to the pony and stroke it and get it to relax. Then he held it while Dora lifted a front foot and set it on the ramp. As the pony relaxed more, she was able to put the other foot on. Barnacle Bill stayed like that for a while, with his eyes half closed, then he sighed, and walked quietly into the horse box.

9

Ron Stryker was as lazy and dodgy as ever. He had to be watched, since he did not instinctively put the horses before himself, as the others did.

Steve came in to supper one evening and found him with his face already in a bowl of Slugger's pea soup that was almost thick enough to eat with a knife and fork.

'I thought you'd done the buckets,' Steve said. 'You didn't give Ranger any water.'

Ron shrugged. 'That's his problem.'

'Get on out there and see to it.' Slugger threatened him with the carving knife.

'*I* did.' Steve sat down with a sigh.

'Don't worry, Slug,' Ron said soothingly, through soup. 'There's always some mug to do it.'

But he was an extra pair of hands, and they were getting back to their old routine, and the farm was straightening up.

'Burnished Bernie can come any time he likes.' Dora looked round the tidy yard, barrows lined up, tools hanging in place, manure heap cleared, and the clatter of Mr Beckett's mower coming up like evening insects from the hay field. 'Perhaps we should invite him before something goes wrong.'

'Never invite trouble.' Slugger shook his head.

'He's sure to come and check on Ron.'

'He'd better come on me day off,' Ron said from the roof of the donkey stable where he was plucking odd chords out of his guitar, 'for he won't like what he sees.'

'Why don't you change the image then?' Dora looked up, and he threw a piece of loose tile at her.

'Can't,' he said. 'I was borned like this.'

'With long red hair and jeans that stand up by themselves?'

'Yus.'

Callie stayed home from school and they worked all next day raking the cut hay into windrows. By the time they had done the evening stable work, everyone was exhausted. But Dora was restless. Ever since they had put Barney into the Bunkers' clean, roomy loose box, sweet with the tang of new wood, she had been worried.

'It's not your business,' Steve said when she worried aloud.

But Dora went on worrying. Every horse was her business. She hated politics, but the only reason she would like to be the first woman Prime Minister was to put through a law that people must pass a test for a licence to keep horses. Dora would make up the test.

'Is it all right if I take Hero out tomorrow?' she asked Callie. Hero, like the others, was a Follyfoot horse, belonging to nobody; but Callie had rescued him from the circus, so she was always asked.

'I couldn't even climb into a saddle.' Holding the brush gingerly in her sore hand, Callie was sitting on the back doorstep brushing hay out of her long hair. Whatever she did, even raking a hay field, she always managed to get it all over her patchy jeans. 'Where are you going?'

'I thought I'd ride over to the Bunkers' and look at that pony.'

'Haven't you got enough horses here to worry about?' Steve called from inside the house.

'Let me go.' She was going anyway, but she wanted to please Steve by asking him. On friendly days like today, when they had all been close and companionable, working together in the hayfield on the side of the hill, with the early summer meadows, patched with buttercups, spreading away to the blue haze of the hills, she wanted to please everybody.

Steve laughed. 'I couldn't stop you. Somebody else's horse is always more fascinating. But for God's sake don't come back with the thing.'

Barney was out in the small paddock at the back of the pre-fab loose box, now smartly creosoted, with a white door and white trim on the window.

'But he's never been in it, the beggar,' Mr Bunker said glumly, 'since Jim turned him out to graze two days after we got him.'

'I can't catch him,' Jim said resignedly.

They stood by the gate, watching the bay pony, head down in the far corner of the paddock.

'You mean, you haven't been able to catch him for two weeks?'

'That's about the size of it,' the father said. 'We tried with oats, we tried with sugar, we tried with carrots. We tried to corner him. We got the neighbours round and tried to drive him, but he puts his head down and comes at you with his teeth, or else whips round with his heels.'

'What was he like to ride?' Dora asked.

'I don't know', Jim said. 'I couldn't get the bridle on. That's why I turned him out. But then I couldn't catch him, and I got sick of it. I don't care whether I ride or not anyway.'

'Oh yes you do.' His mother had come out of the house, looking more human in an apron, with a tea towel in her hand. 'He's longing to ride his new pony, but the animal is mad. I rang up Mr Nicholson. "Nothing wrong with it when it left here," he said. "A deal is a deal".'

'I'll bet I know why', Dora said grimly 'He knew what the pony was like.'

'Then why did it go so quietly with that girl?'

'Tranquillizers. It was drugged.'

'Oh no.'

'Oh yes. That's what they do. Ron Stryker, a boy who works with us, told me. He's been with second rate dealers. He knows all the tricks.'

'I'll sue Nicholson', Mr Bunker said.

'You can't prove anything. The drug has worn off long ago. That's why the pony has gone back to being hard to handle.'

Jim was looking mournful. 'I did like Barney, you know,' he told Dora. 'That first day, when he was nice and quiet, sat in the manger and told him stories about places we'd go, picnics, and wading the ford, and going up the hill to see the Roman graves. He liked it. He put his ears one back and one forward, listening with one and thinking with the other.'

'Would you like me to try and catch him?'

'Yes, please. Perhaps you can make him quiet again.'

'I can try. He must have been badly treated. Perhaps I can get back his confidence.'

Dora put Hero into the new loose box, where he began to lick the heart out of the bright galvanized manger where Barney had had his last feed. With the Bunkers perched on the gate like crows, she walked into the middle of the paddock and stood still with her hands behind her back. Most horses will eventually come up to you if you stand still. When he came closer, she would breathe at him as if she were another horse, so he could get to know her.

He had his back to her. His head was down to the grass, but he was watching her through his hind legs. She took a few steps forward. Suddenly he whipped round and came at her with his ears back.

Dora was not as brave as all that. She turned and ran.

'Join the club.' Mr Bunker moved along to make room for her on the gate. 'That's what he did with us.'

'What shall we *do*?' his wife wailed. 'We can't just leave him in that field until he dies.'

'You could ring Mr Nicholson and tell him to come and take his pony back.'

'I tried that. "A deal is a deal," he said. He was quite rude.'

'Get me some oats and a rope,' Dora told Jim. 'I'll try again.'

She put the bowl of oats on the ground and stood back. The pony was suspicious at first, but at last he moved forward and began to eat. Every time Dora moved towards him, he flung up his head and backed away. Once he spun round and kicked out.

'Be careful!' the mother called unnecessarily.

The kick had just nicked Dora's hip bone, painfully enough to rouse her fighting spirit. Shutting her ears to Mrs Bunker yelling advice and warnings from the gate, she began to move closer, foot by foot. The pony ate and watched her.

Watching him, she crouched and got her hand on the bowl of oats. He would have stayed while she held it, but Mrs Bunker shouted, 'Hooray!' and Barney jerked up his head and backed away.

Dora turned round angrily. 'You wrecked it.'

'Why don't you go in the house, Marion?' Mr Bunker said mildly, and his wife said huffily, 'All right, I will. I don't want to see her brains kicked out,' as if the whole enterprise were Dora's fault.

Dora started again. At last she was standing with the bowl and the pony was eating from it. She took the weight of it in one hand and inched the other round the rim until she—

Got him! She dropped the bowl and clung on to the halter as the pony pulled her all over the field, dragging her feet through the grass.

'Let go!' Mrs Bunker screamed from an upstairs window.

'Hang on!' Mr Bunker shouted from the gate.

Dora kept talking to the pony, and he was slowing and becoming quieter. At last she managed to get the rope through the halter. She pulled him to a stop and he stood, trembling and blowing. So did Dora. Her legs were like a quivering jelly. But he had given in.

She led him to the gate. The first time she put her hand on his neck, he shied away. The second time, he let it stay there. She told Jim to take out Hero, and led Barney into the loose box, stroking him under the mane and telling him how splendid he was.

'I think he's afraid, not mean,' she told Jim. 'You can tell by the eye. And the ears. A mean horse will flatten his ears back all the time, but Barney's are—'

Mrs Bunker had come running from the house, crying out how clever Dora was. Outside the stable, she flung up her hand to pat the pony, and he bit off the very tip of her finger and spat it out into the straw.

Dora stayed with Jim while Mr Bunker took his wife to hospital with a bath towel wrapped round her hand. When she came back with the finger bandaged and splinted, they were in the stable and the pony was licking salt out of Jim's hand.

'He's really all right,' Dora said, adding in thought, but not in words, *Unless you go up to him the wrong way.*

'He is not all right. He tried to kill me. We're going to ring the vet and have the pony shot.'

Jim went white. He dropped his hand and ran out of the stable and into the house.

'You can't,' Dora said. 'I mean it was awful about your finger, and I'm dreadfully sorry, but—'

She looked at Barney, with his honest bay pony head, and felt sorrier for him than for Mrs Bunker. She was in charge of her stupid life. What had happened to him was not his fault. 'Let me work with him.'

'He's got to go.' When Mr Bunker made up his mind, he was unshakable. That was why he was successful in his business. 'I'm phoning the vet. He goes tonight.'

'Then let me take him. Let me try him at the Farm. That family did take Lollipop, so there's room.'

'I don't care what you do with him,' Mr Bunker said, 'as long as he's out of here tonight. Dead or alive.'

Dora snapped the rope on to Barney's halter, mounted Hero, and led the pony down the drive at the side of the quiet old horse.

'Good riddance!' Mrs Bunker called after her hysterically. 'I never did like him anyway. Sir Arthur's boys said he was common.'

10

He was a bit common, with the rather large head and long ears, but not enough to prevent him moving well and freely. He shied at things along the road, and Hero bit him on the neck when he bumped into him. Sometimes he tried to pull away, sometimes he hung back, so that Dora had to drag him along.

It was a very tiring ride. She was glad to see the familiar white gate coming up through the twilight, and the sign: 'Home of Rest for Horses'.

'A home for you, Barnacle,' she told the pony. 'But you're not going to rest too much. You're going to work.'

'What's that then?' Slugger came out of the barn as Dora got off and opened the gate, and walked the horses through.

'I saved the pony's life.'

Slugger sat down on the edge of the water trough and put his head in his hands. 'I give up,' he moaned. 'First that motheaten rug on legs, then that nippy Shetland, and now a perfectly fit pony. As soon as the Colonel's back is turned, in they all come.'

Dora did not pay any attention to him. She was walking forward with the horses, watching Steve.

He was standing in the yard with a pitchfork held across his chest like a pikestaff.

'Oh no, you don't,' he said quietly. 'You're not getting away with that.'

'Steve, I had to.'

He was white with rage. His mouth was set. His dark eyes blazed. 'I told you not to bring him back.'

'They were going to have him shot.' It should not need more explanation than that. Steve knew what Follyfoot was for. To save suffering and to save lives.

'We said we wouldn't take in any more horses unless we both agreed.'

'You would have agreed if you'd been there. Those people were raving.'

'You could have come back and asked me.'

'You'd have said No.'

'Damn right, I would. I told you.'

'*You* told me.' Dora's anger was rising to meet his. 'Who says you can tell me what to do?'

Callie came round the corner of the barn, leading two old horses. 'What's that? What a nice pony. What is it, Dora, can we – oh.' She looked from Dora to Steve and back again, feeling the electric rage between them. 'Come on then, Ginger and Prince. This is no place for us.'

Steve did not appear for supper. Conversation was non-existent. Ron was out with a girl. Slugger was sulking. Callie read a school book. Dora couldn't eat.

She spent the rest of the evening with Barney, stroking him and talking to him to get him used to his new home. He smelled at everything – sign of a clever, inquisitive horse. He ate only snatches of his feed, going constantly to the door to look out. When the Weaver banged a hoof on the wall between them, he jumped and kicked out instinctively.

'Are you still in a mood, or can I talk to you?' Callie's face appeared, ready to disappear if Dora growled.

'I don't care.'

'Can I talk to the pony then?'

'Watch out. He's very nervous.'

'What of?'

'I don't know. He's been mistreated by someone. That dealer probably got him cheap.'

'He's nice.' Callie came in and stood by the door with her hands out low, to let Barney get the smell of her.

'If we work with him, he'll be a good ride for you.'

'But Steve says he's got to go.'

'Steve doesn't give the orders here.'

'Someone has to,' Callie said sensibly. 'He's trying to be like the Colonel, you see, saying we can't keep a fit horse when the old wrecks need us. Only the Colonel doesn't get into tempers and charge out of the gate in the truck and nearly kill a woman on a bicycle.'

'Where's he gone?'

'I don't know. He wouldn't speak to me.'

'Nor me either. I hope he hasn't gone to the Bunkers. Callie, we can't let them destroy Barney. Why doesn't Steve see that?'

'He does.' Callie was rather young for her age, but sometimes she was very shrewd. 'But it's got to be his idea.'

Dora could not sleep. She lay awake in the dark, her thoughts going round and round in pointless circles. Very late, she heard the noisy engine of the truck, and the headlights passed across her bedroom wall as Steve turned into the shed.

She heard him bang the door that led to the attic above the tack room where he slept, and heard his feet go up the bare wooden stairs. A horse coughed. Ranger. Another. Lancelot. Wonderboy snorted into the night. She knew the sounds of them all.

Going to the window, she saw the light go on in Steve's

room. She wanted to run downstairs and across the yard, and call up the steep stairs to him, 'I'm sorry. Let's be friends again.'

Her mind saw her imagined self doing this, but her real self stayed obstinately by the window.

She and Steve did not talk to each other for two days. It was the worst row they had ever had. Worse than the time the donkey scraped him off against a fence post, and Dora laughed at the donkey and Steve thought she was laughing at him. Even worse than the time his beloved old grey Tommy died when he was away, and he said it was Dora's fault.

They communicated through the others.

'Callie, ask Steve where he put the liniment.'

'Slugger, tell Dora I've ordered the linseed and horse nuts.'

Ron Stryker really enjoyed it. He invented messages from both of them, and carried them back and forth to annoy.

'Dora dear, Steve says your stables are a disgrace and you've to do them over.'

'Steve, old fellow, the little lady wants you to come out and see how well she rides the bay pony.'

'Dora, you and his young lordship are wanted in the house. Slugger's made boiled tripe with chocolate sauce and pickles.'

Barney had a lot of fear to overcome and a lot of bad treatment to forget, but Dora worked with him slowly and patiently.

She could see why Jim had not been able to get a bridle on him. First he walked round and round the box so that Dora could not even get the reins round his neck. When she did, he backed into a corner and threw up his head. Being taller than Jim, Dora was able to get her hand between his ears, holding the top of the bridle. Her other hand held the bit against his clenched teeth. She put her thumb into the gap between the front teeth and the tusk and pressed on the gum, but his teeth were still tightly clamped.

'Try sugar.' Callie was watching.

'If I start that, I'll never get the bit in without it. Come in and pinch his nose.'

Several times, Barney managed to jerk his head away, but at last Callie held his nose tight. He snorted, opened his mouth, and the bit went in.

'I'm sorry, Barnacle,' Dora said, as she adjusted the buckles of the bridle. 'But you're too good a pony to be left to rot.'

The first time she got on him, he bucked her off (that was the time Ron called Steve to come and watch).

She got on again, kept his head up, and sent him forward with her legs, and though he jibbed and side-stepped and did not go very straight, he did trot across the field.

Any pressure on the bit made him throw up his head, expecting a jab in the mouth. Winning him back to confidence was going to take time, but he had a comfortable, easy way of going, and Dora thought he had been well schooled once.

11

Steve, who normally would have been as enthusiastic as Dora about retraining the pony, would have no part in it. Even after the row died down and they began to talk to each other again, he still would not listen to her supper time prattle about the progress of Barnacle Bill.

'You spend too much time with that pony,' he said, 'while we do the work.'

'That's a lie!' Dora pushed back her chair and stood up. 'I do all my work first.' The chair fell into the fireplace.

'Might do that in the winter,' Ron remarked, 'when we're short of firewood.'

'Sit down and finish your supper,' Slugger said.

'I'm not hungry.'

'The pony should be turned out anyway,' Steve grumbled as she went to the door.

'But Dora might not be able to catch him,' Callie said.

As she slammed out of the door, Dora heard Steve say, 'That'll be her bad luck then, won't it?'

The row was still on.

The next day when Dora came back from shopping in the village, she got off her bicycle by the gate at the top of the hill, as she always did, to look out at the stretch of meadows where the Follyfoot horses grazed, or dozed in groups under trees like old men in clubs, stamping the ground bare, flicking idle tails.

The usually peaceful scene was broken up into movement. In the largest field, Barney was chasing round without a halter, nipping and kicking at the other horses.

Dora hurried home, dumped the shopping bags in the kitchen, and tried for more than an hour to catch the bay pony.

The field was too big and the grass was too sweet, and Barney did not want to go back to work. He was not afraid of Dora any more, but he teased her, letting her come near with the rope, even letting her slide the end half way up his neck, then jerking away and galloping off, bucking and kicking like a prairie horse.

Hopeless. Dora sat down on a tree stump and gloomily tied knots in the rope. After a while, something bumped her hunched shoulders. It was Barney. He kept his head down and let her put the rope round his neck and lead him back to the stable.

Steve was shovelling gravel from the cart into a muddy gateway. Dora had to pass him. She didn't know what to say, so she didn't say anything.

'Took you two hours to catch him.' Steve said it for her. 'Well, he's got to go out, same as the others. No one gets special treatment.'

That was a lie. All the horses got special treatment, according to their needs and natures.

But Dora said, sick of the row, hating the stupid barrier of stubborn pride that had grown up between them, 'I found out how to catch him. Turn my back. Ignore him.'

'You're very good at that, aren't you?'

'What do you mean?'

'Ignoring people.'

He drove his shovel into the gravel and threw it with a rattle and clatter that made Barney jump and pull Dora away.

The row was still on.

It was still stupidly smouldering when Bernard Fox strode into the Farm the next morning, bathed and shaved and laundered and pressed, looking all about him with the bright, critical air of a Lord of creation.

He had come to check on Ron Stryker.

There was a nip in the air today, and Ron had gone back into the tent-like garment which had once been a military greatcoat, years and years ago. The cloth was worn and torn. The ripped pockets flapped like spaniel ears. The buttons were gone and the coat hung open, the trailing bottom edge raking up a line of dust and hay seeds as Ron moved slowly about his work.

From the back, it was hard to see exactly what was moving. Bernard Fox had to ask. Dora looked at Steve, who turned away and whistled. He would not help her out.

'That? Oh – it's Ronald Stryker,' she said. 'The new stable hand I told you about.'

Ron turned his head at the enchanting sound of his own name. A cigarette hung on his bottom lip. His red hair was held down by a piece of baling twine.

'How do?' He set down what he was carrying and came up with what he fancied was a winning smile. 'Pleased to meet you.'

'And I you,' said Bernard Fox, whose manners were as polished as his boots. I'm keeping an eye on things here, for the Colonel. 'He is expecting my advice about employing you permanently.'

'No he ain't,' said Ron cheerfully. 'Dora's already wrote and got the reply, "*Good old Ron Stryker, best news I've heard for months*".'

'In those very words?'

'Well – in the Colonel's words. Set him up no end.'

This was a slap in the eye for Bernard Fox, and put him in the mood to find fault with everything.

Ron's coat went first.

'It's nippy today.' He clutched it round him. 'I suffer with me chest.'

'A little hard work will soon warm you up.' Bernard Fox rubbed his hands, and started in on Slugger. The old man was scouring out buckets with hot water and soda, wearing an apron made of a bran sack.

'Looks like hell,' Bernard Fox said. 'What if visitors came in and saw you like that?'

'We run this place for the horses, not the visitors,' Slugger muttered, but Bernard went on, 'Haven't you got overalls?'

There were a couple of brown work coats in the tack room which nobody ever bothered to wear. Slugger was forced into one of them, too big for him, too long in the sleeves. He went on scouring and rinsing, getting himself much wetter than when he was wearing his comfortable sack.

Bernard Fox had the morning to spare, alas, and stayed 'to give you a hand'. He found the work of the Farm grossly disorganized, and sketched out a timetable and rota of duties, which he tacked up in the feed shed. He did not exactly hammer in the tacks himself. He supervised Steve hammering.

He supervised the horses coming in from the top field. The Follyfoot way was to open the stable doors, put the feed in the mangers, open the gate of the field and let each horse walk into its own box. They never went wrong. It was a splendid sight to see them come into the yard as a herd, and split up, each with his mind set on his own manger. But Bernard Fox nearly had a fit when he saw this beautiful routine.

'Each horse must be led in and out separately. You can't have them charging about like the Calgary Stampede!'

Anything less like a stampede than the orderly disappearance of hindquarters into doorways would be hard to imagine.

Callie got into trouble for mounting Hero by her patent method of standing astride his neck when his head was down to grass, and sliding down on to his back when he lifted his head. When Bernard Fox objected, she dismounted by her other patent method of sliding down over his tail.

'You are the child who is supposed to be breaking the colt?' Bernard's marmalade moustache was stiff with disapproval.

It stiffened again when he heard about Barney. 'The Colonel has often told me this farm is only for horses in need.'

'He is in need.' Dora's heart sank. Steve was listening. Now he would side with Bernard Fox and Barney would get thrown out. 'He's in need of retraining. He's a good pony, but he's been terribly messed up.'

'That's not your job, even if you were qualified.' Bernard Fox did not like to be argued with. 'He should go to a professional.'

'We can't afford it. Anyway, he needs love too.'

'You talk like a stupid girl.'

'I am a stupid girl,' Dora said desperately, hanging on to Barney's halter as if it were her only support.

'And a rude one too,' Bernard Fox said curtly. 'I'd never employ you, and I wonder the Colonel does. Phyllis Weatherby told me a lot of things about you. I've given you every chance, but now I see that it's my duty to write to the Colonel and tell him what's going on.'

'Oh, please—' Dora could hardly speak, but suddenly Steve was there between her and Bernard Fox.

'Don't,' he said. 'Leave her alone. Dora's all right. She's the best worker we've got.'

He was so aggressive that Bernard's boots stepped two paces back. 'We'll see. I'm keeping an eye on all of you, and don't forget it.' He jerked his head at Barney. 'What are you going to do about that pony?'

'Keep it,' Steve said. 'Dora's right. He does need us. There's more than one way of saving a horse. A good one is happier working properly. And so will Barney be.'

As soon as Bernard Fox had driven away in his car with the silver throughbred on the radiator, they undid all his reforms.

Slugger took off the brown overall and threw it behind the rain barrel. Steve tore down the rota sheet, crumpled it up and threw it at a cat. Callie mounted Hero by sliding down his neck. Ron shrugged himself into his greatcoat again, although the sun was out in warmth. They opened the doors of the horses that had been fed and let them stampede out to graze.

'Yuh-hoo!' Ron gave a cowboy yell as they clattered round the barn and down the grassy track between the fences, stiff old legs stretching gladly, heads forward, snorting, tails up like ancient parodies of colts.

Dora and Steve watched them go.

'Thanks,' Dora said, 'for saving my neck. And Barney's.'

Steve hedged. 'I'm not going to let that Fox come in here and muck us about.'

'But thanks.' They smiled. The row was over.

12

When Dora got Barney's confidence enough to start jumping him, she saw what he really was. He jumped wide and clean, judging his strides to the take-off, and cantered on with his eyes and ears on the next jump.

He was a good pony hunter, a bit slow, but a miniature horse without any pony habits. He was still nervous of new fences, but when he knew them, and knew that Dora would not jerk his mouth, he obviously enjoyed jumping. Callie's summer holidays had started at last. She and Dora made a small course of jumps round the outside of the field – gorse stuffed between two fallen logs, sheep hurdles, a couple of old doors for a wall, dead branches piled wide for a spread jump – and schooled him round it with great joy. Not since the days of the grey horse David had they had anything so good to ride.

And then of course the Bunkers had to ring up.

They had not bothered to come over and see the pony, but the father rang up after weeks of silence and asked if they had sold Barney for him yet.

'That wasn't the idea.' Dora was taken aback. 'I'm working with him.'

'We're getting another pony for Jim. His riding teacher, Count Podgorski, tells us we should, and Nicholson says he'll get rid of that brute for me. I want you to take him back there right away.'

'Look, Mr Bunker.' Dora's brain did not always work fast in emergencies, but now it whirled. 'Give me a bit longer.'

'Waste of time.'

'He's shaping into a good pony hunter. You'll get more money for him.' That argument had worked when Dora and Steve wanted to stop the Colonel selling the grey horse David.

'I'm prepared to take a loss.'

'The Nicholsons took the profit,' Dora said bitterly.

'They've been very decent about it. They're going to find us a top grade pony to make up for our bad luck with this one.'

'Very nice of them.' The sarcasm was lost on Mr Bunker.

'So you take him over there.'

'Not just yet.'

'I'll pay you.'

'Oh God, it isn't that!' The stupidity of the whole thing made Dora explode. 'I can't let the Nicholsons sell Barney to somebody else who hasn't a clue.'

'What do you mean, somebody *else*?'

'Somebody. He's doing so well. Give me a bit longer, please? Come over here, and I'll show you how he—'

'I've no more time to discuss it.' Mr Bunker had exhausted his capacity for talking about horses. 'Sometimes I wish we'd never got into this lark.'

So do I, Dora thought, but she said, 'Then you'll leave it to me?'

'Just don't bother me, girl. I'm a busy man.'

Dora and Callie had been riding Barney in one of the old junky saddles. When she heard nothing more from Mr Bunker, Dora went to the local tack shop and bought a second hand saddle on credit.

'What security?' the saddler asked.

'My wages,' Dora promised. 'I'll pay you something each

month.' When she got home with the saddle on her handle-bars, she found Ron Stryker fussing with his motorbike. He was wearing his purple jacket with the fringes and his cow-boy boots with the white trim. The toes were too tight, so he walked on his heels with the pointed toes turned up.

'What you got there?'

'Grand piano.' Dora lifted the saddle from her bicycle. 'What you got?'

'Three-decker bus.' Ron spat on the rear view mirror of the motorbike and polished it with his sleeve. 'Want to come?'

'Where are you going?'

'See my mates.'

'What to do?'

'Oh – hang around. Have some laughs. Nothing much. Mystery tour. Come on.'

Dora did not like Ron's mates, but she had nothing to do this afternoon, and she enjoyed riding on the back of the bike with the wind in her face and hair and the speed seeming faster than it was.

Ron wore his flashy helmet with the stars and stripes in front and a skull and crossbones on the back. Dora wore the crash helmet that Callie's father used to wear when he rode Wonderboy in steeplechases, before he died.

The mystery tour turned out to be a horse auction on the outskirts of the town in the valley, a sleazy place of broken down sheds and cattle pens patched with tin and barbed wire.

'I don't want to stop here.' Dora had heard about these second-rate auction sales to which no one would send a good horse, and no horse lover would send any horse at all.

'Suit yourself,' said Ron. 'I've got a date with one of the boys.' He got off the bike and propped it on the stand, leaving Dora sitting on the pillion in the steeplechase helmet.

Some boys stopped and whistled at her half-heartedly, but

in shirt and slacks and the helmet, they were not sure if she was a girl or a boy, so they walked on.

A man in town clothes, who did not look as if he had any-thing to do with country animals, was leading a skeleton that had once been a horse into a long shed. Dora took off her helmet, shook out her hair, swung her leg over the bike and followed.

Tied along each side of the shed were twenty or thirty of the most miserable horses Dora had ever seen, even in her experience at Follyfoot. Each bony rump had a Lot number on it, like a parcel. There were no partitions between most of the horses. There didn't need to be. None of them had the energy or heart to make trouble.

Dora walked sadly between the skinny hindquarters. The tails seemed to be set unusually low, because the muscle above sloped away.

'Who will buy them?' Ron was down at the end, talking to a lanky boy with pimples, whom Dora had seen at the Nicholsons when the Bunkers were buying the pony.

'Dog food makers, some of 'em.'

'I wish we could take them all back to the Farm.'

'Yeah. You would.' Although he pretended to be tough and cynical, Ron had worked long enough at the Farm to have more feeling than he admitted. But not in front of his friend.

'Some of them have been good horses. Look at that head. It could even be a thoroughbred.'

'Oh well,' Ron said, 'we all come to it.' He and his friend from the Nicholsons turned away, guffawing about some-thing.

Dora stood at the open end of the shed and watched a man in breeches and gaiters and bowler hat lead a proper horse out of another building where the better stock was. It was a well-bred chestnut, **very** attractive to look at. It must have had something wrong with it to be sold here, but the crowd gathered round the sales ring as it came in, and the bidding started.

Dora was going out to watch, when she had that feeling that someone was looking at her, concentrating on her from behind, almost like a spoken summons. She turned and saw a rangy cream coloured horse with an ugly freckled muzzle and enormous knees and hocks, his head turned as far as the rope would allow, looking at her.

'Hullo, friend.' She went back and pushed between him and the next horse to reach his head. It was a big scarred head, fallen in over the pale eyes and nostrils. His tangled white mane flopped on both sides of a heavy neck. The scars on his shoulders showed that he had been driven in a badly fitting collar.

Dora found crumbs of sugar in her pocket, worse than nothing, because the horse lipped and licked at her hand desperately for more.

'I would if I could, old friend.' She answered the summons the horse's eyes had sent to her back. 'Mon ami. Amigo. I'd take you home and call you Amigo.'

'You like that old skin?' Ron's lanky pal had come back into the shed. 'One of ours.'

'The Nicholsons'?' She had not seen any horses like this at the dealers' stables.

'He gets bunches in and sells 'em where he can. You can make quite a bit of money, dead *or* alive. This ugly old hay-burner has got a few pulling years left.'

'What will he sell for?'

'About sixty quid. That's the reserve Nicholson puts on all of them. If he can't get it here, he'll get it somewhere else.'

'Oh dear.' In her pocket among the sugar crumbs, Dora did not think she had sixty pence.

'Going to move along then?' Ron's friend watched her

suspiciously, as if she might nobble the poor old horse, already nobbled by the years, and by working for man.

She patted Amigo on his strong, hardworking shoulder, and went out to the sales ring.

13

There were several young horses up for sale, unbroken, or still very green. One of the best that came out was a strawberry roan, polo pony type, with an exquisite square-nosed head and a straight, springy action. Among the crowd, Dora spotted the Nicholsons, father, mother and Chip, watching it from the rail, sharp-eyed.

'New Forest-Arab cross,' the auctioneer described it. 'Rising four, well broke, but green. You'll never see a likelier one, ladies and gentlemen.'

'Likely to go lame,' said a grumbly man next to Dora, who had been crabbing about all the horses.

He was evidently a well-known character here. People laughed, and the auctioneer said, 'I'd back his legs before yours, Fred.'

'Back 'em to kick,' Fred grumbled.

The young roan was very nervous. He threw up his head and stared and snorted. He pulled in circles round the girl who held him. When she lunged him to show how he moved he put down his head and bucked round the ring, squealing.

'I wouldn't take a chance on him,' the grumbly man said, but the bids were going ahead. You could not always see who made them, because they did not call out. They nodded, or raised a finger without raising their hand from the rail, or coughed, or moved their catalogue slightly. When the roan pony was sold, fairly cheap for what he might become, Dora did not know who had bought him, until she saw Mrs Nicholson lead the pony away, jerking his head down hard when he threw it up in fear of her and the crowd. Dora thought of a slave sold at auction to the highest bidder, powerless over his life, his future unknown.

When she went to get a cup of tea, she found herself standing next to Chip in the line waiting at the greasy snack bar.

'That was a nice pony your parents bought,' she said.

'Mm-hm.' Chip's deadpan gaze considered where she had seen Dora before.

'Is it for you?'

'Till we sell him. I'm going to train him for the race. If he wins, he'll fetch a big price.'

'What race?'

'The Moonlight Steeplechase. At Mr Wheeler's. You know.'

Dora had heard of the Moonlight Pony Steeplechase which the rich old man at Broadlands organized every year. But it was a posh social affair, with all the Best People in the neighbourhood invited to a champagne buffet before the race, far removed from life at Follyfoot.

But now she found herself envying Chip with the lovely roan pony to train, and the excitement of racing him under the moon over the fences and fields of the pony steeplechase course at Broadlands. And she boasted, 'We may be entering too.'

'You're much too old,' Chip said, as if Dora was fifty.

'We have a rider.'

'What on?' Chip was not really interested, but the snack bar woman was pouring beer and jokes for a lot of men, and it was a long wait for tea.

'That bay pony, remember, that you sold to those people for their boy. He's jumping like a stag, you wouldn't know him.'

'That thing!' It was the first time Dora had seen Chip

smile. She overdid it. She exploded with laughter, slapping her knees, clutching her stomach.

'Well, that's one I won't have to worry about,' she said rudely.

'That's what *you* think,' Dora said, and when Chip got her tea first by pushing ahead, Dora jogged her elbow and spilled most of it into the saucer.

It had started as a boasting joke, but the idea took root. Barney in the Moonlight Steeplechase ... Dora's mind raced ahead. Callie would have to work hard. They'd make bigger jumps, get him very fit ... would Steve and Dora be invited to the buffet supper? She had no proper dress ...

She was jogged out of her ambitious dream by the sight of Ron's friend bringing the big cream horse out of the shed and into the sales ring. She pushed through the crowd and stood by the rail, wondering if he would look at her again, trying to send him a thought message as he had done to her: 'Good luck, Amigo.'

The auctioneer described him as 'a big strong horse with a lot of work in him yet. Some Clydesdale about him, I'd say.'

'So's your grandmother,' grumbled Fred.

Some man bid a small amount for the awkward-looking horse. He was somewhat over at the knees. He had huge feet like clogs, turned inwards in front and out behind.

'Must be the dog meat blokes.' Ron Stryker had slid between people to stand beside Dora. 'That's about all he's good for, with that leg.'

'What leg?'

'Off fore,' Ron said out of the side of his mouth.

'He's stiff, but he walks sound.'

'Today he does.' Ron winked. 'Nerve block,' he whispered. 'Pheet!' He moved his fingers like pushing in the plunger of a syringe. 'That's why he's stiff. Tomorrow he'll be crippled again.'

The bidding was creeping up. A bent old fellow in a battered felt hat turned down all round was raising the bids just slightly ahead of the other man.

'You barmy, Norman?' Fred called across the ring to him. 'He'll pull the log cart.'

Dora remembered seeing the old man once or twice with a thin horse and a big cart piled heavy with firewood. If the cream horse was really dead lame when the injection wore off – and Ron should know after his time with the Nicholsons—

Before she knew what she was doing, she had ducked under the rail and run out with her hands up. 'Stop!' she called to the auctioneer, to the old man, to everyone. 'Please stop it. He can't work, he's lame, you can't—'

She was suddenly aware that she was in the middle of the sawdust ring with the old horse and Ron's astonished friend, surrounded by faces and voices.

She swung round. 'Please!' she said desperately. 'Can't you see he's lame?'

Someone laughed. Several people called out. 'What's the matter with her?' the old man complained.

'Go and find out, Norman,' said Fred, and a lot more people laughed.

Dora put her hand on the horse's neck, staring round in fear.

The auctioneer was professionally unruffled. 'The horse is as you see him,' he said smoothly. 'Out of the ring, young lady, and let's get on with it. The reserve is sixty, ladies and gentlemen, or the horse is withdrawn.' He looked at the old man, who shook his head.

'You pig.' It was not said loud enough for the crowd to hear, but Dora heard it, and flinched at the anger in Mr Nicholson's jowly face, scarlet over the rail. 'You pig.'

'Sixty is reserve, I said. If there are no more bids—'

'Sixty pounds.' Dora wanted to speak bravely, but her voice came out in a squeak. 'I bid sixty pounds.'

'And I wish you joy.' Fred's grumble came through the surprised, amused murmur of the crowd.

14

When Dora reached for the halter rope, Ron Stryker's friend said, 'Oh no, you don't. You pay the auctioneer's clerk first. You got the money?'

'Yes,' Dora lied. What on earth was she going to do? She looked for Ron, but he had disappeared. He had probably gone home in disgust.

She went out of the ring to the accompaniment of hoots and whistles and a few corny jokes. In the crowd, a voice said, 'Well done, good girl,' but when she turned – to ask for help, for money, what? – she could not see who had spoken.

She had bought the horse with nothing. What happened now? Would they sue her? Arrest her? The auctioneer's clerk was looking her way, so she turned her back and found herself face to face with Ron, arms folded, head nodding, mouth pursed up tight, appraising her.

'You done it now,' he said.

'Yes.' She could not even make excuses.

'What a spectacle. Christians and lions. Better than Ben Hur.'

'Ron, help me. You know these people. What shall I do?'

'Search me.'

'What will happen when they find I can't pay?'

Slowly, very slowly, Ron put his hand into the pocket of his bell-bottom denims. Slowly, very slowly, he pulled out a fistful of something that looked like money. It was money. A tight roll of five pound notes.

Sometimes Ron had nothing. Sometimes he was loaded. You didn't ask how.

'Ron, you wouldn't—'

Very slowly, licking his finger, he peeled off twelve five pound notes from the roll, Dora held out her hand. Slowly, licking his finger again, he counted them off into her palm. She closed her fist.

'I can't ever thank you.'

'Shut up.' He would not have it that way. 'It's only a loan, don't forget.'

'I won't.'

'I'll see you don't. You pay me in a month, with interest, or the horse is mine. Agree?'

Dora nodded. There was nothing else to do.

'All of it back in a month, or the horse is mine and I'll sell it cheap to that chap with the log cart.'

The old horse came with her, not willingly or unwillingly. He just came. His enthusiasm for life or any new scene had long ago been extinguished.

As Dora walked away over the trodden grass, she heard a lot of shouting and clatter and saw the Nicholson family shoving the strawberry roan into their trailer by brute force. The ramp banged up and they pulled out of the gate, with the pony neighing and kicking.

Dora and the horse turned into the road and began to plod along. Ron roared past them on the bike as if he did not know them. He had promised to tell Steve to come back with the horse box, but you never knew.

And she did not know if Steve would come.

Dusk came down as she and the horse walked along, and the light slipped away into lilac and green over the line of hills, and stealthily it grew dark.

They were quieter roads now, where the cars did not

swish by in an endless stink of noise. Going up hill, Amigo slowed, and she had to walk slower. Would they ever get home? He seemed to be favouring the off foreleg already. If he went really lame, it would take her all night to get back to the Farm. All night and all day. Would Ron tell them where she was? A normal person would, but he might think it a joke not to tell. His sense of humour wasn't normal.

Dora was walking on the right of the road. Lights came towards her and she pushed Amigo over on to the rough grass. The headlights grew and she saw the small roof lights of the horse box and its familiar bulk, slowing, stopping.

Dora stood blinking in the lights, and leaned against the horses shoulder, waiting for Steve to get out.

'All right.' He stood behind the light. 'Better make it a good one.'

'The horse is old and lame. Ron thought they'd doctored him to sell. He was being bought to pull a heavy cart. So I – so I bought him.'

'What with?'

'Ron lent me the money. For a month.'

'Then what?' Steve stepped out into the light. He looked at the horse for a long time, and then blew out his cheeks. He and Dora were perhaps the only two people in the world who would not say the cream horse was ugly. He was a horse.

'Which leg?'

'Off fore.'

He stepped round and ran his hand down the canon bone and fetlock. Amigo dropped his head and mumbled at Steve's hair with his loose freckled lip.

'Feels like a splint. And the scars, that knee could have been broken at some time. But who's going to pay? The Colonel said absolutely no buying. The Farm can't pay for him.'

'I will.'

222

'How?'

'Somehow. I'll save up my pay.'

'You already owe me most of that on the saddle.'

'I'll sell something.'

'What?'

'Oh – what does it matter?' Dora began to cry. She hid her face in the tangle of white mane that flopped on the wrong side of Amigo's neck, but Steve came round and put his hand behind her head to turn her face towards him. 'What does it matter, Steve?' A cobweb of tears glistened between her face and the lights. 'It's the horse that matters.'

'Dora—' With his back to the lights, she could not see his face.

'What?'

He suddenly put his arms round her and held her very close and tight, so that she had no breath to cry, and did not need to, because she was not afraid any more.

'It's going to be all right. We'll think of something. Come on.' He let her go and took Amigo's rope. 'Let's get this old buzzard home and fed. Get up, horse, you're going to be all right.'

15

The cream horse Amigo did go quite lame within a few days, and the vet said there was not much more that could be done. He did not seem to be in pain. They crushed aspirin with his feed to help the stiffness, and turned him out to graze with the more peaceful horses who would not bother a newcomer.

The old horse behaved as if he had not been out to a proper bit of grass for years. When Dora took him to the gate and let him go, he trotted off, dot and carry, his big feet stumbling over tufts. He even tried a canter, pushing his knobbly knees through the tall grass in the corner.

'He looks almost graceful,' Dora said to Slugger, who had come along to help her if any of the other horses were aggressive.

'Well – almost like a horse, let's put it that way.'

'Look, there he goes.'

Amigo had stopped at a muddy place much favoured for rolling. He pawed for a while, smelled the ground, sagged at all four corners, thought better of it, turned round to face the other way, pawed again, then let himself go, knees buckling with a grunt and a thump as his big bony body went over on its side.

He rolled for five minutes, teetering on his prominent spine with four massive feet in the air when he could not quite roll over. At last he sat up like a dog, lashing the ground with his tail and shaking his head. Prince nipped at him from behind, and he staggered to his feet.

'Poor old Flamingo.' Slugger and Dora turned away.

'His name's Amigo. I told you.'

'That's what I said.'

'No, Amigo. It means friend.'

'Then why don't you call him Old Pal?'

Now Dora had two special projects. Caring for Amigo, and continuing to work with Barney, who was improving every day.

One evening when Callie had jumped the pony well and was pleased with herself and him, Dora confided to her the crazy dream about the Moonlight Steeplechase.

'I'd be terrified.'

'You wouldn't, Callie.'

'The jumps are big and they go flat out for that money prize. Millie Bryant told me. She rode in it last year. She fell off at the water.'

'Barney could do it.'

'*He* might. I couldn't.'

'You could. I'd ride him myself if it wasn't fourteen and under.'

'Just because you're safely out of it,' Callie said cynically, 'don't pick on me.'

Dora put the idea back into being only a dream. Anyway, Callie was more interested in Folly than in Barney. The colt belonged to her, and she took him everywhere, like a dog, determined that they were going to grow up to have the best horse-human relationship ever achieved.

The relationship was still rather erratic. He would do things for her if he wanted, but if there was an argument, he often won.

'He still thinks he's boss,' Callie said when Folly pulled away again and again to the gate when she was trying to lunge him in a circle.' How can I explain to him that a horse is supposed to be stupider than a person?'

Sometimes when Dora and Callie were out for a ride with Barney and Hero, they let Folly run with them, if they were not going near a road or sown fields. Hero was his mate, because they shared Callie, and the colt would follow quite well.

They rode one evening down the hill and along a turfy ride at the bottom of a climbing wood. Folly trotting in and out of the trees as if he were a deer. Near the corner, Barney pricked his ears. Dora heard the faint sound of hoofs on the firm, chalky turf.

'Better get off and grab Folly,' she told Callie. 'There's another horse coming.'

Once, the colt had followed two children on ponies home. Once, he had got into the middle of a hunt. Callie did not want to remember that day. The language still burned in her ears.

A boy on a dark grey pony came trotting round the corner of the wood. Before Callie could get to him, Folly jumped out over the bank. The grey pony shied and the boy fell off.

Dora held Hero while Callie caught Folly and snapped on the leading rein. 'I'm awfully sorry.'

The boy was sitting on the ground, rather dazed, but hanging on to the reins of the grey pony, who stood with its body arched away from Folly, but its neck and head curved round to inspect.

Dora came up. 'Are you all right?'

'I think so.' He took off his riding cap and rubbed his head to see if it hurt. The boy was Jim Bunker.

With the encouragement of Count Podgorsky and Mr Nicholson (naturally), his parents had bought this pony at vast expense so that Jim could ride in the Moonlight Steeple-chase.

'Do you want to?'

'No. But my mother wants an invitation to Broadlands.'

Jim was a bit scared of the pony. Her name was Grey Lady, but he called her Maggie, which sounded less scary.

She was a lovely pony, and might give Chip and the roan some hard competition, except for her rider. His lessons with the Count had improved him enormously, but he was still rather sloppy and vague in the saddle, which was why he had fallen off when the pony shied. He had been trotting idly along with a loose rein, admiring the view, quite far from home and totally lost, but expecting eventually to come to a road or a landmark he knew.

After he found out that he had come quite near to the Farm, he often rode the grey mare over to Follyfoot. He would arrive in the morning, trotting on the hard road, or walking through growing wheat, or riding with the girths loose, or doing something else wrong, and liked to stay most of the day, working with the others, or just mooning about. Tennis lessons, swimming, Pony Club rallies, 'meeting nice new friends' – all the things his mother had planned for his holidays were abandoned, once he discovered Follyfoot.

He had always liked Barney better than Grey Maggie Lady, and he loved the old horses, especially Amigo, who was a dreamer like he was. If the cream horse was lying down in the field, resting his old bones in the sun, he would not bother with the effort to get up when Jim came near. Jim would stretch out behind him with his head against his bulky side, and the two of them would doze off together, under the song of a rising lark.

16

One day when it was too wet to ride, Jim persuaded his mother to drive him over to the Farm. She dropped him at the gate, because she did not want to risk seeing Barney. Even thinking about him made her healed fingertip throb. But when she came back for him that afternoon, Jim was in the barn helping to store bales of hay, so she had to get out of the car and look for him.

She stood in the wide doorway and watched her lanky son heave at the hay with all the strength of his thin arms, which was not as much strength as Callie, even though she was a girl.

'I wish he'd work as hard as that at home,' she told Dora.

'He's good in the stables,' Dora said.

'Not on his own. He has to be *driven* out to take care of that valuable pony. Boys. Isn't it always the way?'

'Oh yes.' Dora nodded wisely, as if she had been a mother for years.

Mrs Bunker called Jim to come down from the top of the hay. 'The Drews are coming for dinner. With their daughter.'

'That fink. Why can't I stay here?' Like every other child who became involved with Follyfoot, Jim would rather be here than anywhere.

'Come down, Jimmy,' his mother said mildly, which was how she always talked to him.

'I'll show you all the horses.' He jumped down.

'We haven't the time, and I don't—'

But Jim was already half way across the yard and waiting

for her by the first loose box. He gave her the grand tour, with histories of each horse, which he had learned by listening to Dora and Steve and Callie when they showed visitors round:

'This is the Weaver, who used to be with the Mounted Police until he got the habit of crib-biting. He led all the parades and once he knocked over a man who was going to shoot a politician in Trafalgar Square. This is poor old Flypaper who used to pull a junk cart. This is Hero, rescued from a fate worse than death in a circus . . .'

If Slugger was here alone when people came, they got a very skimpy tour, because he would say no more than, 'This here is an old police horse, ruddy nuisance. That's a donkey, been here as long as me – too long. Out in that field, there's a lot of lazy eating machines . . .'

When Jim had dragged her, protesting, round the stables, he insisted on riding Barney in the rain, so that his mother could see how quiet he was now.

Sheltering under a tree with a newspaper over her hairdo, she couldn't believe it. 'Is he drugged again?'

'No, he's himself. I wish I still had him, instead of Maggie.'

'No, you don't, dear. Grey Lady is worth twenty of that common pony.'

'She's got less sense.'

'She'll be the best at the races. Even Sir Arthur's boys with their fancy ponies looked a bit glum when they saw her.'

Dora was in with Amigo when Jim took his mother to see his favourite, bandaging the leg which she was treating with a new liniment.

'What a hideous horse.' Mrs Bunker recoiled as he stretched out his pink freckled nose. Since the accident with Barney, she approached a horse very cautiously, with her hands in her pockets, which meant sugar to Amigo.

'Ssh. He's got troubles enough without hearing that.' Jim

knew about Dora's money problems. Everyone knew. Ron Stryker teased her about it all the time, counting up the days until he would, as he said, 'foreclose the mortgage'.

Kneeling in the straw, tying the tapes of the bandage, Dora had one of her wild, impossible ideas.

There seemed to be plenty of money for buying ponies, loose boxes, recently a trailer for Grey Lady, an Italian saddle, expensive breeches and boots for Jim. The Bunkers had taken up horsiness in quite a big way. Mrs Bunker wore a Pony Club badge on one lapel, and on the other a glittery horseshoe brooch. Could Dora ever find the nerve or the words to ask her for a loan of sixty pounds?

While she was searching for them among the jumble of ideas and impulses and half-formed sentences scrambled in her head, Jim told her, dreaming with his shoulder against Amigo's wide chest, 'If Maggie and I win the steeplechase, we'll give you the prize money for Amigo.'

The prize money was a hundred pounds. Colossal largesse from colossally rich Mr Wheeler, who did not think in figures of less than two noughts.

Dora sat back on her heels. 'You wouldn't.'

'Why not? We wouldn't want the money, would we, Mum?'

'For you to win that race will be reward enough for me.'

'I don't much want to ride in it, you know,' Jim said.

'Of course you do,' his mother said firmly. 'It's the chance of a lifetime.'

For her to get into Society at Broadlands. As the parents of a competitor, she and her husband were sure of an invitation to the champagne supper. As mother of the winner, she would be the equal of anybody. If Jim and Grey Lady were first past the post, it would be the crowning triumph of her life.

Grey Lady had a chance. She was a marvellously built pony, very fast and a bold jumper, though she made mistakes sometimes with Jim, because he was nervous.

Now that Amigo's future hung on the race. Steve began to train the grey mare when Jim brought her over to Follyfoot. They had built some larger jumps and a longer course. It included jumping the stone wall on to the lawn, over the rose arbour which had fallen in the last storm, and out again by way of the trench they had dug from the drainspout so that rain and sinkwater would keep it wet and boggy, good practice for the notorious Broadlands Water jump, uneasily nicknamed Becher's Brook.

Steve was in his glory with such a good pony to ride. Jim let him do the training. He would rather ride Barney, or potter about on the donkey, or sit high on the ridge of Amigo's back as he ambled about the field.

Dora too preferred to ride Barney. Although she wanted Grey Lady to win the money for Amigo, she still wanted Barney to be in the race, for his experience and her pride.

'You still think I'm going to ride him?' Callie asked, after the ponies had completed the course, with Dora a hundred yards behind by the time she lurched over the drainwater jump and into the last stretch over the hurdles to finish at the dead tree in the orchard.

'I know he hasn't a chance, but still.'

'If he hasn't a chance,' Callie said, 'I don't mind so much.'

'What do you mean?' Dora slid off the sweating bay pony.

'It was the idea of having to try and win I couldn't face. You know I hate contests.' Callie suffered tortures in exams or on School Sports Day, or at the kind of parties where they played competitive games. 'But if it's just for fun, then I wouldn't mind so much.'

That evening, they sat at the kitchen table to make out the entry for the Moonlight Pony Steeplechase.

'Give us a bit of paper,' Ron said. 'I'm entering me old pal Amigo.'

'He's as good as mine.' Ron never lost an opportunity to make a joke about the loan that was not really a joke.

'If you're riding that Flamingo,' Slugger saw Dora's face and tried to make it into a real joke, 'I'm entering the mule.'

'Too old,' Callie said, without looking up from what she was writing.

'What do you mean, too old?'

'He must be nearly twenty.'

'Oh.' Slugger sat back. 'I thought you meant me.'

On a clean sheet of paper, Callie, whose handwriting was the best, copied out the entry:

'Barnacle Bill. Bay gelding. 14.1 hh. 7 years (he was nine, but seven looked better). Rider: Cathleen Sheppard. 12 years. Colours: Blue with gold cross' (her father's racing silks, much too big, but Dora would take in the seams).

Callie read it out.

'Disqualified already.' Ron was picking his teeth with a chicken bone. 'Warned off the course.'

Callie and Dora stared at him.

'Barnacle still belongs to the Bunkers. Ponies must be ridden by owner. Chip told me when I was down at their place last week to see how she's going with that roan.'

'How is she going?'

'Lovely.' Ron made a circle of his thumb and forefinger, and kissed it into the vague direction of the Nicholson's stable. 'Makes Grey Maggie whatsername look like a plough horse.'

'We'll see,' Steve said.

'But if I'm not going to win,' Callie was working carefully

on the flourishes of her signature under the entry form, 'it won't matter cheating. It's just for fun, isn't it, Dora?'

'Yes.' But secretly, crazily, Dora had never stopped dreaming that the bay pony might win the race. 'Just for fun.'

17

He was too slow. Dora gave him plenty of oats and plenty of galloping, and also walked him endlessly uphill to develop his muscles, but he was not built for speed, and he did not have the speed.

She thought he was galloping faster, until she went with Steve and Ron to a meeting at the race course near Bernard Fox's stables and saw the thoroughbreds run. That was really galloping.

It was a flat racing course a mile oval of beautiful turf, with the double line of rails newly painted, and the red brick stands and buildings bright with white paint and window boxes. There were flowers everywhere, and neat trimmed evergreens. Even the bookies, on a lawn by the grandstand, looked more colourful than usual, with gay umbrellas up not for the rain today, but the sun in a dazzling sky.

Ron Stryker went to every race meeting and came back a plutocrat or a pauper, usually a pauper. Steve and Dora did not go often, because they had no money to lose, and if you followed Ron's tips, you lost, even when he mysteriously won. But on a fine day this course was attractive and the races were exciting, and easy to see all the way round without buying a grandstand ticket.

Dora stood by the rail of the paddock all the time the horses were being led round before the race. She could never get enough of watching that marvellous swinging thoroughbred walk, the arch of the fine-skinned neck as the horse caught impatiently at the snaffle, the muscles moving under the shining skin, the whole bloom of a perfectly fit horse from the tip of the slender curved ears to the brushed tail swinging like a bell.

Dora envied the stable lads and girls who led the horses, but they looked quite unexcited. So did the owners and trainers as they chatted in a sophisticated way in the centre of the paddock. Only the jockeys, when they came out, gave a hint in the eyes and mouth of being tense and excited, although some of them who had been riding for years joked casually, as if riding a race at thirty miles an hour were no more than going to the cinema.

When the horses went out to canter down to the start, Dora pushed through the crowd to get a place on the slope of grass at the side of the stands. From here you could see the whole race streaming round the course like a train, turning the bend, and head on into the straight, pounding, thudding, the leading jockey glancing back, each horse's head going like a piston, its hoofs reaching for the turf and flinging it behind, a galloping marvel.

They were made for speed, and made for a course like this where they could gallop flat out. The pony course at Folly-foot was full of odd quirks and corners, rough ruts and soft patches, muddy wallows through gateways, short stretches of grass where you could let your pony go if you were sure of stopping him in time for the bend round the tree and the tricky hop onto the bank, with a drop into the lane. If Barney could only gallop here, he might learn to stretch and reach and gallop out, as the thoroughbreds did.

Dora was standing among the cheering and clapping people round the unsaddling enclosure, watching the pretty woman owner in a white dress and sandals who was holding her horse's bridle, when the idea came to her.

'Good race, Jessica!' someone called, and the owner waved to them in the crowd. She patted her horse's dark soaked neck and smiled for a man with a camera, wrinkling her eyes against the sun.

When the Pony Steeplechase was run and won, it would be moonlight, not sunlight, in which the winner would stand, with the cheers of praise all round.

Mr Wheeler always picked a date when the moon would be full. If it was cloudy, the race was put off to a clear night. The course was lit by the moon, with floodlights in the trees at the start and finish, and the headlamps of cars positioned to light jumps without dazzling.

This was the great risk and venture of the race, which some people (not invited to the supper) said would need to have a huge prize to get anyone to enter. No one, they grumbled, but an old fool like Mr Wheeler, who had been a daredevil rider in his day and was said to have broken every bone in his body, would dream up a night-time race. Although horses, like all animals, can see better than people in the dark, ponies who galloped and jumped well out hunting or in training would be much more uncertain and nervous under the moon.

But if Barney could gallop here on the race course, if he could learn to gallop by moonlight, flat out with confidence on the smooth turf . . .

18

Dora did not tell anyone her plan. She could not even tell Callie, because if she knew how serious Dora was about training Barney, she might refuse to ride in the race.

'Just for fun,' she had insisted. But there was nothing funny about sneaking Barney out of the small field at night, and riding him down the moonlit lanes into the valley and up the other side to the race course.

This was serious. Dora had turned him out tonight, so that Steve would not hear him come out of his box and across the cobbles. She had taken his saddle and bridle from the tack room where Steve slept above, and hidden it in the woodshed. She had gone upstairs with Slugger and Callie, and then dropped silently from her window into the tomato bed, using a branch of lilac to swing herself down.

Barney was easy to catch these days, as long as you pretended you did not want him. If you stood still in the field, not looking at him, he would come up and drop his mealy nose into your hand and practically beg you to take hold of the halter.

The moon was three quarters full, bright and pearly. A fairly strong breeze blew small clouds across it, but they were quickly gone. Barney trotted quite happily in the half dark, his big ears alert to the unfamiliar black and white landscape, but without shying or stumbling Dora would be able to let him gallop flat out. Neither of them would be afraid.

The main entrance to the race course would be shut and locked, but Dora knew that she could go round to the far side, where there was a gate used by the man who grazed a couple of horses on the grass in the middle of the course. They lifted their heads as Barney came in, and one of them called, but as he trotted down the side of the course to the stands, they dropped their heads again, well used to seeing horses gallop here.

Dora went through a gap in the rail, dismounted, and took Barney into the paddock. Walking casually with a blade of grass in her mouth like one of the stable girls, she led him round and imagined that thoroughbreds walked in front and behind her, and that the knowledgeable crowd were standing round with astute comments, and people like Ron were giving people like Steve unreliable tips about what and what not to back.

Her other self was there too, at the rail, watching herself with envy.

She was also there in the middle of the paddock as an owner, chatting easily with the woman in the white dress, and with her trainer, who bore a resemblance to Bernard Fox, except that he was polite to Dora, and with her jockey, who nodded briefly as she wished him Good Luck.

Then she was the jockey, coming out a bit bow-legged. She mounted, touched her cap to her invisible self as owner, nodded at a last minute instruction from Bernard Fox, rode out and cantered down to the start.

Barney trampled as she collected him, and closed her legs against his sides.

They're off! He bounded ahead, and settled down to drum the turf in a steady gallop that seemed, that was, faster than he had gone before.

He galloped so fast that the wind roared in Dora's ears as if she were flying in an open plane. He galloped half way round the course before he slowed to a canter, and finished with his head down, blowing, the streaks of foam on his dark wet neck white in the moonlight.

The crowd went delirious. They cheered and shouted in the stands. They threw caps in the air, and crowded round Dora as she came off the course, reaching out to touch Barney.

Well done! Good race! The winner, the winner!

Dora got off Barney, and invisible hands slapped her on the back. She led him into the small unsaddling enclosure with the little room where the jockeys weighed in after a race.

She stood there with Barney, his neck steaming under her hand, his nose squared, in and out, to get his breath back, and peopled the rail with admiring faces, and imagined the applause and the excited voices and the click of cameras.

'Oh, my God. Oh, good God, I can't believe it. I absolutely and finally will not believe it.'

The vision fled. The cheers of the crowd faded. Dora and Barney stood alone in the empty unsaddling enclosure. Behind them at the gate were three men. One was Bernard Fox.

'Get that animal out of there.'

Dora led Barney out, feeling more foolish than ever in her life, which had already included many foolish moments.

'I dread the answer,' Bernard Fox said, 'but I'll have to ask you to explain.'

'I didn't think anyone would be here.'

'We happened to have a late committee meeting, and that's a better explanation than yours. A thief climbs a drainpipe and gets in through a bedroom window. He's at the jewel box when the woman pops up in bed. "A burglar!" '

Bernie was showing off for the other men.

'The thief shoots her dead and takes the diamonds. When they catch him, he explains, "I didn't think anyone would be there." '

239

The other men, one tall, one small, laughed. Dora did not crack a smile. Barney put his head down and cropped the short clovery turf.

'You'll have to think up a better excuse than that, Dorothy.'

'You know the girl?' The tall man looked at Dora down his long nose.

'She works for the Colonel at Follyfoot Farm. Mad as hatters, the whole lot of them. And the Colonel's the maddest to leave them on their own. I'll have to write to him again,' he told Dora, 'so let's hear your reason for trespassing.'

Dora shook her head, 'There isn't any.'

She could not say, 'I'm training the pony for the race.' They would say, 'What race?' and laugh when they heard. She thought of the marvellous big horses streaming round at thirty miles an hour. They would laugh at poor little Barney with his burst of speed that ended in a canter.

'I don't make sense of it,' the small man said.

'These young people,' the tall man said, 'they just want to barge in to other people's property as an act of rebellion.' He put on the voice with which grown-ups who can't remember what it was like to be young tell each other what the young are like.

'A revolutionary, eh?' The small man was quite twinkly and nice.

'Nothing so dashing.' Bernard Fox would not let it improve to a joke. 'She's a trespasser, and should be prosecuted. I shall write to the Colonel and warn him, in case the committee decide to tell the police.'

'Please don't.'

He did not answer, so Dora got on Barney and walked away. Before she turned out of sight behind a clipped hedge, Bernard Fox, delivered his parting shot.

'And you're too big for that pony.'

19

As the night of the race approached, excitement grew. Stories kept coming in about the other competitors, mostly exaggerated for good or bad.

Mrs Bunker reported that Mr Bunker had been up at the squash court at the Manor and had seen one of Sir Arthur's ponies jump almost five feet. The carpenter had measured it.

Jim reported some highfaluting claims that Count Podgorsky had made for one of his other pupils.

But Jim had also seen the pupil fall off. 'For nothing. She rides worse than me, if you can imagine it.'

Steve had heard from the feed merchant that Mrs Hatch from the Pony Club was buying cough medicine for her daughter's pony.

Ron was still hanging about with his pal at the dealers, keeping out of sight of the Nicholsons, but watching the roan pony, now fancifully named Strawberry Sunday.

'That's your competition,' he told Jim. 'The Nicholsons have made up what they like to call their minds that they're going to win. When they go after something, that lot, they get it. It's not only the money and the sale of the pony, see. But people round here don't think so much of them. They gotta win, see, and show who's best.'

'That's that, then.' Jim was sickeningly defeatist. 'If they're the best, they'll win.'

'*You've* got to win.' Steve made a fist and held it under Jim's pointed chin. 'Think of Amigo. Get out of here, Ron. You're bad news.'

'I'm only saying what I see. Just thought you'd like to know, that's all. I seen that strawberry roan last Saturday gallop alongside their big thoroughbred, and she was right there with him all the way.'

Steve groaned.

'Just thought you'd like to know.' Ron went across the yard, chucking a pebble at a swallow swooping under the barn roof, and out to his motorbike.

'I thought you were going to help me hang that gate,' Dora called. 'Where are you going?'

'Down the Nicholsons. I got everybody here all sweated up about the roan. May as well get Chip into a lather by telling her how good our grey is.'

The excitement began to build up in the neighbourhood. Among people involved with the race, who talked of little else, it became clear that Strawberry Sunday and Grey Lady would be the favourites.

Poor Barnacle Bill. If he could not even gallop a mile on the flat, he would be lucky if he finished the steeplechase course at Broadlands. But he needed to work, so Dora went on training him and Callie, if only to keep herself from worrying about what Bernard Fox and the committee were going to do to her.

What had he written to the Colonel? What would the Colonel write to Dora? She still had not told anyone about the moonlight gallop. One morning, she almost told Steve, but when she opened her mouth, the words sounded foolish before she ever got them out.

'Steve.'

'What?'

'Nothing.'

'Get a move on then. Maggie's all tacked up. I'm going to race you and Barney across the big stubble field.'

'Let Callie ride him.'

'Why not you?'

'I think I'm too big for him.'

'Since when?'

'I just think so.'

Why care what Bernard Fox had said? But when someone you don't like tells you something you don't want to hear, you do care. You even begin to believe it.

After Steve and Callie had ridden off, Dora heard his bossy voice.

'Anyone about?' He was calling out of his car window, as if he expected a reception committee.

Dora ducked into the tack room. She heard the car door slam and his boots in the yard. No escape. Bernard would be sure to snoop in here to see if they had cleaned the tack, so she nipped up the stairs and hid in Steve's room.

Crouching by the window, she heard him talking to Slugger.

'Where is everyone? The place is deserted.'

'No, it aint. I'm here.'

'Where are those lazy kids at this time in the morning, with all the work to be done? Look at the bedding. Hasn't been mucked out for days, by the look of it.'

'Well, you see, it's like this.' Dora heard Slugger go into the slow, maundering voice he put on to annoy people who annoyed him. 'That there is the Weaver's stable, that is.'

'It's a dirty stable. I don't care whose it is.'

'Ah, but if you knew the Weaver. Very messy, he is. I knew a horse like him once, long ago, before the war, it must have been. Big brown horse with sickle hocks. Name of – name of – what was that beggar's name?'

'Where's Dorothy?' Bernard interrupted.

'In the tack room,' Slugger said. 'Cleaning tack.'

'I'm glad to hear it.' Dora heard him open the door and shut it. 'If she was, she isn't now, and from the look of the tack, she ought to be. I can't stop any longer. I came to tell her I'd heard from the Colonel.'

'Oh yes?' Slugger was interested. Dora's heart fell into her stomach like a stone.

'He said he'd written to the Farm and settled the matter. I wanted to know what he wrote.'

The stone leaped out of Dora's stomach, suffocatingly into her throat.

The Colonel had settled it. How? The sack? When the letter came, she would not be able to read it.

But after she heard Bernard's car leave, and turned to go down, and saw the letter with the familiar writing and the foreign stamp on Steve's table, she had to pick it up. It was addressed to Steve, but she had to read it.

'*Dear Steve,*

I owe you a letter, so I'll send this one to you.'

Sitting on the unmade bed, Dora glanced through the first pages, which were about the villa and his health and some people they had met who used to breed hunters, and some details about the Follyfoot horses, and the forms from the Ministry of Agriculture.

On the next page, her name stood out from the Colonel's scrawly handwriting as if it were up in neon lights.

'*So Dora has been having some fun. Never a dull moment, eh? I've calmed Bernard Fox down, but tell her to watch her step, like a good girl. We don't want any trouble at the Farm. The old horses come first.*

When Steve and Callie came back, with Barney very blown, Grey Lady still on her toes, Dora said, before Steve had even got off, 'I read the Colonel's letter.'

'In my room?'

'I was making your bed.' It was still unmade. 'No, I wasn't. I was hiding from Bernie.'

'Oh God, is he—'

'It's all right. He's gone. He wanted to find out what the Colonel wrote. So did I. So I looked.'

'You read other people's letters.'

'You don't give other people's messages. Why didn't you tell me what the Colonel said?'

He turned away from her to dismount. With his face to the pony, putting up the stirrup, loosening the girth, he said, 'I didn't want you to know I knew.'

'But you don't know what I did.'

'No, but I thought if you wanted me to know, you'd tell me.'

He did not ask a question with his face or voice, so Dora said nothing.

He led Grey Lady away. Dora went back to work.

Steve was the best friend Dora had ever had. He had told her once that she was the only real friend he had ever had. But sometimes they could not talk to each other.

20

Three days before the race, Mrs Bunker came over to Folly-foot, white and shaken.

She had been woken in the night by the barking of her miniature poodle, who wore a jewelled collar and slept on her bed.

'Mimsy was quite hysterical. I knew she heard something. So I put the sheet over my head and sent Mr Bunker down to investigate. He took his gun. I told him not to, because it's worse to kill someone than to be burgled, but he took his gun, and when I heard the shot, I thought my heart had stopped.'

She put her hand on it, to make sure that it was working now.

Mr Bunker had seen a figure in the shadows by the gate of Grey Lady's paddock. As he came closer, the gate swung open. He shouted, and the figure – man? boy? girl? He couldn't see – ran off. He fired a shot after it.

The shot had woken all the neighbours and, as Mrs Bunker had predicted, caused more trouble than the intruder. Mr Bunker was to pay a fine for possession of a shotgun without a licence, and Mrs Bunker had been embarrassed by stares in the supermarket, because the word had spread round like a bush fire that he had shot her.

Worst of all was the knowledge that someone was trying to sabotage Grey Lady.

'I think they were either going to kidnap her, or turn her loose to get killed on the road.' Mrs Bunker's eyes were round with horror. 'Who would do such a dreadful thing?'

Ron snickered. 'I got a good idea.'

'The Nicholsons?' Dora said. 'Oh, that's absurd.'

'I told you they were desperate to win the race.'

'And you've been scaring them about Grey Lady.'

Ron laughed. 'Shook 'em up a bit, didn't it?'

'Better put a padlock on the gate,' Dora told Mrs Bunker.

'I told Jim to keep the pony in the stable,' Steve said.

'She bangs her foot on the door in the middle of the night.'

'Hang a sack full of gorse on the door,' Steve said, 'and put a dirty great padlock on the bolt.'

'And on your oat bin,' Ron added darkly. 'There's some people will stop at nothing.'

How much did he know? The curious thing about Ron was that he could seem to be on everybody's side at once. He was mixed up in all sorts of things without ever actually taking part or getting caught. He lived on the fringes of many worlds – the Farm, the race course, horse trading, the motorcycle gangs – without belonging completely to any of them.

It was even impossible to find out whose side he was on to win the race – Strawberry Sunday or Grey Lady. He was taking bets on it, illegally. Ron would take or make a bet on anything. How many palings in a fence, or red cars passing in the next mile, or grains of maize in a handful. What time the rain would stop. What tin of soup Slugger would open for lunch. 'Two to one against tomato. What'll you bet me?'

Dora found him looking thoughtfully over Amigo's door as the rawboned old horse dozed in a shaft of sunlight, resting one back leg, his hip bone sticking up like the peak of Everest.

'What will really happen if Grey Lady doesn't win the money and I can't pay you back?' she asked.

'I told you. The old skin will be mine.'

'You don't want him.'

'He'd fetch a bit. The firewood chap still hasn't got no horse for next winter.'

'You wouldn't really—'

'You think I'm soft, don't you girl?' Ron made his tough face, jaw twisted, eyes narrowed, talking what he thought was gangster American out of the side of his mouth. 'You might get surprised one of these days.'

Ron was away from home that evening, 'checking on a few situations'. He never said exactly where he was going, or who he was going to see.

'I'm still worried about Maggie,' Steve told Slugger. 'We're going down to check the padlocks and make sure everything's all right.'

'And get a load of bird shot where it hurts,' Slugger said. He began to push aside the clutter of mugs, letters, ornaments, combs, books, pebbles, hair clips on the wide shelf above the fireplace.

'What are you doing?' Callie asked.

'They'll be needing to eat breakfast off the mantelpiece tomorrow.'

Dora and Steve left the truck down the road from the Bunkers' house, and walked barefoot up the drive. All was dark and quiet. No lights in the house. Padlocks on the loose box door and on the oat bin in the shed.

Grey Lady had been lying down, but she got up nervously, and watched them over the door as they padded about, looking in sheds and behind bushes, up into the trees and down into the non-existent depths of the ornamental well.

Often they stopped and listened to the normal noises of a suburban night. Two dogs barking back and forth. A rooster who had set his alarm clock too early. A radio. The throb of drums from some distant cafe, the beat without the music. The endless faint roar of cars on the main road beyond the hill whose edge was rimmed with brightness from the stream of lights.

Nothing to see. Nothing to hear. In the paddock, Dora stopped again. Something to smell? She raised her face like a dog and put her hand on Steve's arm.

'I smell smoke.' She gripped him tightly.

'A chimney?'

'No, nearer.'

They were by the bottom fence, looking for the footprints of the intruder at whom Mr Bunker had fired. As they ran back to the stable, the smell of smoke grew definite, grew stronger.

Steve shone the torch round the outside of the loose box. The grey pony was banging against the gorse-filled sack on the door. Dora pushed her head aside and saw, at the edge of the straw, a billow of smoke that burst, even as she looked, into a crackle of fire.

Uselessly she pulled at the padlock, bruising her fingers and yelling for Steve.

'Get her out! We've got to get her out!'

As smoke began to fill the stable, Grey Lady plunged against the door, wild-eyed. Steve wrenched at the padlock, and swore.

'Get up to the house,' he told Dora. 'Wake them. Get the key.'

Dora ran. She beat on the door of the Bunkers' house and shouted. It seemed an eternity before a window went up and a head in a sleeping net looked out.

'Go away. You're drunk.'

'The stable's on fire!' Dora was gasping for breath, her throat full of smoke fumes. 'Get the firemen – give me the key!'

'Oh, my God.' The head went inside and shouted, 'James – James! Where's the key?'

'Key, what key?' A sleepy rumble.

'Grey Lady's stable is on fire Oh, my God. Oh, my heart.'

'Hurry!' Dora yelled. The fire would take hold fast in the straw bedding. She might already be too late to save the pony.

When the key came sailing out of the window, she scrabbled for it in a flower bed and ran, choking with fear and the acrid fumes ahead. Gasping and sobbing, she turned the corner of the stable and saw Steve raise a huge stone in both hands and crash it down on to the bolt. Something snapped. The door splintered open, tearing away at the hinges, and fell with a noise like a cannon as the pony trampled over it and off into the night.

Running behind her, Steve and Dora heard the tattoo of her hooves on the road. They followed as far as they could in the dark, but she had run on the hard road and left no traces. They did not know where she might have turned.

'Let's go back and ring the police. Someone will stop her.'

A fire engine was in the drive, pumping water into the stable. The Bunkers stood desolately in their night clothes. The father chain-smoked nervously. The mother in her hair net clutched her shivering poodle. Jim was crying.

He ran to Dora. 'Where's Maggie?'

'She ran off, but she's all right. We'll find her.' She put her arms round him. His thin body was trembling, although it was a warm night.

Neighbours had come from all round. Raincoats over pyjamas. Mothers carrying babies. Barking dogs. Old men coughing. Children frantic with excitement. It was not until

250

the fire was almost out, and smouldering sullenly in the wreck of the stable, that Steve and Dora saw that one of the people in the watching crowd was Ron Stryker.

'What on earth?' Steve grabbed him from behind and spun him round.

'Hands off. I didn't start it.'

'Who said you had?'

Ron always made excuses before he was accused.

'The fire engine passed me on the road. When I saw where it went, you could have knocked me down with a—'

'How did you know who lived here?'

'I didn't. I saw poor old Jim. What are you two doing here, for that matter?'

'We came to check. We were here when the fire started.'

'Oh yeah?' Ron leered.

What did he know? Was he mixed up in this himself?

Dora pulled Steve back into the shadows. 'He couldn't possibly—?'

'He may know who did.'

'If anyone *did*. It could have been an accident.'

One of the firemen, who had been looking for clues, came out of the loose box with something in his closed hand.

'People who smoke in a stable,' he said, 'shouldn't be allowed to keep horses.'

'I'm always careful.' Mr Bunker ground out his cigarette under a foot, but almost at once his hand went to his pyjama pocket and he lit another.

'But you were out here late this evening, you said.'

'To make sure the pony was all right before I went to bed.'

'Excuse me.' The fireman went up to him. 'Is that a filter?'

Mr Bunker took the cigarette out of his mouth and showed him the filter tip.

'Thank you.' The fireman opened his hand and showed

what he had found in the straw. The white plastic filter of a cigarette.

'It couldn't have been me.'

His wife and son were looking at him. Jim was still crying. Mr Bunker was blustery and red, as if he would cry too.

'I told you. I'm always careful.'

'Someone wasn't,' the fireman said.

Dora looked at Ron Stryker. Under the lank red hair, his face showed no expression. If he did know anything, he would never tell.

Accident or arson? To Steve and Dora it did not matter. All that mattered now was finding the terrified grey pony.

21

In the morning, the police had heard nothing. Dora and Steve spent all day until dark driving round asking people, following up false leads, getting nowhere. Grey Lady had vanished.

'She'll never come back.' Jim was heartbroken. The pony meant much more to him now that this terrible thing had happened.

'I'll get you another,' his mother said automatically, but she was desolate too, her dreams of the race and the party and the glory all shattered.

'I'll never ride again,' Jim said, with a long white face of tragedy.

His mother was too upset to tell him, 'Yes, you will.'

Next day, the day before the race, Dora rode Barney out alone all morning, following the way Jim used to ride between his house and Follyfoot, turning into farms where the grey pony might have gone looking for other horses, searching woods and thickets where she might have run blindly in and got caught up in the undergrowth.

'How do you expect that poor little beggar to run tomorrow?' Ron asked when she brought Barney back at midday, tired and sweating.

'We're not going to the race.'

'Don't be daft. I may get my money from you yet. He and Callie will have a better chance.'

'Not against the roan. They've got what they wanted.'

'You're not thinking—?' Ron looked shocked.

'I'm not thinking anything,' Dora said wearily. 'I don't know what I think any more. Come on, Barnacle, if you've finished your lunch, we're going out again.'

'Take it easy,' Ron said cheerfully.

Steve was out with the truck, looking hopelessly round the roads, while Dora rode hopelessly on the field paths. They met in the lane that ran along the bottom of the gorse common. Dora came down the bank with Barney, and found Steve sitting on the bonnet of the truck eating a sandwich and staring moodily across the broad valley, where cows and sheep and distant horses grazed, and tractors moved across ridged fields, and you could not have recognized a grey pony even if it was somewhere there.

'Any clues?' Useless to ask it.

'Only negative. I've just rung the Bunkers,' Steve said. 'The police still haven't heard anything.'

'It's hopeless, isn't it, Steve?' Dora got off Barney and let him tear grass off the bank.

'Not yet. If she'd been hit on the road, the police would know.'

'Suppose we never hear anything?'

'Then we'll never know. It will be like that poor dog Roger, who went away when he was ill.'

'I hate that. It's better to see an animal dead than not know.'

'No.' Steve shook his head. 'It's better to go on hoping.'

'I wish you had the horse box instead of the truck,' Dora said. 'Poor old Barney could get a lift home.'

'He's all right. He's so fit. It's a shame he can't do the steeplechase course.'

'I couldn't go, could you, Steve?'

'Not without Maggie. Not without at least knowing where she is.'

254

It was quite a long way home. Dora pushed on, trying to keep out of her mind the terrible visions of the beautiful grey pony smashing into a speeding car, lying out somewhere with a broken leg, stolen, abused perhaps, chased by shouting boys with stones, running into wire in her panic.

Barney was fit enough to trot steadily along, but at a cross-roads where they should have gone straight on, he stopped and tried to turn left, and would not answer the pressure of Dora's legs.

'Come *on.*' He was never like this now. He had become a calm, trusting pony who never shied or stopped or whipped round.

He stood like a mule, listening with his big ears.

'All right.' Dora heard hooves too. 'So there's another horse somewhere. There are about ten thousand horses in this country. If you stop for every one of them, we ll never get home.'

It was a grey pony. It moved from the shelter of some overhanging trees. Barney called. The pony lifted its head and broke into a trot, its rider wobbling bareback, hanging on to a halter rope with one hand and the mane with the other, red hair flopping.

'Told you to take it easy, didn't I?' Ron grinned. 'Whoa, Maggie.' He hauled the pony in and slid off, wincing. 'I'm as sore as the old lady who rode the cow.'

'How on earth did you find her?' Dora could speak at last.

'How on earth?' Ron mimicked her. 'Not, Thanks, Ron dear, or, Oh you clever boy. Just, How on earth did *you*, a dope like you—'

'Oh, shut up.' Dora was so relieved that laughter came easily. Or was it tears that wanted to come? 'Oh Ron, I don't care. I'm just so glad she's all right. You don't have to tell me anything if you don't want to.'

'Like what? You accusing me of something?' Ron's eyes

were sharp. 'Just because I've got a lot of good friends who keep their eyes peeled and their ears to the ground – contortionists, they are – and know everything that goes on, I'm always getting accused. Going to have it on my tombstone. "Ronald Arbuthnot Stryker. Always Accused".'

'Where was she?'

'Man found her over Harlow way. Run herself into the ground, she had, and he got a halter on her. Seeing she was classy looking, he was going to keep her in hopes of a reward. I persuaded him different.'

'How?'

'I have my methods.' He closed one eye. With Ron, you never knew whether to believe the whole story, or part of it, or none of it.

Dora asked him no more, and he told her no more.

22

Steve was wild with joy. Everybody was. Apart from a few nicks and scratches on Grey Lady's legs, and a piece of skin torn off her shoulder, she had not suffered from her terrifying adventure.

The run across country and the long jog back with Ron had calmed her down. The Weaver was turned out, and she walked peacefully into his loose box and put her pretty head straight into the manger to lip up the chaff the finicky old horse had left.

'She'll be all right to race tomorrow.' Steve brought her a big feed. 'Ring up the Bunkers, Dora, and tell them she's here. They'll hit the ceiling.'

'Are you mad? After all I've been through to get that animal back. There's still tonight, you know. There's still *danger*.' A word Ron loved.

'He's right,' Steve said. 'Let's keep her hidden.' He came out of the loose box and shut and bolted the top door. 'Don't trust a soul.'

'I must tell Jim, and put him out of his misery. He can keep a secret.'

'It wouldn't need words to give it away. He's got to keep his misery, right up to the last moment when we tell him he can put on his new boots and his Mum can put on her new dress and meet us at Broadlands. And *then* watch some people's teeth gnashing!' Steve gnashed his own like castanets.

'You still don't think it was Mr Bunker's cigarette?'

'I'm not taking any chances. I'm going to see that pony win tomorrow if it's the last thing I do.'

Dora went to tell Amigo. 'All is not lost, old friend.'

He had never thought it would be. He hung his heavy head over Dora's shoulder and dreamed of an eternity of easy living.

'Even if Grey Lady doesn't win,' she told him. 'I'll get your money somehow.'

She heard Steve call Callie to go and clean Barney's saddle and bridle. There was that too. The saddler was getting a bit restless. She ought to be worrying, but somehow, standing in the stable with her kind old horse, sharing his content, it was hard to worry.

No time for worrying the next day. No time for anything except finishing the work of the Farm and then starting to get Grey Lady and Barnacle Bill ready for the Moonlight Steeplechase.

'Since it's going to be run in the middle of the night', Slugger grumbled, 'it hardly seems worth using all my washing up liquid on the manes and tails. "*Makes your dishes sparkle like the dewy morn*".' He picked up the empty bottle and read the label. 'Fat lot of good it's going to do Maggie and old Barn to be sparkling like the dew when there's thirty ponies kicking mud in their faces, all shoving together at Becher's Brook with the banks like a sponge.'

'They won't get mud in their faces,' Dora was plaiting Barney's wet mane, and spoke through a mouthful of rubber bands, 'because they'll be in front.'

'I don't like it.' Slugger shook his head and stuck out his lower lip. He had never liked it. 'If the Colonel was here, he'd not let you go.'

'If the Colonel was here,' Callie said from underneath Barney, where she was trimming his heels with Anna's scissors, 'he'd be at the front of the crowd yelling, "Legs, dammit, legs! Where's your impulsion?"' Memories of her jumping lessons with the Colonel.

'It's all right for them that can watch the race.' Slugger sniffed. 'But how'd you like to be left here biting your nails and wondering who's coming home on a stretcher – you or that pony?'

'Oh *thank* you for minding,' Callie said.

But Dora, realizing what was behind the grumbles, said, 'Of course you're coming, Slugger. You've got to come.'

'Didn't get no invitation, did I?'

With Callie's parents away, Dora and Steve had been sent their invitations to the supper party.

'You're the groom,' Dora said. 'We've got to have a groom. All the posh people will.'

'What about me?' Ron asked. 'If it wasn't for me, there wouldn't be no Grey Lady.'

'So you'll be her groom. Two ponies, two grooms. I told you we were going posh. You can wear Steve's jodhpurs.'

'Like hell he can,' Steve objected. 'What'll *I* wear?'

'You'll wear *the* suit.' Steve had only one set of garments that could reasonably be called a suit.

'Only if you wear *the* dress.' Dora had only one dress that could reasonably be called suitable for Mr Wheeler's party.

Two hours before it was to start, Dora rang up Mrs Bunker.

'Yes?' Jim's mother had been answering the telephone with this dead voice ever since the disaster of the fire, expecting no good news.

'Put on the red dress, Cinderella. You're going to the ball.'

'What ball? Don't play tricks with me, Dora, I've got a splitting head.'

'Take an aspirin. You're going to Mr Wheeler's champagne supper.'

'It's only for people who have a child in the race.'

'But you *have*! You *have*! Grey Lady is here and we're taking her over to Broadlands with Barney. I can't explain now.' Dora cut short a babble of excitement from the other end of the wire. 'Just get yourself and Jim dressed, and we'll see you there.'

'He's gone to bed. He's exhausted.'

'Wake him up. Give him some vitamin pills. Tell him he's going to win!'

23

Steve's jodhpurs were too big for Ron, who was less muscular. He reefed them in round his waist with his gaudiest tie, and put on his pointed cowboy boots and a sinister long black sweater. He added an Indian headband and a tin Peace symbol – Peace, for someone like Ron who was always making trouble! – on a thong round his neck.

Slugger looked less sensational, but more correct. He had brushed and pressed his Army breeches, and Dora had sewn a leather patch on the frayed elbow of his tweed jacket, and found him a check cap of the Colonel's. They stuffed it with newspaper to keep it off his ears.

Callie, with her hair in two tight pigtails, wore her father's blue and gold racing silks proudly. Steve borrowed Ron's orange shirt to go with *the* suit. Only Dora was still in her old bleached jeans as they loaded the ponies, rushing Grey Lady into the box as if there were spies everywhere.

Dora had the yellow dress and sandals in a paper bag under the front seat where the five of them sat crushed together, singing 'One Meat Ball' to keep their nerves calm. The moon was up and full, its mysterious face half smiling in a cloudless sky.

'I wish it was raining.' Callie shivered.

'Nervous?'

'No. Yes. No.' Callie looked at Steve. He was nervous about Grey Lady. He did not want her to be nervous about Barney. 'I'm excited, that's all.'

'He'll go well for you.' Dora squeezed with the arm that

was round Callie to make more room. 'He's a good pony. The best.'

'If everybody else dropped down dead,' Ron said. 'The waiter *roared* across the *hall*, "We don't serve bread with one meat baw-haw-hawl..." '

At Broadlands, Dora changed into her dress in the horse box, combed her hair and put on the sandals. Barney was being walked round by Slugger, bow-legged, very horsy, eyeing the other ponies under the peak of the Colonel's cap. Grey Lady was still in the horse box. They would not take her out until just before the race.

On the terrace in front of the big pillared house, the local socials were drinking and chattering. Coloured lamps hung in the white portico and along the windows of the great house. There were candles in glass bowls on the little supper tables. Yellow flares streamed dramatically from the balustrade.

Floodlights in the trees lit the wide sweep of parkland that was the start of the course, and its finish. Beyond, at the bottom of the slight slope, you could see the first fence, a brush jump, clear and black in the moonlight, and beyond that the post and rails, and then the corner of the copse, where they would turn across a stony road and over the bank. Headlights of cars parked to light the tricky take-off silhouetted the young trees.

Dora had walked the course twice with Callie. She knew every jump, every turn and stretch of rough going. It looked very different now, the fences bigger, the rails more solid, the grass waiting white and challenging for the charge of galloping hoofs.

Steve and Dora managed to get themselves on to the terrace by climbing over a dark corner of the balustrade, to avoid coming up the main steps in the light and the stares. They stood shyly in a corner, and a waitress brought them something on a silver tray which she said was ginger ale, but which tasted in Dora's excitement as if it might be champagne.

They saw Sir Arthur and his wife, very much at ease, talking about 'the tribe', as they called their three sons, who were indistinguishable in looks and behaviour, except that the youngest was even ruder than the others.

They saw the local Master of Foxhounds, a television personality who would rather be behind his pack than in front of the cameras. They saw Mrs Hatch of the Pony Club, with her picket fence teeth, and the famous horsemaster Count Podgorsky, slim and elegant, with shining hair and shoes apparently made from the same material.

They saw the Nicholsons, beefy and too loud in this company, talking up 'fantastic' horses they had for sale, and putting down a great deal of champagne with their little fingers crooked, to show they knew what was what.

They saw – help! – Bernard Fox's crinkly ginger hair moving through the gathering towards their corner, an amused smile lifting his marmalade moustache.

'Dorothy?'

'Hullo.' The yellow dress had felt all right, but instantly it felt all wrong, and Dora knew it was too short.

'I hardly recognized you. You look very nice.'

'Thanks.' Dora tried to move behind a small table, because he was looking at her legs.

Bernard Fox stayed, smiling at her, twirling his glass. He was obviously trying to find some slightly less insulting way of asking 'How on earth did you two get here?', so to get rid of him, Dora said, 'We brought the bay pony. The Colonel's stepdaughter is riding him.'

'Done any training gallops lately?' Burnished Bernie was mellower tonight. It must be the champagne.

'Oh yes.' Dora glanced at Steve. She still had not told him about the race course, in case he thought it was silly. 'At the Farm.'

'Good girl.' Bernie laughed at her, and then wagged his head and chuckled to himself, 'Couldn't believe my eyes,' remembering Dora in the unsaddling enclosure.

'What did he mean?' Steve whispered when he finally moved off.

'He couldn't believe seeing us here,' Dora said.

'I didn't like the way he looked at you.'

'Nor did I.' But Dora took a quick look down at her brown legs, and could not help feeling a bit pleased that Bernard Fox had admired them.

The Bunkers had still not arrived...

Suppose they never came. Suppose Jim refused to ride. Suppose Mrs Bunker refused to come to the party because it was too late to go to the hairdresser. Suppose Mr Bunker had put his foot down because he was still upset about being suspected of causing the fire.

Steve and Dora went through a dozen anxieties. Below the terrace, the young riders were having a picnic supper, on the grass, their coloured shirts and jerseys vivid in the light of the flares. They looked over the edge and saw Callie eating stolidly. Saw several girls in a group, giggling. Saw others sitting alone, too nervous to eat. Sir Arthur's boys throwing food about. A tall boy in glasses who looked too old to ride. Mrs Hatch's daughter with her teeth spaced like her mother's. No Jim.

'If they don't show up, I'm leaving,' Steve fretted. 'Ron can drive the box home. I'll hitch-hike.'

'May as well have the supper,' Dora persuaded him. But although the guests had begun to help themselves from the long buffet tables at the back of the terrace, piled with marvellous looking food, she and Steve were too shy to push through the chattering crowd, who juggled plates and forks and glasses, looking for places at the tables.

'Come on, come on, you've got no supper.'

A short old man, twisted like a dune tree, limped up to them, leaning on a knobbly stick. He had thick white hair, eyebrows like fluffs of cotton wool, and a pointed white beard. His face was aged and lined, with faded blue eyes that smiled at them, a more simple, direct face than many of the others here.

'It's – you're Mr Wheeler, aren't you?' Dora asked, embarrassed because they had been too shy to speak to him when they arrived.

'Forgive me for not greeting you before,' he said, removing her embarrassment. 'You're from Follyfoot Farm, aren't you? Steve and Dora. Good. Good.' He had a way of looking at you closely, not staring insolently like Bernard Fox, but attentively, as if it mattered to him to know what you were like. 'Come on. Get some food before the savages devour it all.'

He went with them to the buffet, and even asked the butler, who looked more like a bishop, to take special care of them.

The butler carved beef paper-thin and delicate rolls of ham, and helped them to pile their plates with chicken, salad, pastry shells filled with creamy shrimp, something in aspic, pickles, olives. He invited them to come back for more, and when he had turned away to open bottles, Steve managed to sneak a plate of food and two glasses of champagne out to the far corner of the terrace, so that Slugger and Ron could reach up for them later.

24

After the ice cream and little coloured cakes, Mr Wheeler stood at the top step of the portico, leaning on his stick, and made a short speech about the Moonlight Steeplechase.

'I stole the idea,' he said, 'from those famous Cavalry officers of some hundred and fifty years ago, who were sitting round after dinner one night, drinking brandy and wondering what kind of lunacy they could think up to pass the time.

'They all had good horses in the stables, and as the moon was bright, they set out to race each other across country for the tall church steeple which stood up miles away in the moonlight. Using a steeple for a landmark gave us the name Steeplechase, as you know.'

He beamed down on his audience, who nodded and murmured, whether they knew or not, to show that they did. The Master of Foxhounds said, 'Jolly good luck to 'em,' and Mr Nicholson belched a champagne bubble and said, 'Hear, hear.'

'With white nightshirts over their Mess uniforms, and white nightcaps over the brandy fumes in their heads, they rode straight and reckless, taking everything in their path, over, under or through. Tonight, we have the more civilized course over my land, but the young riders will take it just as hard and straight and courageously as those first Midnight Steeplechasers.'

'For a hundred pounds, who wouldn't?' muttered Mrs Nicholson, the same shape all the way down from her square shoulders to her hips in a dress like a sack. She looked at

Steve and Dora. 'I know you, don't I?' and turned away, not caring whether she did or not.

Mr Wheeler was announcing that since the young riders were the most important guests tonight, he would introduce them all to the rest of 'this brilliant company.'

He called out the names, and they stood up in their colours, Callie blushing furiously, caught with a piece of cake in her mouth. 'Cathleen Sheppard on Barnacle Bill.'

Dora cheered, and Mrs Nicholson turned round and gave her a look.

'Betty Hatch riding My Pal' – applause. 'John Deacon,' the boy with the glasses ('How old is *he*?' from Mrs Nicholson), 'riding Challenger' – applause. 'Linda Murphy with Lassie' – applause, loud from her own family. 'Chip Nicholson, riding Stawberry Sunday' – applause, and a whistle from her father, made socially bold by champagne.

Chip stood up unsmiling, disowning him, chunky and workmanlike in good boots and white breeches and a red and white striped racing shirt.

'John So-and-so on Geronimo. Joan This-and-that on Black Velvet . . . Jim Bunker . . . Where are you, Jim?'

A slight figure idled across the grass, pale-faced under the flares, swishing a thistle with his whip, flop of hair over his narrow forehead.

'Just in time. Good boy. Jim Bunker, everybody, just in time.'

'My mother got her zip fastener stuck,' Jim said unconcernedly.

Laughter.

Poor Mrs Bunker, arriving so flustered and late in her red dress with the sequin top, the laughter met her as she came up the steps, Mr Bunker close behind, as if to stop her from turning tail and running.

But Mr Wheeler who was terribly nice to everybody,

came down from the portico and greeted them warmly, and took them to get food and wine. She must have broken the zip. The back of her dress was sewn up with big stitches, perhaps by her husband. Poor Mrs Bunker. Her night of glory.

But there was still Grey Lady.

All the ponies were to parade in a circle of turf marked off below the terrace. Steve got the grey pony out of the horse box, while Slugger put Dora's saddle on Barney.

Jim ran up, carrying his saddle, dropped it on the ground, and flung his arms round Maggie's neck.

'Don't make a fuss,' Steve told him. 'We don't want the Nicholsons to know she's here till the last minute.'

He saddled her up behind the box, while Slugger took Barney and walked round with the other grooms and stable girls and big sisters and mothers of the riders. Barney looked his best, mane neatly plaited, tail plaited at the top because there had been no time to pull it. Heels and head and ears trimmed. White star and hind socks washed and rubbed with chalk, gleaming in the moonlight. Slugger plodded with his head down, because that was the way he always walked, but he wore a grin of pride.

Callie stood in the middle with the other riders, riding cap jammed down tight, biting her lip, arms folded over the blue and gold silks.

'I wish the Colonel could see them.' Dora nudged Steve.

You could tell which family owned which pony. They each watched their own. Only the Nicholsons were shrewdly assessing the field.

There were twenty-eight of them. The roan had not come in yet, and Ron had been told to bring Grey Lady in last. He passed behind Steve and Dora with his mouth full and a glass in his hand.

'Where's Maggie?'

'Tied back of the box for a moment while I got the supper you left me.' He wiped a hand across his lips. 'Ta.'

'Bring her in now.'

Strawberry Sunday had joined the parade, with Ron's lanky friend leading her. Then Ron brought in Grey Lady, on her toes, jogging, reaching at the bit like a little race horse.

Dora and Steve watched the Nicholsons. If they were shocked, they did not show it. They stared at the grey as they stared at the other ponies, with a dealer's eye, shrewd, calculating, not giving away admiration or contempt.

The television M.F.H., who was in charge of the race, gave the order to mount. The riders joined their ponies among the trees at the edge of the floodlit strip of grass that swept down to the first jump.

Dora, more nervous than Callie, gave her last minute instructions to which she did not listen. 'Don't push him at the start. Take the bank turn wide, give him room to stand back. Remember there's a ditch on the other side of the cut-and-laid. Watch that little chestnut – he kicks.'

Chip was up on the roan, point-to-point saddle, stirrups very short, rubber racing reins.

'That same bay pony?' Under the pulled down peak of her cap, her face was deadpan, like her parents. The jeer was in her voice.

'Looks a lot better, doesn't he?' Callie said, naive and friendly, but Chip had moved on.

Dora saw Jim go over to Grey Lady among the people and ponies by the trees. There was a flurry of excitement. Someone shouted. She ran, and pushed through the crowd. Grey Lady's saddle had slipped round, and Jim was lying on the ground, whimpering and holding his wrist.

'Who did up the girth?'

'Don't look at *me*.' Ron, with his headband and his Peace symbol, was holding the nervous grey pony.

'I did. I know it was tight.' Steve was kneeling by the boy on the ground, but was pushed aside by a sobbing woman in a spangly red dress who flung herself on her son.

'My boy, my boy! I knew something like this would happen.'

Although the whole thing had been her idea: buying the pony, teaching Jim to ride, entering for the Steeplechase.

'It's all *right*, Mum.' Jim stopped whimpering and sat up.

'He put out his hand as he fell,' Steve said. 'The wrist is either broken or badly sprained. There's a doctor here. Someone's gone to fetch him.'

'It's all your fault,' Mrs Bunker said hysterically, on her knees in the tight dress, trying to get her arms round Jim, who was trying to keep her away from his hurt wrist. 'Who asked you to bring the pony here?'

This was so fantastically unfair that Steve did not answer. He got up, took Grey Lady from Ron, and went with Dora out of the crowd, as the doctor came to Jim.

'I *know* that girth was tight, Dora.'

'Ron left Maggie to get his supper.'

'And his pal was late bringing the roan in.'

'Because he was loosening the girth?'

'By God,' Steve said bitterly. 'By God, I hate to see them get away with it. This pony could have won.'

He hunched his shoulders, looped Maggie's reins over his arm, and slouched towards the horse box, swinging Jim's riding cap by the elastic.

News of the accident had spread among the riders, who were collecting for the start. Callie trotted back, her eyes dark with anxiety in a white face.

'They said it's Jim.'

Dora nodded. 'He's all right. But he can't ride the pony.'

'Oh, poor Maggie.' Callie thought of horses first. 'Poor Jim. And – oh Dora, the prize money – poor *Amigo*!'

'Listen, Callie.' It all came into Dora's head at once, just as if it was written down in a book and she was reading it. 'Grey Lady can win. You ride her. Jim can pretend he gives her to you before they take him to hospital. Mr Wheeler won't mind, because of the accident.'

'But you wanted me so much to ride Barney.'

'That doesn't matter now. Winning matters.'

'I can't. Maggie's too fast. I can't ride to win.'

'You can. You must. Think of Amigo, Callie, we can't let the Nicholsons get away with this.'

'They did it?'

'I think so. Are you going to let them win?'

'Steve!' Callie shouted, her voice shrill with excitement. 'Bring Maggie back!'

25

'A bad start,' the television personality called out in his voice
that was familiar in the homes of almost everyone there. 'But
it's going to be a good race. The moon is up. The ponies are
fit. The riders are shaken, but not unstrung.' Only one girl,
who was a mass of nerves anyway, had got off after what
happened to Jim, and refused to get back on. 'Five minutes,.
everybody, to get settled down again. Five minutes till line
up.'

Callie was on Grey Lady. 'Jog her round,' Steve said. 'Get
the feel of her.'

'I know her.' Callie gathered up her reins, confident now
and not afraid. 'Sorry Barnacle. He would have liked to run,
Dora.'

'He's going to.' Once more the book of ideas was open in
her mind. 'Hold him a minute, Steve.'

She ran to the horse box, pulled on her jeans, stuffed the
short yellow dress into them, kicked off her sandals and trod
into her old shoes. Steve was still holding Jim's riding cap.
Dora grabbed it and shoved it on her small head, tipping it
down over her face.

'Who's that child in the yellow shirt?' someone asked as
she joined the others, letting down her stirrups as she went.
Dora did not hear the answer. But they thought she was a
child. All right, Barney. You shall have your race.

The television star was holding up a flag, while he tried to
get the twenty-nine ponies into some sort of line.

'Back the brown pony, bring up the little chestnut, come
on, that boy in the green shirt. Look out, no barging. Yellow

girl on the bay, get on the end there. All right, all right everybody—'

At the end of the line of stamping, jostling ponies, Barney
was wildly excited. His days of lawlessness came back to him.
He trampled, grabbing at the bit. Dora shortened her reins.
He reared up slightly, pulling, and just when she thought she
could not hold him, the flag came down and he plunged
forward in the galloping surge of ponies.

Whatever instructions had been given to anybody not
to go flat out at the start of the race were forgotten, or
impossible to obey. Big ones, small ones, Welsh, New
Forest, cobby ones, they all went full tilt down the
floodlit stretch of the park, and by some miracle were
over the strong brush jump and pounding towards the
post and rails.

Someone refused and swerved into someone else, who
swore like a grown up – Sir Arthur's youngest. Dora had to
pull Barney sideways. He got too close to the rails and had to
cat jump, landing short and losing ground. Dora gathered
him together and he settled down to gallop his own steady
pace in the middle of the field. Grey Lady and Strawberry
Sunday had pulled out ahead. Some of the smaller ponies
were already falling behind.

Wide at the turn into the bank, Dora had told Callie, and
she told it to herself now as they came to the corner of the
copse where the lights of the parked cars illuminated the grey
and the roan with haloes for a moment as they reached the
top of the bank together, and dropped down with a switch
of their tails.

To get up the steep bank, you had to take off from the
stony road, not put in a stride on the grass. Dora swung into
the light, saw people standing by the cars, a man on the roof
with a film camera – one stride into the road, and then she
gave Barney a kick that propelled him from his strong

quarters to the top of the wide bank. He changed legs and jumped out into the drop, wide and safe.

Beside him, a pony stumbled and fell. Its rider pitched forward, and one of the people scrambled up the bank with a shout.

Don't look back. Never mind the others. It was a dangerous race, but even if they all fell, Dora and Barney must keep going, their own line and their own pace. That was how she had planned it with Callie.

As each jump came up – the cut-and-laid, the narrow brush the hedge with the guard rail, the little ditch – Dora only had time to see that Callie was over, and then it was she and Barney. He took off too soon at the cut-and-laid, dropping a leg in the ditch. He was bumped at the brush, stirrups clashing, by the tall boy, who turned his head and shouted at Dora, although it was his fault, glasses spattered with mud. He stood back beautifully from the guard rail, clearing the hedge by miles. He tried to stop at the dry ditch, because the moonlight looked like water in it, which he hated, but Dora forced him over by strength of will as well as legs, and he jumped straight into the air, much too high, and landed stiff-legged, with Dora hanging on to his mane, because she knew he would jump it like that.

Several ponies seemed to have dropped out, or else they were far behind. Dora was in a middle bunch, Grey Lady and the roan and about half a dozen others were ahead. Jumping well, Barney gained ground at the fences, but lost it in the fields between. But the pace was fast, and the others were slowing too. Dora passed the Hatch girl, floundering across a ridge and furrow, and someone else on a long-tailed black, who ran out at the low wall. Barney was still going steadily, but he was tired. Anything might happen at Becher's Brook.

It was the last fence but two of the Steeplechase course. It came after the final turn towards the home stretch, a stream with sticky banks, which ran across a corner of the park, in view of the spectators at the top of the slope.

After the brook, there was a hurdle jump, then a low rail between two trees, nothing much. But Broadlands' Becher's Brook had floored many ponies who were galloping home to win, and Dora, as she cantered across stubble, hopped a double rail into the park and saw the water gleaming, thought that it would floor her too.

Callie and Chip were still yards ahead of anyone else. Grey Lady did not mind water, and if the roan jumped badly here, as most ponies would, Callie could pull ahead and Chip might not catch her.

Headlights of cars gilded the surface of the running brook. Grey Lady went fast at it, and almost stumbled in the soft footing. Callie checked her for the take off, and she was in the air when the roan came sideways into her and they fell together on the other side, floundering in the marshy ground.

Dora saw Grey Lady struggle up. She must get to Callie. Barney stopped in a bunch of ponies, trampling the sticky ground suspiciously. Barney, you must! Dora held tight for the enormous jump that he would make over the hated water, and almost fell off when he suddenly dropped his head, and charged through the water into the mud on the other side. The dreaded brook was only a few inches deep here, and he was clever enough to know it.

And there was Callie standing up, hatless, filthy, waving to show she was all right, waving Dora on, as the other ponies splashed and floundered over the brook behind her.

Someone was alongside her at the hurdles, and hit them with a rattle. She was alone over the low rail. Barney pecked, recovered, and plodded into the floodlights, to pass the white post at the top of the slope in barely a canter between the cheering, whistling crowd.

Barney stopped of his own accord. A riderless pony crashed into him, and the rest of them pulled up in a tangle.

Slugger was running bandy-legged, his mouth open in a shout.

'Barney!' Crumpled newspaper flew out as he tore off his cap to wave it.

'Dora!' Steve jumped down from the balustrade of the terrace, and as Dora dropped off Barney, he flung his arms round her in a hug that nearly broke her ribs.

'You won.' He held her off and grinned at her before he turned and ran down the slope to Callie.

26

A lot of people were running. Callie was walking forward with Grey Lady. Chip was sitting on the muddy bank, and Strawberry Sunday stood with her head low, one foreleg dangling.

'My God, it's broken!' someone called, and Dora saw the Nicholsons' lanky boy, Ron's friend, throw down a cigarette and run towards the brook.

She left Barney in the crowd and broke away from the congratulations and the flashbulbs, and walked to where he had dropped the cigarette. It was still smouldering. Dora trod it out, then bent and picked it up, looked at the white filter, and put it in her pocket.

'Who is it? Who won?'

Mr Wheeler, fieldglasses round his neck, limped down from the terrace steps.

'Run down to the brook,' he told a boy, 'and tell me what's happened there.'

The crowd separated. As Mr Wheeler reached out to shake her hand, Dora took off her cap and shook out her short hair.

'Dora?'

'I'm sorry,' she said. 'I'm too old to be in the race, but I didn't mean to win.'

'It was a great race anyway,' Mr Wheeler began, but parents and riders were clamouring at him with protest and argument.

'She's too old.'

'She's disqualified.'

'My boy was second.'

'No, I was.

'Tortoiseshell was second.'

'Without a rider, stupid.'

'Mr Wheeler, Mr Wheeler, it isn't fair—'

'Quiet, everybody!' he bellowed with surprising volume for so old and small a man. 'Dora won, but she can't win. We know that. So whoever came second—'

'I did.'

'It was me.'

'My daughter was well ahead.'

'I saw it, I tell you, it was Bazooka.'

'I was in front of him.'

'*I* was.'

'Bazooka . . . me . . . my daughter . . .' But since the race had no second prize, nobody had really seen, in the excitement, who was next in the bunch behind Dora and the loose pony.

Mr Wheeler took her arm and walked with her and Barney under the trees, away from the lights and the squabble.

'I can't give you the money,' the old man told her, leaning on her arm, 'so I'm going to give it where it's needed. I'm going to give it to Follyfoot. You won it, you can spend it how you like. For the old horses.'

The boy he had sent down to the brook panted back.

'The roan pony pulled a tendon. Not a break, but it's pretty bad. The Nicholsons are wild. They say the grey jumped across her.'

'*She* knocked into the grey!' Dora was furious. 'I saw it. It was delib—'

'I saw it too.' Mr Wheeler cut her short. 'But let it go. The pony's badly hurt.' He sighed. 'A sad ending to something that perhaps I never should have started. I'm not going to run any more Steeplechases, Dora. Not at night. Not for money, anyway. Money spoils everything, doesn't it?'

Dora didn't know. She never had any.

When Dora gave Ron back his sixty pounds for Amigo, he pulled a bulging wallet out of the inside of his jacket and added the money to a considerable wad of notes.

'Ta,' he said. 'And for the rest of it. Always a picnic for the bookie, when an outsider wins.'

'But the race was a washout,' Steve objected. 'Those people may want their money back.'

'They can sue me then,' Ron said smugly, 'and admit they placed illegal bets.'

'Money spoils everything.' Dora echoed Mr Wheeler.

'Speak for yourself.' Ron put the wallet back inside his jacket and swaggered off.

By the time Jim's broken wrist was healed, and the plaster cast off his wrist, Grey Lady had been sold to a hunting family who would use her well. Jim was to have Barney back.

'But don't worry,' he told Dora. 'I'll ride him over to the Farm mostly, and he can see all his friends. I'd let you keep him, but Steve says he knows you can't keep a fit pony here.'

'*I* know we can't,' Dora said. 'Steve's not the boss. We both are. We both know what Follyfoot is for.'

It was very sad when Mr Bunker rebuilt his stable, and came for Barney with the trailer behind the red minibus.

Dora watched it pull through the gate, and went out into the road to see the last of Barney, rounded bay quarters, black tail hanging over the ramp, the net up front swinging as he pulled contentedly at the hay, with a horse's trusting ignorance of parting.

The trailer disappeared round a corner. Dora went back into the yard and got a wheelbarrow and fork and joined the others at work.

As she backed out of Amigo's stable, a man's voice behind her said, 'Excuse me, miss.'

Dora set down the barrow.

'I've got my cattle truck outside,' the man said. 'I found this wretched horse. Belonged to a neighbour of mine, who went away for a bit. I thought he'd told somebody to look out for the horse, but when I went by his place, I saw he'd simply left him. In a little yard. No grass. No more hay. Water all gone.'

'How *can* people—' Dora started out with him towards the truck.

'They do.' The man shook his head. 'I've been abroad. Egypt, South America, India. I've seen how they treat horses. But this poor fellow . . . I can't take him, so I thought of you. When I couldn't get an answer on the phone, I pushed him into the truck and brought him over. I know there is always room here for a horse in trouble.'

'Yes.'

Dora called Steve, and they went out to the horse. He was so starved and weak, they could hardly get him out of the cattle truck. He walked with them slowly on his shaky legs into the loose box that used to be Barney's.

'Here!' Slugger was filling a bucket at the tap. 'I just cleaned that stable out.'

He brought the water over, and they watched the horse suck it in through his wrinkled lips, and then he sighed, holding the last of it in his mouth, and dribbled it slowly over Dora's hand.

'One day,' Slugger picked up the bucket and turned to fetch more water, 'one day we'll keep an empty loose box here. That'll be the day.'